To Minnie and Saxo, the truest of friends.

Places Reversed

Robert Braithwaite

ONE

Liquidation days tended to follow a familiar pattern. No matter how much you'd prepared, no matter how much you'd managed out the risk, something unforeseen always happened. And pulling off a coup at the bloodstock sales, it seemed, was not so far removed from doing the same in the financial markets; they both came to fruition in the same short, sweet, scary, climax.

Freddie Lyons stood at the gates of *Etablissement Elie de Brignac,* studiously composed. He wet his lips with his tongue then crossed the threshold into France's principal bloodstock trading arena. No matter how many times you'd been in similar situations, there was always a moment before the day began when your mouth dried and your legs went hollow. Suddenly, a rush of emptiness travelled up from his feet and went to his head. His breathing turned shallow. He stood stock still for a moment, then feeling no better, went to sit at a nearby bench until the sensation had passed.

He completed his time-out with two minutes of regulated breathing: eight seconds in; hold for six; breathe out for four. Then he shook himself awake, checked his catalogue against the nearby TV monitor, calculating that it was still an hour before his first horse went through, and set off to face the day again.

As he did, he heard his phone ping. He glanced briefly at the screen and saw that it was a message from Edward Hamilton, his bloodstock agent. Here they were, finally arrived at the day that had been eighteen months in the planning, and there was Edward, still wanting to dole out last minute notes. His heart sank. Edward's contribution had been vital, but he had this intellectual zeal about him that could turn ordinary conversations into lectures and cross examinations. He went back to the bench and opened the message, resigning himself to another unwanted conversation.

Joy of joys, Edward was running late, 'could we put the get-together back by half an hour?'

Of course we could! 'Text me on the way,' he replied.

It would mean rejigging his schedule before the first horse went through, but that was fine – he'd take advantage of the extra time to prepare better for their final run-through, and dismiss Edward all the sooner for doing that. Then as soon as they were finished, he'd go and tackle Penny, calling Felix on the way over to see her, to update him with any last-minute news. He'd still be able to clear his obligations before the day got going.

As he left the avenue to enter the fray, he saw straight away that he'd been spotted by Jonny – Jonny Antoine Müller, 'JAM' of the bloodstock journals, his wife's new beau. Flabby, continental, slightly effete, with an air of sneering haughtiness about everything he did, and nothing whatsoever like Freddie.

He watched him put up his hand to cut short a conversation with a client, then turn towards his office. It was tucked away in the quiet backwater at the far end of the semi-circular building that housed the sales ring, next to the exit chute where the horses were led out once sold. Knowing that a confrontation was coming, Freddie decided on the spot that he might as well get it over with.

He went to stand in the no man's land twenty or so yards from Jonny's office door where there was no passing trade to overhear their exchange.

Penny appeared. Five feet and a bit, light to the point of being frail, she peered out from behind her kohl-blackened eyes with an expression set somewhere between inscrutable and furious. Instinctively he reached out his hand to her, then stopped as he saw that it wasn't reciprocated. Jonny followed her at a short distance. Separated this last year, mainly because of the things that were about to happen today, they were now just a financial settlement away from being cut adrift from each other forever; he braced himself for the onslaught.

'So, you're not dead then? I hoped you might be when I saw the house shut up,' she said.

'Charming,' he replied. 'I'm here and I'm still slim and beautiful.' He couldn't stop himself taking a sideways glance at Jonny.

'Good. Well, I'll have my three million quid then.' She stuck out her hand.

He smiled at the simple juvenile gesture. 'I've told you, if the worst comes to the worst, you can have the house. But if you give me some space, get off my back and let me get on with my business, there's a chance I'll be able to settle up with you in cash sometime soon. Please?'

Penny continued to stand squarely in front of him. She uttered a single syllable: 'Ha!'

Both men exchanged silent looks with each other. Then she said it:

'You haven't got a clue, have you?'

'About what?'

She sighed a deep long sigh, trying to keep the lid on her temper. Her hands were on her hips as she looked down at the ground for what seemed like an age. 'You,' she shouted, pointing at his head, 'are delusional. How many horses have you got in this sale? And DO NOT lie!'

'None. Look in the catalogue, do you see my name in there?' His words sounded more apologetic than he'd intended.

'Who bought them for you?' she asked. 'Gay Gordon and that fucking idiot savant you've been hanging around with?' She meant Edward. He wasn't everyone's cup of tea. Freddie liked him, he was just like him in many ways, if a little more analytically inclined.

He was a maverick; a bit of a genius who knew that he was miles smarter than almost everyone else he met, so he never compromised his behaviour in the cause of getting-on. She was right, he was a bit *special*.

Her description of Edward made him laugh.

'You are lying then, now we know. Those two have bought at least ten horses that are in this sale. How many of them are yours?'

They were all his, plus a few more in other names. He shrugged, as if to say, 'So what?'

'Tell him, Jonny,' she said, pointing at Freddie again.

Jonny dropped his perma-smirk for the first time, ever maybe, then told him.

'For Penny, I research all the horses that Edward buys this year. There may be twelve of them in this catalogue, I think. I have seen these horses now, here. Some of them, all maybe, very nice on the outside, OK looking pedigree too, but not good horses Freddie. They all have a fault. An early fracture perhaps, surgery to correct a fault, but not to make good racehorses. No X-rays in the office. They hide something about them Freddie, I'm afraid. Expensive, yes, as foals, I see that, and the correct price too if the horses are correct, but they are not. They are most definitely not. I am sorry my friend.'

Freddie's stomach turned a somersault. He bit hard on to his bottom lip as he tried to master his composure. There'd been no warning. It didn't compute.

Edward Hamilton? Yes, he was smart but there was just something so honest about him too. And he was potless. Freddie had always thought that he had been Edward's first proper client. He had been drawn to him by the same instinct that took him to parts of the market that his former colleagues dare not go – his sportsman's nous that sniffed out chances where they saw only risk. Edward? Edward with his shiny jackets and worn-out Hush Puppies? No. Not him. Or Gordon, his little Sancho Panza with his twenty-acre stud in a remote part of Scotland. They couldn't afford to run a decent car between them; they didn't have the money to coordinate a coup like that.

Penny simply nodded her head as if to say, 'It's all true and there's nobody to pull you out of the mess you've got yourself into this time.'

Jonny stepped forward and put a hand on his shoulder.

'It doesn't make any difference to you,' Freddie dredged up from somewhere. 'It's nearly all client money.' But his voice lacked conviction and he could hear it as well as they could.

'Oh yeah. Well, you'll be able to pay me the money we've agreed then.' Penny began to wave a clutch of formal looking documents at him before thrusting them into his hands. 'Read them and do what it says by the end of next week, or we're coming after you.'

'I've told you. It's client money,' he tried again. 'Just give me some time now to get over today – please don't make it any more difficult than it already is. I promise you I'll get you your money. You've got the house as a guarantee. If the worst comes to the worst, you've got that. Just give me some space now.'

'I am not waiting for that fucking folly to get sold to get my money, Freddie.'

'Who did he work for?' he asked Jonny.

Jonny shrugged, embarrassed slightly that Freddie chose to speak to him instead of his ex.

'I don't know, for me Edward has always been someone on his own.' He left him with a final shrug of the shoulders. It meant, 'We don't care, we just want our money.'

It definitely did not compute. It really didn't. And just to prove it, Freddie went to the *English Bar* and waited for Edward to turn up for their meeting. But when an hour later he still hadn't arrived, he knew that it was all true.

Five hours later, Freddie stood in the sales ring as the auctioneer held his gavel high and announced, 'Le marteau se lève.' It was no more than the standard artifice of his trade; a theatrical warning to buyers that this really was their last chance. But this time, it served better as a final warning to the vendor himself as his last horse passed through the ring. It said, 'Here is the final moment in your old life. Enjoy it because it ends when the gavel comes down.' Crack! It seemed to be directed at him alone, and he flinched as he heard the noise.

Now he knew too. He couldn't yet put a final figure on his losses, but within an hour he'd be able to calculate them to the cent. He left the sales ring to call Felix with the news.

TWO

The Normandy Hotel in the centre of Deauville has an old school elegance about it which elsewhere might have started to look at little dated. The bar was the sort you might find in a Pall Mall club, a little haven of casual civility in the middle of formal luxury. The place was almost empty. Freddie walked in and saw Felix nursing a drink and playing with his phone on one of the little tables for two at the edge of room.

'Not here yet?' he asked.

Felix shook his head. 'This is where we stand,' he said, turning his phone towards Freddie to let him read the spreadsheet.

A waiter approached.

'A large anything,' said Freddie, then added, 'err, Chivas Regal,' when the man didn't act on his first order.

'Where are we with the bank?' asked Freddie.

'You know, I'd spent all day with them, and they'd just agreed to extend the facility when I got your text. So, I don't know. I just hope they don't take the line that I've knowingly misled them.'

'What's the client said?' asked Freddie.

'I told him the truth Freddie – well the bit that interests them – thank God it was a small project. I've told him that he can have three point three and put us out of business, or two point five, and give us a chance to stay afloat and make up the shortfall.'

'Did he choose?' asked Freddie.

Felix shook his head. 'We'll find out in a minute. His approach was more *three-point-three* was an unsatisfactory starting point for discussions. That may have been a negotiating strategy, but he didn't sound pleased.'

'Jesus, you don't think he'll want the lot?'

Felix nodded, 'I do. Sixty cents on the dollar, that's where he's headed. To the round four mill.'

'Then what do we do?' said Freddie.

Felix simply regurgitated a truth that was already well known to Freddie. 'Well, we're seven hundred short of that figure, with a bank that will no longer cooperate, so we're heading towards out of business with a massive hole to fill. I'll ask for six months and be prepared to settle for three. Then we go out looking for charitable clients I suppose.'

Freddie hung his head. He didn't speak.

'I've transferred mine, by the way,' Felix added.

'I haven't had time to sort my end out yet,' said Freddie.

'Freddie, don't delay, if this is anything less than an amicable settlement, you know what will happen.'

'I'll do it as soon as I'm home,' he said.

It would take some quick thinking and reorganisation; his share would as good as clean him out. 'At least we'll deliver it in washed funds,' he said.

Felix tried to smile but couldn't manage it.

'Jesus, I wish I could sell that fucking house,' said Freddie.

'Did you have any in yourself?' asked Felix.

Freddie nodded. 'All-in.'

'I knew you had, you fucking idiot,' he said. 'Tell me Freddie, how did we even end up in bloodstock?'

'Because we fell for Hamilton's bullshit. Because of a lack of choice. Because the stock market's oversold and the only direction is down; same with property, especially now that Russian oligarchs are getting flushed out, and China's a busted flush; commercial property too, no one wants to commute now everyone's realised that they can work just as well from home; because the bond markets were beyond too high; because quantitative easing skewed every asset price so that there was no value left in anything at all; because all the go-to alternatives were fucked – fine wine, transport, logistics, fossil fuels. Do you remember this conversation twelve months ago? We thought it was the only market left in which we could hide and potentially make a few quid for ourselves.'

'Oh yeah, that's right. That thing about your know-how giving us an edge.'

'Have you given Hamilton's name to the clients?'

Felix took a long draw on his drink, 'Nah. What are we going to do? Tell them that we had rings run round us by a sociopath? Have them knock him off, so that we can never get our money back? Just leave that be, and we'll go looking for Hamilton on our own terms when we've got out of this mess.'

Two men sat down at the table next to them. Suddenly they became aware that the bar had started to fill up and it was no longer their private office. Instinctively, from years of practice, they each put a halt to their conversation, and looked to the new arrivals to acknowledge their presence and say hello.

'Freddie?' said one of them.

'Ced?' Ced, the salesman from way back when. The man who loved horse racing, and was always chasing rainbows, be they Derby winners, or his rightful inheritance from his aristocratic Polish ancestors before the communists stole it all from them. Ced, who'd looked somewhere between thirty and forty-five for the last twenty years?

There was something familiar about the tall man with him. He wore the brightly coloured trousers, country-gent, uniform favoured by a certain sort of racegoer. Perhaps he'd seen him at the races?

'This is Alan Halliday, a very good friend of mine. Alan's the leading English bloodstock agent over here. Perhaps you've met already, I'm sorry.'

Felix and Freddie seemed to shake heads simultaneously, but Alan Halliday did the speaking. 'No, I don't think so,' he said.

Alan, no more than Freddie and Felix, could claim to be long-lived in the bloodstock markets, but he was practised at not surrendering any advantage to unknown foes. With his height advantage too – he stood all of six foot five – he liked to try and imply an easy authority over most new people he met.

Freddie smirked as he drank him in.

'Been at the sales, boys?' he asked.

There was a delay while Felix and Freddie decided between them which of them might address this idiot. They were used to dealing with bigger fish than Alan Halliday, and none of those people ever referred to them as boys. It was people like him, loud-mouthed adherents to the playbook, compliant eyes-on-the-prize bonus hunters, that had caused them to find each other at the bank in the first place.

'I have,' said Freddie. 'Have either of you ever come across an agent called Edward Hamilton?'

'No,' said Ced, shaking his head.

'Can't say I have,' added Alan, distracted by the waiter. Freddie was suddenly struck by the sense that Edward Hamilton might arrive. He turned in his chair to face into the room expecting to examine the sparse and scattered clientele, to see who he might, or should know, and was surprised to see that the place was really quite full already. It was as if the bell had been rung at the Sales and all the British people had grabbed their satchels and filed out to the Normandy. Yes, that was it, that's what was odd about them, most of the people in the bar were British and you could see it. *Maybe I've become French*, he thought. Smiling he remained in the same position, not caring to explain his absence from the conversation. He started to look closely at each individual person in the room, to examine what it was that gave them away. *Something about their manners perhaps?* They seemed to have this collective deference about them: only too eager to jump out of the way of the new person coming through; only too ready to say sorry to the person they bumped into as they did. And they clung on to their coats as if they weren't quite sure of the etiquette. He scanned them more thoroughly still to try and pick out a single person that he knew to be French so that he could test out his theory, but he could only find the smarmy vet in his customary bow-tie, and he was the most dedicated Anglophile he knew.

Felix coughed to attract his attention, and Freddie turned back to face the group again.

'So, horses, that's what you're doing just now is it?' Ced asked Freddie.

'You're going to have to excuse me for a moment please,' said Felix, 'my client's due, and I need to grab that space while it's still free.' Then turning to Freddie, he said, 'We'll chat when it's over.'

A response formed on Freddie's lips, but Felix cut him off.

'If there's no compromise on four,' which he spoke quietly whilst making the sign with his fingers, 'I'll call you over. See you in a while.'

'Horses, finance, I can turn my hand to anything and make a mess of it,' said Freddie turning back to Ced again, 'though I've got a feeling I'm going to be at a loose end for a while now.'

'If you're back in Newmarket for the sales, come and see me, I've got something you might want to have a look at,' said Ced, pushing a business card towards Freddie.

'It's not one of those massive cheques with light bulbs round the edge made out to me for four million quid, is it?'

Ced smiled at his friend from the old days and gripped his thigh. 'So lovely to see you, old boy. Hey, I thought I just saw Penny outside. Dressed up to the nines. It must have been. It'd be lovely to...'

'Ced,' Freddie interrupted. 'We're not... anymore, it's...'

'Oh. I'm so sorry, I didn't know... that is terrible news. Really? I can't believe it.'

'Yeah. She's back on the game, mate.'

Freddie laughed after a little silence to give Ced permission to do the same.

'What went wrong?' Ced asked. 'Do say if I'm prying. I don't mean to. I'm just shocked. That really is the most...'

'Oh, you know, cherchez la fucking disaster. I think I just brought too much of the job home. You know what a dirty job banking is – and believe me it's worse when you're running your own *boutique investment house*,' – he decided to omit the part about washing criminally acquired funds to return sixty cents on the dollar, 'and now, I'm into a pretty messy settlement with her too. If she comes in here, I'll have to peel away and talk to her for a minute.'

Ced understood. Of course, he did, he always knew the right thing to do and say. He turned to Alan, who like Freddie had been distracted by the busy crowd. 'Alan's our...' said Ced, but Freddie didn't catch what *our* ... it was.

'Oh yeah,' he replied, 'are you based in France too?'

It bore no relation to what Ced had told him, but Alan answered nevertheless. 'I've got a little apartment up behind the racecourse,' he said, 'it serves as an office when I'm here. You?'

'I've got an enormous house up in the hills over there,' he said, casually pointing behind him. He was going to add, 'But I wish I had a small apartment behind the racecourse instead,' then changed his mind, and decided to leave the statement as it was so that Alan might start to understand which of them was the Alpha-male in their little circle.

'Will you stay for another?' asked Ced.

Why the fuck not? he thought. 'I need a drink,' and he moved to Felix's seat so that he could look out into the room.

Penny came into the bar. Freddie drew in his breath and said, 'Excuse me chaps, she's here now. Sorry Ced, do you mind?' She wore a short, lightweight, black shift dress, a pair of Christian Louboutin shoes, with a chunky platinum necklace and bracelet. She was ready for a date with Jonny, and Freddie knew that he wasn't yet here.

'Penny.' They weren't scheduled to meet but he didn't want her to get away without a reconciling chat. 'Don't run away. He's not here yet, come and talk to me sensibly. That was all wrong today. If I'm not going to see you again for a while, I don't want you to go away from here with the wrong impression.'

Her heady musk gave him a jarring memory of being in places like this with her when life was simpler and sweeter.

'It's Jonny you're meeting, is it?

'Err, yes. Who else do you think it'd be?'

'You might have had second thoughts about me.' He smiled, but his contrived cheekiness didn't cut it any longer. He beckoned her to come with him for a moment, out of the bar, to a quieter area. 'There's too many people in there, I don't want to risk being overheard.'

They walked through the corridors of the hotel until they found a space off the main lobby. 'You see Freddie,' she said, 'this is exactly the way I no longer wish to live.'

He shushed her. 'You're right, we got taken. Mea culpa. But it wasn't our money, it was all client's money. That's what Felix is doing now. Please Penny, you've got to trust me about that. You can see that, can't you?'

'But they were all in your name, weren't they?'

'Yes,' he whispered, 'our clients don't like to be noticed. And everything you're doing is bringing attention to it. It's not helping.'

She stopped and turned back to the bar, but he reached out and grabbed her hand to stop her. 'Come on Penny, don't take offence at everything I say. What went on at the sales today was not good, I admit that and it will be costly to me, it will impact my cash flow – I'm being honest with you about that, but long term it just means a lost client, no real lasting damage. Look, whatever happens, there's our house. Even if we take a bid on the price, your money's safe.'

'Well stop talking about it, and do it.'

'Please, Penny, I can't just conjure up a buyer out of thin air. Give me a chance to get it organised.'

'I've told you; I'm not going to keep hanging on until the house is sold. We both know that it could take years.'

'If it takes that long and my cash flow is still bad, I will take a mortgage on it. How's that?'

She stopped for a moment. 'Who'd give you a mortgage? Admit it, you haven't got it, and you've no got no chance of getting any time soon? You've spunked your... you've spunked our money. That's the truth, isn't it?'

'Listen to me. I have not. But you can't just take a lump sum like almost three million in one go, it'll cripple me.'

'The judge said you could afford it.'

'Oh, come on, I didn't get to give evidence in person. That judgment was ridiculous, you can't expect me to...'

He held out his hands to plead to her. She ignored the gesture and took a few steps backwards along the corridor towards the bar. Then she turned to speak.

'I no longer have any expectations of you. What about all those bonuses you've paid yourself? For goodness' sake Freddie, you bought that ridiculous house for cash.'

He exhaled an exasperated sigh. 'And what about all those years we posted a loss? Where do you think I make up the shortfall?'

'You told me that it was your client's that had lost,' she said.

'I did, I was talking about business in general. But this time it is their loss. It's not ours... but you know how it works Penny, don't pretend you don't.' He began to whisper the words at her, 'We disguise that it's their assets. You know that.'

'You lent criminals my money!' she shouted back at him. He tried to shush her, edging closer to her. 'For God's sake Penny, not so public, you'll get me...' He reached out to try and hold her, to calm her, to try and persuade her to take the intensity down a notch or two, but she resisted. Pushing him away, she turned and walked briskly back to the bar.

He didn't follow immediately. A group of six or so women made their way along the corridor looking for the *Ladies*. He didn't want to barge through them to bring more unwanted attention to their little spat.

As soon as they passed, Freddie quietly followed her as she weaved her way through the crowd to the end of the bar where he'd left Ced and Alan. As she approached their seats, he noticed that it became increasingly difficult for her to find a way through, until eventually she was forced to stop. He caught her up, touching her hand lightly to let her know that he was there, and made a gesture with his finger towards his mouth to say, *don't say anything inappropriate.* She returned a puzzled look, not so much in reply to his unsaid request, more to say 'what's going on'?

The crowd in front of them seemed to stand in concentric circles as if trying to observe a captivating event at its centre. He couldn't locate Ced but he could see Alan, standing alone in the middle of it all, peering out like a long-necked bird casting around the room. When he picked out Freddie, he made straight for him.

'Good God, what a thing to happen,' he said.

'What thing?' asked Freddie.

'I thought you were here,' he said, reacting as if Freddie had made a joke in bad taste.

'No, we were discussing something in the back rooms, what is it?'

'I'm sorry,' he said, 'it's Felix. I think he's dead. A heart attack or something.'

Freddie immediately pushed his way through the crowd. In a little clearing he saw someone tending to his partner, who was lying prone, lifeless, seemingly out cold.

'What, just now?' asked Penny.

'Yes,' said Alan, 'he was just along from me at the bar, and I noticed that someone went down on the floor. I thought whoever it was must be drunk at first. Then I saw it was him; he just crumpled in front of our eyes.'

Freddie returned a few moments later. 'Oh God Penny, you should see him,' he said.

'Is he...?' said Penny, not daring to say the word.

'I don't know. I'm not sure. I was sent away. They were doing stuff to him but... I don't know... I just don't...'

He leant on the table and lowered his head to hide his tears, then just as quickly, as if an inner voice had told him to pull himself together, he rose up, dried his eyes, and said, 'That could have been me. I've got to go. Are you coming?'

'Freddie, what's happening in here, right now, that chaos, is you and your life. That's why I'm waiting for Jonny. I'm sorry for Felix, and I'm sorry for you, but you are on your own.'

Penny left, and Freddie sat alone, bereft, in the crowded bar. Eventually, a police officer approached him, and requested that Freddie follow him.

'You came quickly,' Freddie said.

The policeman gestured towards the door, as if to say, 'I came from across the road.' 'Does he have a next of kin?' he asked.

'No, maybe a sister or brother somewhere. I was the closest person to him that I know.'

Freddie was scared but felt some security at the idea of getting into the back of an ambulance with a policeman sat alongside him.

'Is that why I'm here?' he asked. 'Does it mean that he's... gone?'

The paramedic tending to Felix shook his head, his focus on the patient. The policeman said, 'No, but he is very vulnerable.'

'Vulnerable?' *What an odd word.*

The policeman seemed implicitly to understand that he had used a word that hadn't translated well. 'Sir, it is a very serious matter. We must keep him stable until we reach the hospital.'

'What is it? A heart attack?' asked Freddie.

The paramedic thought for a moment then described it as a *sudden event*, and left it at that.

They rode along in silence for a moment. The paramedic working, the policeman stoically silent, Freddie, a million different things racing through his mind. Then his mobile pinged – an anonymous number had sent a message. It read, '£4M – ASAP.'

'Best if you err... sir,' said the paramedic indicating the phone.

As soon as the ambulance arrived at the hospital and the paramedic had disappeared with Felix, Freddie went back to his phone and replied: 'Believe settled at 3.3? Will send that Monday.' But he knew from previous experience that if his response took any longer than a few minutes, the likelihood was it would never be read.

On Monday morning Freddie accessed his work accounts remotely from home. He transferred his contribution to that which Felix had previously sent, and then sent the whole of it to his client's account. It was seven hundred thousand short of the four million owed, but it was as much as he had, and it at least equated to the offer Felix had told him he'd made when he last spoke to him. Last spoke to him. When he'd finished, he packed a bag, locked the house, and took a cab to the police station to attend an interview with an Inspector Grandcollot. From there, he intended to go next to the hospital to check in on Felix and hopefully pick up from him any details that were discussed before the almost fatal moment.

'Don't tell me…' said Freddie, as Grandcollot denied his request to visit Felix, but the detective soothed his concerns with a shake of the head.

He was a gentle-faced man possessed of a charming, almost over-rehearsed geniality. His greying hair and whiskers belonged to another time, but Freddie could discern beneath them lurked a face which revealed intellect and patience.

'Your friend is isolated, away from visitors, and will be treated by a small team of specially selected staff.'

As if to answer the puzzled expression he saw on Freddie's face, he went on, 'He has been poisoned we believe,' then, talking over Freddie, 'by an agent which is very potent, and can remain a threat to anyone who is in contact with it, for many, many years.' Still, he wouldn't let Freddie intercede. 'That is why access to the place where he is being treated is strictly controlled.'

He looked at Freddie in silence for what seemed like a never-ending moment, and just as Freddie changed his facial expression to speak again, Grandcollot re-started and said gravely, 'He is very ill. You should be prepared.'

'Novichok?' he asked.

'The newspapers refer to it in that way,' Grandcollot replied.

'They think he'll die?'

'He is gravely ill,' Grandcollot said, 'his treatment will take a great deal of time, and should he respond to it well, the recovery still longer.'

Freddie's head dropped.

'It is wrong of me to speak of recoveries, it will give you too much hope.' It sounded harsher than he'd intended. 'I have here the contact information for the *medecin*, who you must call for full details. But you may not visit. He is in a facility which is not for the public. You do understand?'

'It, it, it... sounds...'

Grandcollot waved him down theatrically, 'I am advised to tell you that part of the treatment perhaps, in fact likely, is that Monsieur Felix will be placed into a medical coma. That is what I know, for the rest, you must talk with this *medecin*.'

Freddie resisted the temptation to ask any more questions and gestured with his head to say that he had heard and would comply. He smiled weakly across the desk.

'You do not ask me who could do such a thing,' Grandcollot said.

'No, I think, I, err, I, no, I think I'm in shock,' Freddie replied.

Grandcollot's expression indicated, *I thought you'd say that.* 'I must ask,' he said, 'if you and Monsieur Felix were on good terms.'

'What? The best. We're the best of colleagues and friends, we trusted each other absolutely.' It's funny, he thought, that the more you assert something, the weaker it sounds. For some reason he started talking again, and added, 'We'd die for each other.'

It was only when Grandcollot smiled that he realised the import of the words.

'But you had debts?'

'We, err, the company? No, that traded solvently.'

'So, from where does this mystery enemy come, we must ask?'

Freddie could not summon a convincing response and settled for a slow despondent shaking of his head.

'You will provide for us access to your client lists?' Then he added, 'Your management accounts, the travels of Monsieur Felix, his err, how do you say this, you both were salesmen of the company, or was this just him?'

'Both,' said Freddie instinctively, then qualified it to, 'him mainly, but both.'

'But he was the Russian speaker?'

They both spoke Russian, but Freddie answered, 'He was a level above me, yes.'

'Again, you don't ask if the attack has the hallmarks of a Russian conspiracy.'

'No, no, I just assumed.'

'Well, you are right to assume. It does.'

Freddie took a long, slow, tremulous breath.

'Can you translate this word, *Novichok*?' asked Grandcollot.

'It just means *new thing*. That's it.'

'Interesting,' said the detective. 'It means, of course, that we always associate it with Russians. But really, any criminal gang with the funds can find it.'

Freddie didn't reply as he forced himself to extract a morsel of positivity from the thought that *anyone could have done it*. It might have been an accident.

'Could it have been an accident?' he asked.

'Unlikely,' the detective said eventually. He paused again, then said, 'Can I ask you, whilst we investigate this matter that you do not leave the country. Or in fact this region? It is as much for your own safety.'

For a while he complied with Grandcollot's request. He moved the remaining personal items he needed from the main house to its *dependence* a hundred yards away, telling himself that it would present better that way and sell sooner. Then he set up his work from home office, bringing all his files from the temporary office he and Felix had rented. He felt safer locked into a small cottage that had one point of entry at the end of a long path, and he felt much safer being able to control which version of his and Felix's company he presented to Grandcollot.

He stuck it out tolerably well for a little while, but then the trees went bare and his vista from the hills above Deauville revealed a desolate view, without another house between his and the main road a mile or so away. Before long, he'd barely get through the night without jumping at the tiniest noise outside, and when he wasn't terrified, he drove himself mad trying to trace back the clues in Edward Hamilton's behaviour that he'd missed; then the same of his clients, and those last moments in the Normandy. Then he stopped going out altogether. He couldn't visit Felix and was secretly glad of that. When the grocery van came, he took to watching them drop the order on the steps of his cottage from an empty horse box two hundred yards away.

Eventually Grandcollot started to drop by less and call more, and so one night, he packed a case and drove to Calais.

THREE

Newmarket, like so many other market towns in England, spilled outwards in all directions from what was essentially its only commercial street. From parts of the town, you could see that it was entirely enclosed by countryside, but from the clock tower at the top of the High Street, all you could see in front of you was a meandering patchwork of tatty shop fronts that gave it a forsaken look, as if this moment in its history was just to be endured until somebody came along with a new idea to turn it into something better.

The first time in more than twenty years since he was last here, Freddie looked at the town through French eyes now, and fought to suppress the sinking sensation as he stopped to drink in the scene for a moment. Then, that sense of being the farthermost frontier town in civilisation – not yet quite disappeared behind the plastic awnings of the new world coming – still hung in the air. *Boots* was somewhere else then and in the place it now stood, there once was a hotel. In those days, when you entered by the permanently open French-window style doors, how far you then progressed towards the billiard room at the back was determined by the place you occupied in the hierarchy of locals who derived their living otherwise than by having a job. In those days, before the internet and ubiquity of television screens, they still chalked up results as they came in on the board outside the Telegraph Office.

If only England could be more like France he thought as he made his way between the Bedford Lodge Hotel on Bury Road, to Tattersalls on the other side of town; or France a little more like England perhaps. One of the two anyway.

No matter. He turned the corner from the High Street onto The Avenue and crossed the road towards the main gates of Tattersalls. An unnoticed motorbike shot behind him, almost clipping his heels, and as he jumped up onto the kerb, he smiled a misty smile recalling his father's entreaties about two-wheeled transport – a fear he shared with Felix. He breasted the rise towards the original boundary wall of the citadel, paused for a moment at the Fox Rotunda, then took a deep breath, lowered his sunglasses, stood up his collar and went in. It was the first time since that night in the Normandy that he'd gone into a venue which was open to the public. It would be the first time since then that he'd be without a constant three-sixty degree awareness of everyone and everything close by.

He'd had occasion to be amongst this bloodstock crowd in recent times too but knew himself to be at a remove from most of them now: the professionals; their clients; each of their respective acolytes; the evangelists and all the other spongers, flunkies and liggers who found a way to extract an income from these markets, whether they were up, down, in favour or out.

He made his way as directly as possible across the busy terrace into the main building and headed straight for the back bar where Cedric Sadowski was waiting for him.

'Freddie, Freddie, dear Freddie,' said Ced getting up to greet his sometime friend. 'So glad you could make it. Come and sit down. Conrad Wilson and Warren Parry,' he added, indicating the two men sat with him at the round table in the bay window furthest from the bar.

'That was a nasty business in Deauville, are you all right old boy? How is Felix?'

'Felix is now in an induced coma,' said Freddie.

Ced's open-mouthed response invited more from Freddie, but he declined, 'We've been told he'll be very lucky if he pulls through,' was all he'd say.

'Was it a *Novichok* thing like they say on the news?'

Freddie nodded his head and gave Ced a grim smile.

It was early evening. The action in the ring was relayed over TV screens dotted about the place, and in the corner of the bar, a bank of six screens tuned into that, a rolling news programme, and live races from around the world.

'So, this is Freddie, a great friend of mine,' Ced told Warren and Conrad.

He passed him a glass of red wine filled from the last of the bottle.

'I was telling the boys that you used to be Champion Amateur.'

'They gave it to the one who turned up most,' said Freddie, 'and there were only about six races a year.'

Warren laughed, but Conrad chose to ask a question about prize money which Freddie didn't hear over a loudspeaker announcement, so he gave the usual answer: the one about twice winning the Gentleman Riders' Derby at Epsom on August bank holiday, and thereby securing the amateur riders' title for those years, as well as his weight in champagne, but never any money unfortunately.

'You'd be surprised how much a case of champagne weighs,' he answered Warren, as Conrad and Ced conferred quietly over a text message. 'Well, that's what they told me anyway. I was an undergraduate at the time and didn't account for much once the lead was taken out of my saddle. But there never seemed to be very much left at going home time.'

'So, Freddie, Conrad and Warren run this company, HRC,' said Ced, 'You may have heard of Warren's dad, Derrick Parry, the Premier League CEO?'

'Yeah, I have. That would make you about the same age as your mum, wouldn't it?'

'He got us going,' said Warren. He didn't laugh but his eyes smiled, 'his background is casinos.'

Conrad interrupted to take over the anecdote, 'All casinos have the same issue; they're all chasing down the same set of high rollers. But whereas every rich person knows that they can join any casino whenever they want, very few of them can get a large bet on with a bookie.'

'What, horse racing?' asked Freddie.

'Any sport. But yeah, horses mainly.'

Is that the story or am I supposed to tease the details out by asking interesting questions? he thought.

'Have you always done that?' he tried.

'No, the business is only a couple of years old. We used to be in insurance, that's where me and Warren first met, then when we'd put some money together, we set up this high-roller gambling thing.' Freddie looked sideways at Ced, Salesman Ced, Slippery Ced, holding court, trying to pretend like they were lifelong friends, and not just some people he met when he was drunk on the train on the way home. Freddie was trying to convey, 'You brought me here for this?'

'Happy to stick with this?' asked Ced, getting up and waving the empty bottle. Receiving no reply, he left them to talk as he wandered over to the bar.

'I'm not really a high stakes gambler,' said Freddie.

'No,' said Conrad laughing, 'Ced was just telling you what we did. Our clients are the petro-chemical boys, that sort of thing. The trick is to get enough of them together in one place so that you can persuade the big four bookies to make a dedicated department for them. We've got an app.'

Freddie had only ever had one job interview in his life, but this didn't feel like the way they should go.

'Sounds fascinating,' he said, 'how's it all going?'

Conrad told him that they'd launched their venture on Derby Day two years ago and had decided that they would pause for thought and weigh up the situation when turnover hit two million. Their first ever bet from their first client, taken by Conrad on the train on the way to Epsom, was in fact for two million, on the favourite in the Derby. He started laughing like one of those creeps Freddie knew too well from the bank, *I can't believe how successful and lucky I am. Aren't I great?*

'You face some pretty big liabilities then?' Freddie asked, trying to show an interest in it all and find a way into the meeting. Perhaps their clients included the sort of former KGB agents, now billionaires, that he was used to dealing with?

'No, not us,' said Warren, 'we're on profit share.'

'So, Freddie,' said Ced, setting down a new bottle and four fresh glasses, 'you're into bloodstock trading, aren't you?'

'Ah, here it comes,' thought Freddie. 'I have been,' he said. Not that it was a great success, but who cared, if it got him a salary and an opportunity to get active in the market and chase down his losses.

'And now, we're setting up a bloodstock investment scheme,' said Conrad.

'As well as the gambling stuff?' asked Freddie.

'Yeah,' said Conrad. If he didn't roll his eyes, he at least exchanged a long, tired look with Warren.

'What's your angle?' asked Freddie.

'We buy yearlings that need time, introduce them to racing slowly, showing them to be capable and progressive, but, unlike other horses of their age, not ruined by being forced too early. Then, the very people who did not have the patience to deal with them as yearlings, are queuing up to buy mature, lightly raced, fresh horses on their way up, ready to reach their peak. You know, as Cup horses, or recruits to jumping.'

Ced chipped in, 'We've got a little private syndicate of our own to test the model, which is going to run this year, but we're having a raise now for the first proper scheme to launch in August.'

'Can't your clients just do it for themselves?' he asked.

Conrad laughed, 'No, not them,' he said, 'they're the people that we'll eventually sell the horses to. That's why it works so well for us. Tara Fitzsimmons could buy and sell our scheme on her own and wouldn't notice the difference. This is a new business, separate from all the gambling stuff – it's just for us… and our friends.'

'So, what's my in?' he thought. Maybe they want to keep the French horses in France? The pitch was coming – they were going to ask him to do it for nothing for points in the scheme. That was the way that these things normally went.

A P.A. announcement cut across their conversation. It asked for a bloodstock agent, an O'Riordan, something or other like that, to come to the office to collect an envelope. Freddie laughed and shook his head. He looked around the table but his amusement wasn't shared.

'They steal from you in plain sight,' he tried, but he might as well have said it in a foreign language. Still, it was a chance to switch the conversation away from the pitch. 'You represent Tara Fitzsimmons, do you?' he asked.

Warren seemed to sigh as he said, 'Yeah.'

'Tell me something that's always puzzled me about her,' said Freddie. 'She must have about two hundred national hunt horses. The economics don't work. They'd cost about five million a year to train, plus she'll have to buy them in the first place, and mostly she buys expensive ones, so that takes her to about ten million. In a good year, she'd get at most say three million back in prize money. She never sells a horse. How does it work?'

'Do you remember her horse, the one that won the first race at Cheltenham this year? The Supreme Novices?' said Conrad.

'Yeah, Caspian something,' said Freddie.

'Caspian Fish. Well, she had five hundred grand on at sixes.'

'Oh,' said Freddie, 'that's how she does it. That's the different scale you were talking about.'

Ced coughed. Freddie ignored the hint.

'I don't get it,' said Freddie, 'that's just one client, and she needs to take seven million a year off you just to break even. How can that work?'

Warren said, 'Quite.'

Conrad took the lead again and, slightly impatiently, said, 'It's a numbers game. If we have enough of them, we can balance a book – we didn't really lose much on that Cheltenham race. And, of course, it's shared between a panel of bookies these days. Our app puts the bet up and they can take as much of it as they want, and if there's any left half an hour before the race, they split it four ways. Mostly they're glad of the information. Don't forget for every Tara there's some prick in a dishdasha having two hundred and fifty grand on Arsenal to win two-one. And Tara doesn't get it right all the time.'

'But she doesn't play fair,' added Warren, 'tell him about Ascot last year.'

'We're at Ascot, OK,' says Conrad. He was annoyed with Warren now. They were there to close as many people like Freddie as they could in the two evenings spent in Newmarket, and here was Warren, opening diversions and dragging the whole thing out. 'Tara was having a bad week. Obviously, it's the flat, so she's not backing her own horses, and she's just another mug punter. By teatime on Friday, she was ten million down.'

Freddie said, 'Wow,' on cue, and Warren smiled.

Conrad continued, 'Then there was this five-runner race at Thurles in the evening. She had two runners in it, and guess what? The outsider won at twelve to one.'

'And she had a million on it I guess,' said Freddie

'She doesn't care,' said Warren, 'other people feel guilty, but Tara can't. She calls them jockeys' races, where everyone in the race is riding to her instructions. If they don't, chances are they'll never get another ride in public again.'

'I see,' said Freddie.

'You must have had offers like that when you rode didn't you?' asked Warren, 'not to lose, but to ride a certain way to give another horse a better chance?'

Conrad raised his eyebrows at Ced.

'They didn't do it with us,' said Freddie. 'We weren't good enough to follow instructions.' And finally, all four of them laughed at the same time.

'So, Freddie,' said Ced, topping up his glass, 'is this the sort of thing you might be interested in? We'd really love to have someone like you involved.'

He replied with an elongated, 'Yeah,' which didn't convince him, let alone his audience.

'Take this away with you to read,' Ced said, 'tickets are twenty-k each, and most people are buying two or three. We're aiming to raise one point five million by the first yearling sales in August – that way we can get five or six horses; above a million and it's a go-er. We really want the right people in this Freddie. The upsides are unbelievable and look at our clients from the other business – it gives us a pretty good safety net. Have a read, it's all in the document.'

'Marlborough Thoroughbreds? How tacky,' said Freddie, but only Warren laughed.

'You'll see other schemes like this,' said Conrad, 'now that the Melbourne Cup has made long distance races all the rage again. But we thought of it first, we've got the right man buying the horses for us, and the difference with us is, as we keep saying, we own the end clients.'

'Plus,' added Ced, 'we're proving ourselves this year. You should come and watch one of our horses work on the Cambridge Road gallop tomorrow. Would you like that?'

'We're very confident about this,' said Conrad.

'That's the sort of positivity I've been waiting to hear,' said Freddie. They weren't sure whether he meant it to sound as sarcastic as it did.

'So, what do you say?' asked Ced.

'Put me down for a ticket,' said Freddie. 'And I'll have a read of this to see if I'm in for anymore.'

There was an invitation to hang around for a while, but Conrad's barely suppressed frown when the offer was made told him that it was time to go.

'No thanks, I count it unlucky to meet the other candidates,' he said.

Another P.A. announcement asked for an envelope to be collected. 'And I've got to go and get my wages.' said Freddie getting to his feet.

'If you're sure,' said Ced, still not quite sure whether he'd been told a joke or not. 'Meet us at the viewing platform at seven thirty.' Then he got to his feet, told Freddie again how much he cared for him and worried about him, and drew him forward into a tight clinch.

Freddie felt uncomfortable submitting to Ced's embrace. He found himself with his arms trapped, looking eye to eye with Warren over Ced's shoulder, and short of anything else to do, he winked at him.

Once undone from Ced, he looked directly at Conrad and Warren, signed off by saying, 'Paka-paka,' then turned quickly and left before he saw their reaction.

FOUR

Freddie headed first to the impromptu car park made by the dead end of the access road to the *July* racecourse, but as he turned from the roundabout, he saw that a crowd had already gathered. He stopped immediately and reversed his car, and drove instead to the golf course car park, half a mile back along the road into Newmarket. That was closer to the viewing platform rendezvous they'd made the previous evening, though he knew from past experience that Ced's coterie of newly arrived bloodstock investors would park where he'd intended to, then congregate just after the bend in the Cambridge Road gallop, unprepared to take on the dewy morning walk of three furlongs or so along to the designated meeting place.

He picked a moment in the sporadic Cambridge rush hour commute and jogged across the broad straight road that ran from the High Street. He swerved through the zig-zag chicane of post and rail fencing designed to allow ridden horses through but keep loose horses from escaping, then entered the great vastness of the training grounds set between the two Newmarket racecourses.

Seven thirty in the morning, by no means early by Newmarket standards and not a single horse visible in the whole of what, three thousand acres? He crossed the dusty red path along which horses walked, walking to, or returning from their morning's work, through the lush grass and to the edge of the all-weather gallop that hadn't existed in his day. In those days they just watered the grass and dolled off fresh strips as the old piste became too worn.

He walked along the gallop to save his shoes, and up to the raised viewing platform where Ced should have been waiting. Looking down the gallop to its bend, he just discerned a group of men as they appeared through a gap in the hedge from his intended car park. He waited to see where they finally settled before setting off to join them and checked his phone for messages as he did. Ced would have contacted him if he'd moved the meeting place, wouldn't he? Perhaps he'd already filled up his scheme with investors and Freddie was not quite as crucial to it as he'd made out yesterday evening? Who knew? Who cared?

They eventually stopped a hundred yards or so on from the bend, and so Freddie descended from the platform and went back to the dusty red path to make his way to join them. He noticed a single horse coming his way along the path. Checking every now and again to make sure that he gave it right of way as it passed, he stepped back towards the perimeter hedge fifty yards or so before it did. As the rider came closer, Freddie could just discern his tiny, worn and grooved, mahogany face between his hat and raised collar, and he readied himself to say, 'Hello' in case it was one of the old boys he ought to know. The face came closer into view, wearing that familiar dead-eyed grimace set at the horizon.

Freddie's jaw dropped.

'Birdie?' It was Birkett Coward, his old boss. Birdie to everyone who knew him well.

'Ferdyshenko! What brings you back?'

'I thought I was coming for a job interview, but it turned out to be a twenty-grand scalping.'

'By who?'

'That lot down there,' he said, nodding his head in the direction of Ced's group.

'What happened to the old job?'

'Don't ask. I found out the hard way that it wasn't forever.'

'That wasn't what you said when you didn't take the job with me.'

Freddie waved away the comment and started walking on towards Ced and his followers. Side by side they chatted and laughed about the old days.

'What you here for anyway?' asked Birkett.

'I told you, this lot are selling a scheme, I thought they'd got me up to run it for them.'

'No, here, this morning.'

'I don't know; they're watching a horse canter. The usual bullshit, it's just an extension of the marketing. It'll be another hour of my life I won't get back.'

'Make it worth your while, stay on and watch this lad work,' said Birkett.

'The horse you're sat on? I thought it was the hack.'

'What makes you say that?'

'His size, for one.'

'You're as bad as that lot,' he said, indicating Freddie's new friends, 'this horse is going to win the Hunt Cup.'

Freddie laughed. 'What, next year?' he asked.

'No, this,' said Birkett deadpan.

'You do know it's May already, don't you? You haven't been hibernating again, have you?'

Birkett shook his head as if feeling a deep pity for the ignorant fool and said no more.

'What's he called?' said Freddie eventually. Birkett leaned back on his horse, turning sideways to take a good look at his former protégé. The look that conveyed, *interested now, are you?* But Freddie wouldn't play and kept his gaze straight ahead. After another fifty yards or so, Birkett, without turning to speak, quietly said, 'Milksheikh.' Something about the transaction was chastising, and it brought to mind the silent bollockings that he'd handed out to Freddie as a young jockey on the way home from the races. The sting of the recall reminded Freddie that it hadn't always been great fun.

'Here I am then,' said Freddie, as they arrived closer to Ced and his new clients.

'Yep, here you are,' replied Birkett, going ahead as Freddie crossed the wake behind him.

'If you need an out, go and wait at the end of the gallop for me.'

'You're serious, aren't you?' said Freddie.

Birkett stopped his horse for a stride and said, 'I've never been more certain of anything in my life,' then he gently moved the reins again and continued to walk on towards the bottom of the hill and the start of the gallop.

'Morning Freddie,' said Ced, breaking from the crowd to welcome him, 'I thought that was you coming along.'

'Was that Birkett Coward you were talking to?' asked Conrad arriving with him.

'It was,' he told him, 'My old boss when I worked here.'

'No way,' he said, 'does he always just wander about like that on his own?'

'Yeah, he's got dementia,' said Freddie, 'he thought he was on his rocking horse, and I was his nanny.'

'Oh.'

'Am I on time?' he asked, 'I thought we were meeting up at the viewing platform.'

'Absolutely perfect, old chap,' said Ced, 'that's them, just arriving at the bottom of the gallop now. We're coming up third.'

A string of horses cantered steadily by, two abreast. Once the last had disappeared into the distance all eyes turned to a man in the centre of the crowd so that they might hear his judgment before they gave their own. But the tall man with his back to Freddie was only interested in telling anyone he could persuade to listen that a routine piece of work like that was of no matter to a hard knocking professional like him.

'Is that Alan?' Freddie asked Ced.

'Yeah, our bloodstock director,' he replied, 'do you want to have a chat?'

'Not this time, thanks,' he said, 'it's already beginning to feel too much like a banker's field trip for me. I think I'll get going.' He began to walk away from the group.

'We're off to breakfast at the Rutland once we've watched the string back, won't you join us?' Ced called out to Freddie's back. Freddie turned round to shout back, 'I've promised Birkett to take him for a milkshake, he mightn't be around for much longer, so I should really.'

'What about... '

'The money?' thought Freddie. 'You'll have to ask again for that my friend,' he said to himself, and he left them to walk steadily back towards the end of the gallop.

He turned occasionally on his way, so that he wouldn't miss Birkett, coming like *Famine* on his black horse down the long straight of the gallop. Another string had got itself in between him and Ced's lot, and Freddie was already beyond the viewing platform when Birkett finally came into view.

There he was, the old man sitting on his favourite horse as if they'd always been partners, seeming to control his sweet high-tempo'd canter with just the crook of his index finger. He clicked him as they went past Freddie, and without any other aid from the rider the horse stretched and lengthened his stride to finish the last furlong or so of the gallop at something like racing speed.

Birkett walked back along the dusty track to meet Freddie, and as they met, turned to walk back again towards the grassy corner at the cricket pitch end of the gallop.

'See, he's already come back in his wind, he looks a lot less fit than he is. Just likes his grub, don't you pal?' He gave his horse a loving rub down his sweaty neck.

'What's he all about then?' asked Freddie.

'You don't remember him? I don't suppose you would unless you knew to look. He's four now, won a maiden as a two-year-old, and a little conditions race early on last year. Only run three times. I was thinking of running him in the Guineas, but he threw a splint.'

'Then what?'

'Oh, it was nothing really, next he got a fat joint because of that arsehole in my yard, and kept it half the summer, and when I finally got him back the ground had gone. So, I thought I'd keep him for next year.'

'And?'

'It's next year now, couldn't you work that bit out?'

They'd reached the end of the path, and Birkett jumped down from his horse and threw the reins over his head to lead him quietly for a moment as he continued to talk to Freddie. It put them closer together and so Birkett dropped the volume, just in case what he said carried beyond the hedge into alien ears.

'You know Slipshod, the good miler I've got?'

'Yes.'

'That thing couldn't blow wind up this fella's arse last spring.'

'But now…'

'No, *then*. I took him to Sandown, didn't I?'

'Which one are you talking about, Slipshod?'

'Yes, for God's sake keep up will you. Last spring. He was half fit. You know how I have them first time out?'

'Yes, I do.'

'Well, he was about half as fit as normal, like this lad looks today, and he ran a horse of Stoute's to a head.'

'Go on,' said Freddie, the story was starting to get a little bit interesting.

'You know the one I mean, don't you? The one that won the Two Thousand Guineas a month later.'

'No! Why didn't you put him in the Guineas?'

'I told you, he threw a splint, and he was still a big baby then, I didn't want to spoil him.'

'No, not him, Slipshod.'

'Honestly, I didn't really think he was that good then. But he'd have gone close. I know that now.'

'So Slipshod turned out to be the best in the end then?'

'Yeah well, Slipshod is still good. He won his first group race at the beginning of the month, back at Sandown. Did you see the race?'

'No. I live in France, don't I?'

'France? What are you doing over there? Don't answer, we'll come back to that. Anyway, Slipshod, he won on the fucking snaffle, Freddie. He's a Group I horse, I'm sure of it now. I'm running him in the Queen Anne you know.'

'Yeah, like I was saying, he's getting better with experience.'

'He is. But you know how he couldn't blow smoke up the arsehole of this lad as a three-year-old?'

'He can now, can he?'

'He couldn't catch the cunt in horse box now.'

'What?'

'I'm telling you the truth, son.'

'What's all this about, Birdie?'

'What do you mean?'

'I mean, that you have a well-earned reputation for being tight as a crab's arse. I don't see the rest of the string around you. I don't see anyone. And yet you've just opened up to me about it all? I promise you Birdie, I'm still after the last racehorse swindler that turned me over. I'll burn your fucking yard down if you're trying to leg me over.'

'Oh, that bad, eh?'

'Yeah. Worse actually.'

'Good job we met then,' he said, and smiled quietly to himself.

Birkett continued to lead his horse, widening the circle that had Freddie at its centre.

Freddie started to speak but Birkett raised his hand to stop him. He indicated with his head, something behind Freddie that required them to fall into silence. Freddie turned to see that a long string was pulling up after working close by.

It *was* different in his day. Then, every string looked scruffy. No matter that the individual riders might have the best of kit, the horses too, in those days the whole of the string was mismatched in colours and styles. Nowadays, every saddle cloth, every rider carried the same livery. He'd heard about this; it was to make them easier to identify to the officials who patrolled the gallops. The men and women who watched silently, and reported secretly, and whose intelligence would be compared with the Heath-Tax returns made by the trainers.

The string slowly made its way to a worn circle in the grass, fifty yards or so away from Birkett and Freddie, where the riders seamlessly adjusted their mounts into single file as they accessed the circle. None of them talked, conditioned by years of the same routine, waiting to give the first news of the work to their trainer. They settled to the endless silent circling, only the post-exercise snorting and blowing of the horses could be heard.

The grey and blue stable colours, neat as it made them as a team, leant them a mournful air against the desolate backdrop of the endless Newmarket grasslands. His mind drifted to Dickens' *Yorkshire Schools*. He looked at Birkett wearing the same old *Barbour* jacket that he always wore, perhaps the same one, he thought. Then from there he went to Edward Hamilton, Yorkshireman. Dour young fogey. You could add sneak, liar, fraud, and bully to that now. The bile rose in his chest and for a second or two he became overwhelmed by an intense rage which turned into anger against himself. Birkett, in the background, was gesticulating wildly and it served to distract Freddie and snap him out of his fit of melancholy. He shook off the thoughts and looked over properly at Birkett.

Anticipating a trainer arriving, Birkett was beckoning Freddie onwards into the non-delineated hinterland of the gallops. He walked head downwards, ruling out any conversation, leading his horse in approximate circles each one further and further away from the well-groomed string. Freddie shouted over to ask him whose horses they were.

Birkett replied only that, 'your voice carries much further than you think out here.'

Eventually a boy of about twenty appeared. He went to the centre of the circle and said just a few words, following which the string unwound from its circle and began to file away. It headed towards the gates opposite to those by which Freddie had entered, leading to the back of Hamilton Road and away from the gallops.

Neither man spoke for a few minutes until eventually Freddie shouted over, 'What's he rated?'

'Who? Slipshod, one hundred and twelve, which underestimates him you know,' said Birkett, coming back closer to Freddie again.

'And Milksheikh?'

'At the moment? Eighty-eight.'

'How come?'

'I told you; he's hardly run, the handicapper hasn't had a chance to see him yet. And between what I know, and what the handicapper knows, there's about forty pounds-worth of opportunity.'

Freddie smiled, he'd heard similar stories before, 'Are you serious?'

'More than. I might have underestimated him, but he's at least a stone better than Slipshod.'

'Well, that is… Jesus Birdie, are you sure you're sure? He won't even get in the Hunt Cup with that sort of rating, will he?'

'No, you're right, he won't. I'll have to win a race and then he might just sneak in on bottom weight.'

'How are you going to do that?' He asked, Birkett still circling him, leading his horse, 'Royal Ascot's only a month away. I can't see it, Birdie. He's a nice horse I get that, but look at him, you're asking him to win a decent race in his condition – it'll take such a lot out of him, and you'll never get him right again in three weeks.'

Birkett's plan had been long since formed, and he simply could not entertain an alternative point of view.

'There's a race for him here on Thursday. It's over six furlongs and that's never his trip, so we should be able to make him look a bit more ordinary than he is, especially half fit. If I can get him to win that nice and easy, the handicapper will put us up the seven pounds like they usually do for ordinary winners of ordinary races; ninety-five is guaranteed to get us in the race, and it's somewhere near bottom weight most years.'

Birkett was the time served trainer; who was Freddie to gainsay him? Perhaps though, in his dotage he was getting a bit, you know, looser about things. It would be terrible if he became embarrassing as he got older. And there was no one in his life to rein him in.

'I'm still free for a bit Birdie, do you fancy a milkshake?'

'The shake part is Sheikh, like an Arab leader. And no, thanks, I've got a yard to run.'

'OK. But if you wanted to talk some more…'

Birkett turned to face the horse again before he reached the end of his sentence, then crooked his left leg for Freddie to put him back in the saddle.

'Birdie?'

'Yes, son?'

'What are you telling me all this for?'

'Cos I know you, and 'cos you've got that desperate look on your face. Come and stay with me on Thursday and see for yourself, there's a job in this for you if you're interested.'

Freddie patted Milksheik's near side rump as they rode away.

Left alone he suddenly felt ridiculous, like he didn't have a friend, or for that matter, belong, anywhere. But he stayed put, drinking in the view of his old workplace. As he did, he inhaled deeply on the aroma left on his right hand from patting Milksheikh, trying to savour every last moment until it faded.

Five minutes later he knew. Nothing on earth was going to stop him returning to Birkett's yard next week. Until then, all he had to do was find a quiet place to lie low where Grandcollot, his old clients, his ex-wife, and anyone else who was interested, couldn't find him if they wanted to.

FIVE

Newmarket has two racecourses: the Rowley Mile, for the spring and autumn; and the July Course, for the summer months. From the Rowley Mile it's difficult to make out the July Course, with its original low-rise Victorian stands tucked away behind the Devil's Dyke and settled amongst the trees right on the very boundary of the Newmarket grasslands. The Rowley Mile though, with its garish five story grandstand, is visible from miles away, incongruous in the flat and featureless grass gallops, in the same way that the clubhouse of a remote Scottish golf course stands out in a desolate landscape.

There is no circuit to either of the courses, they just come at you in long straight, mildly undulating lines from miles away – the running track being distinguished from the grass that surrounds it only by the white plastic running rails that stretch so far into the distance they seem to join like railway lines. And so, you watch the races from almost head on. Today there are TV cameras on high cranes relaying the live pictures to enormous screens, but once, not very long ago, you had only your binoculars and the racecourse commentary to guide you; that judgment of when to put down the binoculars and switch to the live action always a bold one, as the horses left the dip and ran the last furlong and a half to the line.

The grandstand forces the crowds to gather from the winning line and spill backwards down the course, and it seems to be every racegoer's goal to get as close to the winning post as possible. That after all is where the action is decided, but it does not take many goes at racing before you realise that the horses are often spent by the time they reach the last few yards and all you get is the sight of them hanging on for all they're worth. Which is why you'd always catch people like Birkett down in the dip more than a furlong away, because that is where the horses change from cruising to hitting top speed, when they make the move that wins them the race, or when they don't, and they're being kept for next time.

He was stood there with Freddie waiting to watch Milksheikh make his seasonal debut. It was one of those Newmarket days, windswept and lonely, as if each race was staged just for the private interests of the owners and trainers without another single paying customer in the place. Birkett had just Freddie for company, and when they first met, he took him to the far end of the paddock, as far away as they could get from that place in front of the enormous paddock TV screen where the horses exited for the racecourse, just in case there was a sudden outbreak of clubby bonhomie amongst the usually sullen ranks of Newmarket trainers.

Only eight runners, which although it didn't overly concern Birkett, made him doubt that he'd be guaranteed the strong pace in the race that he would have liked for his horse. He was a miler, not a sprinter, and he'd need every yard of a strongly run race at six furlongs to be able to do himself justice. A hack canter and a sprint from the bushes would turn it into a little bit more of a lottery; nor did he want to counter that risk by giving his still tender horse the added work of cutting out the running and doing the hard work for the rest of them.

'Only lead if you have to,' he'd told Tolley Woolf, the oldest freelance jockey in the weighing room, 'Drop him in, unless it's desperate.' Then he said, 'You'll win, but you'll have to get after him, he's a bit undercooked,' and following that said nothing more until the bell went and he wandered over to the horse with Tolley to leg him up.

'You should back this horse,' he said to Freddie as they arrived at Birkett's viewing point down in the old stand beyond the furlong marker. But Freddie seemed disinclined.

'What is it?' asked Birkett.

'You're all right Birdie, I don't want to spoil your luck. I just hope he's as good as you think.'

'Luck's got nothing to do with it,' he said.

'Birdie,' said Freddie, 'did you see him compared with those other horses in the paddock? He looked miles behind them.'

'I know,' said Birkett, 'great, isn't it?'

Freddie shook his head.

An announcement came from the stands: 'They're going behind.'

'I've got him worked out you know, through Slipshod, you don't have to worry.'

Freddie looked sideways at him again.

'I've worked them against the same horse – not at the same time, I didn't want that Irishman involved fucking it all up. There's only me and the jockey there when I work him. But I've used the same horse, Bugbear, he's a grand old lad, you could set your clock by him, and he's hard to get by. I've told you he can beat Slipshod already. I know things go wrong in horse races, but they won't today, and even if they do, he can't finish outside the three against this lot. He must be the biggest each way certainty that ever put his head through a bridle.'

Freddie broke out his phone from his pocket.

'What's this, you're not telling anyone are you? Give it here,' and he made a snatch for his phone.

'Don't be stupid, I'm having a bet – a cautious one, because I don't know what you know, but just to keep you quiet I'm having a bet.'

'Don't you have to talk to someone?'

'No, these are the Betting Exchanges, you just go online and take the odds. It's like a web site.'

'It looks like the bloody Stock Exchange to me. How do they work? How do you know that your bets been taken?'

'I'll tell you later. You can get a lot of money on at the last minute – and it's all anonymous. No one knows who you are or what you're up to. I prefer it that way.'

'Just one more out of line now,' said the faraway voice. Birkett shrugged, as if to say, 'Each to their own,' but he might have said, 'Good, that's why you're here.' Then he turned and took a few steps towards the large screen facing the stands on the inside of the course.

A horse crossed Milksheikh shortly after they left the stalls and took the rail position from him.

'There's quite a strong cross wind, isn't there?' said Birkett, not taking his eyes from the screen. 'Don't have him stuck out there in it Tolley,' he said out loud, as the eight runners settled down to run two by two. Then as the race developed into its rhythm, he continued talking, hands thrust deep into his pockets, wandering maniacally, looking at the ground more than he did the screen, muttering, 'There's no pace, there's no pace.' Then: 'Get him tucked in, you idiot!' and after that just curses and grunts. He looked at Freddie for a moment, woe stricken, but Freddie refused to hold his gaze and looked back at the screen.

And as they approach the dip, Crosshatch still leads going well, Salty Dog comes under a ride in second and can't stay with him, and the jockey on Milksheikh suddenly starts to get animated too. Crosshatch still leads, and if anything extends his lead now, and it's hard to see where the dangers are coming from. Only Milksheikh stays on, but he's being ridden vigorously to close the gap and Crosshatch still seems to travel well. Milksheikh, is he getting closer? Crosshatch is asked to go and win his race, but suddenly his jockey looks very busy, Milksheikh is relentless in second, the line is coming, Crosshatch with the rail, Milksheikh down the centre, there's nothing in it, here's the line, and it's… Milksheikh who imposes on the line.

Birkett turned to Freddie, grinning ear to ear.

'Could not have been better,' he said. 'Let's go and see the lad.'

'I couldn't pull him up Birdie,' said Tolley, jumping down from Milksheikh and loosening his girths. 'You've upset them in second, they thought theirs was a good thing.' Birkett nodded sagely. 'Where are you going next with him?' asked the jockey.

'We haven't decided yet,' said Birkett.

'Well don't forget me when you make your mind up,' said Tolley, 'thanks for the ride.' He touched the peak of his cap and made for the weighing room.

'I won't. Thanks for that,' Birkett called behind him, unable to take the grin from his normally featureless face.

'Did you back him?' he asked the girl leading up, now walking the horse in circles as he dried off from the soaking she'd just given him.

'I didn't know you fancied him,' she said.

'I didn't. Didn't have a farthing on him myself, but I'll give you your tenner at sixteens if you come round the office at break time tomorrow,' he said. 'I don't want you falling out of love with him.'

A man with a microphone approached and asked whether Birkett would consent to a few questions.

'It won't do you any good,' he told him, 'but if you want.'

'Where's he going next?' asked the young reporter.

'Well, I'd like to keep him sprinting, but the owner usually has strong views about these things, so I'd better not say too much 'til he's had his say,' he replied.

'Is the owner here today?'

'No, he's been unwell.'

'But whatever the choice, you'll be Ascot bound?'

'Oh, that's a bit quick I think,' said Birkett, 'that's his first race for a long time, and he's been a bit fragile. We'll see how long he takes to recover, and then we'll see what weather they're promising us. He'll not be going anywhere on a fast ground.'

'You're thirty-threes for the Wokingham I see. Not tempted?'

'Maybe next year's Wokingham perhaps, and you'd have to be a bit more generous to tempt me. But none of it's up to me. I'll have to speak to the owner.'

The interview wasn't over, but it was brought to an end by Birkett walking away.

'They're your colours, aren't they?' asked Freddie.

'Yes and no,' he replied.

'Yes and no? What's that supposed to mean?'

'It means yes, in the sense that yes they are, and no in the sense that it's no one else's business.'

Freddie laughed, and the old man put his arm around his shoulders as they walked from the course to the car park, 'Have you missed me Ferdy?' he asked. 'Come on back and I'll tell you a story.'

Back at his house, Freddie crept quietly from the office into the living space that contained the kitchen at its far end and saw Birkett filling the kettle at the sink.

It would have been a nice house in other hands; its furniture not so much inherited, as passed down. Structurally it was desirable, essentially built on an early notion of open plan living, but something about its unlived in portions and shabby contents let it down somewhat.

'Will you ever get a shift on and get in here?' he said, looking back over his shoulder.

'How long have you been here? I was only a few cars behind you coming out of the races,' Freddie asked, but he didn't get a response.

'Tea and ginger snaps, do you?'

He had never known Birkett produce anything other than ginger snaps and cornflakes from his own kitchen.

'Come on Birdie, I've just won a few quid, let me take you out to dinner.'

Birkett stopped drying the dishes and turned round to look at him. He seemed to ponder the offer for a long time before finally saying, 'Good idea. Let's get out before they send the shop steward in. This thing'll work better over a plate of chops.'

At the Packhorse Inn, Moulton, two hours later Birkett looked up from his plate of pork belly and mash and groaned. Wearily, fatigued by too much eating and drinking, he raised a finger towards Freddie, took a quick look around for stray ears, then said, 'That horse,' slowly making a gesture towards his nose, to indicate that he didn't intend to mention its name, 'that horse. I trained his mare.'

He was pissed. He probably weighed about nine stones, and one glass of wine could do a quick tour round all his vital organs. Freddie began to form a question but before he'd got a few words into it, Birkett talked over him: 'She was the best race mare I've ever trained.'

'I don't remember her,' said Freddie.

'Air Hostess, she was called, after your time maybe. She was lightning. The best, just the best.' And he made a gesture with his hand that went within a few centimetres of clearing the table of its contents. It was going to be a long night coming.

'What did you do with her?' he asked.

'Nothing,' said Birkett, shaking his head. 'We got her up to about a ninety odd rating, but we didn't get her anywhere near where she should have been. Never won a big prize.'

'What went wrong?' asked Freddie.

'She was a difficult ride, you know fillies, you've got to treat them just right. But her, she was different again. When you rode her, you had to kid her on that she wasn't in a race. We used to take her to the races all the time, you know, when she wasn't running, then brought her back on the lorry, just try and get her to think that she didn't always have to race when she got there, kidology, you know… Then in the race, you'd do the exact same thing, tell her she wasn't racing, and that it didn't matter – get her switched off cold at the back, and then you had to hold on to her, and hold on to her, and sometimes you'd be giving them ten, fifteen lengths start between the two and the one, and all the time you'd feel this big engine roaring underneath you, then, when all was lost, you'd let her go, bang!' He brought his hand down on the table and made everything on it jump. Heads turned in their direction and Birkett bowed his in case any of them knew him.

'Sorry,' he said more softly still than he had been talking, then continued, 'And you got one run out of her. Devastating, but one run. Oh my God, that run. It made the hairs stand up on the back of your neck. It was unbelievable. It was Group I class. She was the best I've ever sat on.'

'Was she sold on?'

'Naah. No one knew how good she was. That was her undoing. We couldn't trust an ordinary jockey on her, only brilliant men were good enough to ride her. We took her to Goodwood to win a handicap; I fought with myself for weeks whether we should just go straight for the Group III, but in the end, I thought the big field in the handicap would get her the strong pace we needed. God, I wished we'd had gone the other way. Anyway, we had her in the handicap, and she was a good thing. A proper good thing. And we put that little prick up on her – him who's gone to Hong Kong now because everybody rumbled him in the end. We were one of the first, and everyone thought it was sour grapes when I started telling everyone about him – but they knew I was right in the end. Well, we had the crown jewels on her that day, and the bastard stiffed her. He over revved her, drove her into the race, stopped her, started again, and when she came back in, she was bleeding from her mouth. She never put a foot forward from that day. Didn't want to know.'

'Aw Birdie, stories like that make me hate racing.'

'Me too Ferdy. Me too.' He put his cutlery down, shoved his food to one side and took a long moment to consider his thoughts before he came back into the room. 'So that's why I bought him when he came up as a yearling. Her first foal.'

'Who?'

'Him,' he said, looking around the restaurant for eavesdroppers, 'today. Him. He's her first foal, I thought to myself no one else knows what I know, so I grabbed him. Very fair price actually.'

'It's one way of getting back what you deserve,' said Freddie.

'It's a start I suppose,' he said and fell into silent thoughts again about times gone by and missed opportunities.

Freddie continued to eat quietly, thinking to himself that the evening was lost now. He had so many questions he wanted to ask. Birkett was only telling him half the story, he was certain of that, and this had looked like the perfect opportunity to probe and get to the bottom of it, softened up by alcohol, tired from a long day, rarely relaxed and happy by having a plan and a horse go right for once. But just as soon as he'd started, he'd gone over the top into maudlin reminiscences.

Suddenly Birkett snapped out of his reverie and said louder than he meant to, 'How much did you win today?'

'Er, enough to take you out for dinner. Why? How much did you win?'

'For Christ's sake Ferdy, I tried to tell you. I won twenty large. That's my stake.'

'What?'

'I'm having it on him in Hunt Cup. Well, you are – on your stock exchange thing or whatever you do.'

Ah, so that was what it was. Was it? 'Are you nuts?'

'It has been said,' said Birkett, 'but this thing has been planned for a very long time Freddie. And you my friend are a very lucky man, because out of nowhere, you've landed yourself right in the middle of it. Thanks to your pocket computer and whatever ill wind blew you here.'

'I don't know, I've got to sleep on it,' said Freddie.

'What? You know that you can't bet cash anymore? They ring the fucking Samaritans if you have more than fifty quid each way in a betting shop. I don't know how the new world works – you do. Take care of all that for me. You can work for me while we organise it – no wages mind – you'll make enough out of what we're doing.'

'I need more than a winning bet Birdie.'

'Do you? Why? Who else is hiring?' He shook his head at his poor deluded friend, then just as a question began to form on Freddie's lips, he continued, 'He's too good to fuck around with Freddie. We aim him at the Hunt Cup, then I've got to get on with him, and prove that he's a proper Group I horse – a champion,' he whispered the last two words. 'I'll swerve Newmarket and Goodwood, and I'll give him an autumn campaign, then win that race with him on Champions Day back at Ascot in October.'

Freddie smiled at the old man. Why hadn't he just stayed on as his assistant?

'What,' said Birkett, 'don't you like the idea of a million quid? Who else is going to give you that in the next six weeks?'

'A million?'

'Twenty grand at fifties. One million quid. Each.'

Put like that… and one million was three hundred more than he owed his ex-clients. He wasn't so strapped yet that he couldn't dredge up a stake for the bet, albeit that it meant borrowing money from the settlement – what the lawyers would say was not strictly his to borrow. And he couldn't afford to eat if the bet went wrong. But other than that, he was right, who else was offering a gateway to a million right now?

'We'll get out my good whiskey tonight and explore all the details if you like. Then you can think about it while you're having a sleep – though how anyone manages to do that is beyond me,' said Birkett.

'OK,' said Freddie, 'and then perhaps you'll tell me what you're really up to.'

Birkett looked at him coyly, then said, 'Come on, I'll get this, and let's away.'

A long night followed. But it was one in which Birkett did the listening, not the talking.

SIX

In racing stables like Birkett's, you'd normally notice a change in mood on the day after a winner. Nothing about the routine would alter, but you'd detect a certain lightness pervading the air – the collective satisfaction of a mission accomplished and rewards well earned. Not that Birkett would ever broadcast the fact that he'd plotted up a race and the horse was off for its life, carrying his money, but there would be something known and shared, something decipherable about its preparation, something recognisable about the trainer's *MO*. But that hadn't been the case with Milksheikh this time.

Freddie came slowly from the house, having woken up a moment earlier. He joined Birkett as he watched his first lot horses circle, hands behind his back, rocking against the kerb of the fountain, his loose-fitting jodhpurs doing nothing to disguise his wiry frame underneath. Freddie's arrival seemed to make the collective mood a degree sullener as the riders sniffed out a conspiracy from which they'd been excluded.

'There's a man who's done a lot of thinking by the look of him,' he said as Freddie joined him in the centre of the circle. 'There's a horse ready for you, aren't you going to get changed?' he asked, laughing.

'No, please, no movement, no nothing for a moment Birdie,' he said.

'You're going to have to keep better hours than this once you're working,' Birkett said, and turned his attention back to the circling horses.

Liam Williamson, the head lad, arrived on the last horse to join the lot. Most mornings he was the first person to join the lot, and he'd often pull out as the stragglers arrived, before they'd had any chance to hear the instructions. Today he was last.

'Good result yesterday boss,' said Liam through his smile.

'I don't know about that,' said Birkett, and offered no more explanation than that.

As Liam came round to pass in front of Birkett again, he added, 'I didn't think we had him that fit.'

Birkett let the comment go, saying nothing until Liam came by him the next time, then answered, 'He wasn't. The rest just stopped, and he was last man standing. That little prick didn't have the sense to bury him.'

Nothing further was said until Birkett gave his orders, sending them up and away for a long slow canter over Side Hill, and a long walk back.

As the last of them turned and disappeared out of the yard Birkett winked at Freddie and said, 'We'd better get a look at him I suppose.' He shouted for the yardman Davey Flint to put a head collar on Milksheikh and bring him out to be looked over.

They kicked around for a moment while Davey prepared the horse. Milksheikh's box didn't look into the yard like the rest. His was landlocked, requiring the removal of one of his two neighbours from their boxes first to allow him out, and looked out over Birkett's garden alone.

Davey brought the horse out to where they stood, then as he came to a halt, went to stand facing Milksheikh head on to give the initiative to his boss. Birkett bent down to feel his ice-cold legs and said to no one in particular, 'The damage these fucking jockeys do when we're trying to be patient with these horses.'

'Is he oh-right?' asked Davey.

'He was going to be my Cambridgeshire horse,' Birkett said, still crouched examining the horse's legs and feet. If that wasn't an answer to Davey's question, it's all he was getting.

Birkett continued speaking to the air 'Now the world's seen him I'm going to have to do something else with him.'

He asked Davey to walk the horse for them to see how he was moving, then trot him. Everything confirmed what he'd hoped to see, that the race had done him no harm whatsoever.

'Go and give him a pick of grass and send Alison in to see me about him when she's on her break,' he told the yard man.

'But Mr Birkett, I'll be behind...'

'Never mind that,' Birkett said, 'you work for me, not Liam. Send him to see me if there's anything he doesn't like.'

He turned to Freddie and gestured silently with his head to follow him to the opposite end of the yard.

'If you ever want to get the word out quietly in here, tell him a secret,' he said nodding back with his head in the direction Davey had disappeared.

'Did I agree then?' asked Freddie.

'I thought you had nowhere to live?' said Birkett.

'I need a place to lie low. How come you're so chirpy anyway?'

'I'm healthier than you. It'll do you good to work here. Come and have a look at the horses.'

With a quick sideways movement of his eyes, Birkett sent Freddie's attention over towards Davey who was meandering around the yard with the horse, one moment heading back towards Milksheikh's box, the next changing his mind and heading towards the paddock.

He shook his head in resigned amusement then took Freddie to the farthest corner of the yard, where box by box, he gave him a quick pen picture of its occupant.

'I'll take you through the first lot horses when they've gone out on second, and we'll give him a hand while we're doing it,' he said pointing with his thumb behind him. 'I thought you said that you were having your house taken off you?'

'Did I tell you that? I'm supposed to meet Penny next week at Saint Cloud, at the breeze-ups to sort it all out.'

'You said that's when you're going to go and see about the mare.'

'Er yeah. God, you do remember more than me; did I agree to that?

'Well, it's not far out of your way, you might as well go and have a look to see if she's got another Milksheikh.'

'I did say that, didn't I?'

'You were speaking Ferdy,' he said, 'quite a lot.'

'Sorry.'

'No, I enjoyed listening. You've been in the wars lad.'

They went on to the next horse, talked about it for a moment, then reverted to the story of Freddie's woes, criss-crossing subjects in this way as they made their way round the yard.

Out of the corner of his eye Freddie noticed that Davey had let Milksheikh off his lead reign, closed the paddock gate and was skuttling off towards his tack room.

'So, is it one of your horses that's selling at Saint Cloud?' said Birkett.

'No. It was. The bloke that Penny's with now bought it off me for nothing at the yearling sales last year. He's selling it through the breeze-ups now to get his cash back. I think it was only an act of charity him buying it in the first place, or some sort of gesture to Penny, not to see her assets whittled away to nothing.'

'You'll get nothing for it then?'

'Me? No, I've had my pittance from it already. He was the one who told me.'

'What?'

'I thought I bored you to death with all my problems last night – that all the horses I bought were crocks.'

'You never really got round to explaining it properly.'

'Too angry, was I?'

'You might say that.'

'Sorry Birdie. You'll know not to open your best malt next time. No, what it was, I was buying for clients. Wealthy, scary clients, who... look, they wanted their money cleaning up. I was just glad of a bit of professional help in a tough market, and there he was. At first, he just ran the horses up, had some other schmuck pay too much for them, and had an arrangement with their agent to split the difference.'

'We've all been on the end of that deal son. I don't know how they have the brass neck to keep on doing it.'

Birkett looked over towards Davey and as soon as Davey returned a furtive glance, Birkett gestured silently with his hand, pointing in direction of the paddock, ordering him to return to look after Milksheikh.

Freddie picked up the conversation again. 'But I was happy enough I suppose, we turned a nice little profit on the trade that first year when we were finding out. Then we went in heavily the next. Have I already told you this?'

Birkett shook his head.

'Well, that time it turned out that the horses I was buying had a hole in them or had some other issue – they were other people's write-offs that they'd got hold of for nothing. Good pedigrees and not bad looking. You've got to hand it to them really, they were very professional about it. Then, just before they went through the ring, where they were about to be sold for nothing, I got put to the wise, and poof! There was no one there. There was just me, sat on my thumb.'

'Jesus son. Is he the one that put your partner in hospital?'

'No, that was my clients.'

'What?'

'A message to say that we'd messed up and owed them money. I guess they just needed to take one of us out. It could have been me.'

'What have you got yourself into Ferdy?'

Freddie had taken a turn, head down. It was like admitting an act of stupidity that somehow you had not acknowledged until you heard the words spoken out loud to someone else.

'You said you've paid them off now though, didn't you?'

Freddie, still head down, nodded. 'I paid them everything we had so that I didn't end up like Felix. But it still fell a bit short.'

'How much?'

Freddie slowly raised his head, and looked sheepishly into Birkett's eyes. 'Seven hundred.'

'Thousand?'

He nodded.

'So, you are absolutely skint then?'

'Yeah. And some. Because when I've found their money, I've got to settle with Penny. I mean, her claim came first, but you know, she's not a former KGB agent with access to weaponised anthrax or whatever it is.'

Birkett was lost for words.

'I've got left what I used to think of as petty cash – what I escaped the country with.'

'What took you so long to decide to come into the deal then?' Birkett asked.

'I don't know – I keep second guessing myself. And because there's something about this deal that I don't get, and you haven't told me.'

Birkett smiled and shook his head slowly. 'You've forgotten how to trust folk, lad,' he said, then made a gesture to stop talking as he noticed Davey on his way back.

He arrived holding Milksheikh on his lead reign. 'Please Mr Birkett,' he said, 'I'll have to put him in now, I'm a long way behind myself.'

Freddie looked at the horse and imagined him to be smiling conspiratorially as if they were sharing the same observation about the man who stood at his side. Freddie stepped forward to rub his muzzle and share a moment with him.

'Don't panic boy,' said Birkett, 'come and get this lad out for us. I want to show him properly to Freddie.'

'But Mr Birkett, sir...'

'We'll help get things organised. Freddie's dying to get stuck in, aren't you?'

'Can't wait,' said Freddie.

Davey dutifully returned Milksheikh home and rushed back to get the new horse out to be inspected.

'This is Bugbear,' said Birkett as Davey came out of the box with him, 'smasher, isn't he? Walk him away for us Davey lad.'

'What is he?' asked Freddie.

'I suppose you'd say he was a ten-furlong handicapper,' said Birkett, 'but I'm going to run him over jumps this summer.'

'He's big enough,' said Freddie.

'He's been the making of Slipshod and the other horse,' he said, almost under his breath. 'What we would have done without him, I don't know. It's a shame really because it's cost him his own races.'

Davey stopped in front of them so that they could inspect the horse more closely, anxious to get on with his jobs, but ears alert for useful information.

'Keep walking him 'til I tell you to stop,' said Birkett, before turning conspiratorially towards Freddie and continuing, 'But I've got something lined up for him. Have you heard of the Monkey Puzzle Selling Handicap?'

'No.'

'They run it at Sedgefield in the middle of August at their first meeting of the season,' he said. 'It's got to be the worst race in the calendar. It is. It's terrible. You could ride him, and still win.'

'Thank you. You do remember that I pulled off some gambles for you too, don't you? Aren't you scared of losing him in a seller?'

'We'll buy him back out of what we've won. Whatever it takes, even if it turns it into a loss. He's too valuable to me. But I want to give him his day in the sun, and maybe see how far he's capable of going over hurdles this winter once he gets that win under his belt. What a job that'll be. He's hardly ever been on a racecourse; everyone will think that he's always injured.'

He lowered his voice again as he noticed Davey coming back towards him.

'Come on now Davey get him away; they'll be back in a minute.'

'I'll put him straight on the walker Mr Birkett sir,' he said, and led the horse away.

'Do you think he heard what I said?' Birkett asked Freddie, 'I'm going to have to be careful now you're back, I'm used to keeping it all in my head.'

Freddie smiled to himself. It was a long time since he'd attended a morning meeting with someone so smart. He sucked deeply on the fresh morning air and thought of his millionaire ex-colleagues, still not yet on their way to work.

SEVEN

Friday morning came and here he was, on that familiar journey, heading westward on a never-ending piece of straight road in the early hours of what still felt like last night. The journey of a thousand miles he'd made so often with Penny on shopping trips, out to catch the ferry at Caen, or sometimes to the races at Saint-Malo. In his memory, even back then it always had a little air of melancholy about it: the empty N175 delivering you into dead and dying villages one after the other; all of them pretty in parts but somehow imparting something sinister in their sombre desolation. Here an abandoned Cidrerie, there the crumbling edifice of a farmers' cooperative, all reminders that throughout the region the agri-economy had either got big or disappeared. He climbed up and out of Troarn, and ever onwards, and noticed that sign again which indicated an enormous number of kilometres still remaining to Caen, and so yet more to Saint Lô. This was always the point where they started to feel the grind of the excursion.

He should have been on his way to Paris, but here he was, heading in the opposite direction, 'just dropping in while he was there', as Birkett had put it, to check out on Air Hostess, and have a sniff about. As he left, Birkett had changed tack slightly from, 'See if she's got a nice yearling,' to, 'See if they'll sell her cheaply, I'd love to have her back,' adding for clarification that if her owner's assessment of their horse was anything under a hundred, Freddie should allude to being able to get them twenty-k more than their highest expectation. But he was to make it clear that they wouldn't be getting paid until after Royal Ascot, 'You know, it'd be a lovely present to myself out of the winnings,' he'd said.

When Freddie had asked, 'What if there are no winnings?' Birkett had replied, 'We'll cancel the deal. She stays where she is, no harm done.'

He went back to the radio for company. She always said that he locked on to the radio the moment he turned on the ignition. How many journeys like this were passed with scarcely a conversation? Too many.

'At least here you get *Nostalgie*,' he would say to her, 'instead of the never-ending sameness of Radio 4.' It was so well named, *Nostalgie*. It felt as if they had no more than about twenty or thirty records which they played on a loop; each one for them marked with a time and a place that they would always associate with it. 'Just a minute, wait for the chorus. What's this one called?' Then singing the few words that he could pick out, 'Listen... Moi je suis une marionette... that's it isn't it?' That was a Banneville-la-Campagne song, just by the water tower.

'Construis,' she said, 'Moi je construis les marionettes,'

'Oh yeah, he's making puppets out of paper and string, isn't he?'

'Enough listening to Les Années Yeah, already,' she'd said that day. They both spoke good French, but hers was as a native.

'Just one more,' he'd pleaded, 'it's Joe Dassin, don't you love him? It reminds me of hot summer days, corn fields full of poppies, miles of straight empty roads leading to the South of France.'

'You just like living in Martini adverts,' she'd said.

'And what's wrong with that?' he'd replied. 'That's the image of France I really love. Do you remember when you used to come here when you were young and there was that smell in the streets: a mixture of petrol and coffee and cigarettes – all of it so different from England? It felt so far away from home then, didn't it? All exotic and new. What did you call it, Les Années What?'

'Les Années Yeah, means *The Sixties*, you seem to be obsessed with the Seventies now old boy,' and she'd giggled. 'The Seventies doesn't have a name.'

'Oh yeah, but remember those times? Levi's, cowboy boots, cheese cloth shirts, open topped sports cars, eternal summers, cafés...'

'For goodness' sake shut up will you, you really are starting to sound like a Martini advert now. In fact, it's worse, you are *golden-aging*, it was probably just as bad here as it was in England. And concentrate on your driving by the way.' That was as much conversation as they shared, her calling out from the back seat where she felt safer. Perhaps the silences were her doing? Part of the road safety protocols.

As Troarn lay forgotten behind him and nothing new arrived to take its place, he stared distractedly across the bare hard-worked landscape, increasingly desperate to catch a glimpse of sea in the far distance to break the monotony, until finally he left the never-ending road to turn into deeper countryside towards Saint-Lô.

He imagined a lone sniper in a disused barn picking him off as he drove by, no one any the wiser. And with that his thoughts switched back to Felix again. God! He'd known Felix longer than he'd known Penny. They'd first met in the department that ran the French energy company, until it was broken up and sold off. Then because of the languages they shared, French, English, Russian, plus Spanish in Felix's case, Italian in Freddie's', they'd been put in charge of the new department that 'brought on' fledgling international clients – the up and comers with awkward demands and unreliable back-stories, the ones nobody else wanted, and where by degrees they became the bank's money laundering department. Jesus, what sort of idiot would demand seven hundred grand from you, then take out your partner? Unhinged lunatics, that's who.

His father had always counselled him never to fear a bully because they could always be beaten by brains, but this lot, they were a breed apart. They saw the world in a different way. It was the first time he'd broken cover, and suddenly aware of it again, he spent the next thirty kilometres constantly looking for suspicious cars in his rear-view mirror and feeling anxious at every traffic light.

The radio went back on. It was always a better journey when you did it with someone. He'd see Penny in a couple of days. An off the record meeting in a neutral place. No lawyers. If the worst happened, what was he to do? To hand over the keys to the house and ask her to give him about ten percent back when it was finally sold? That was about as flexible as his negotiating position was now. There was no cash left. He'd already ransacked every account they held to mine sweep all the small deposits, and that, about fifty-k, would be his living fund until things changed. Besides that, there were some odd bits and pieces that were difficult or unpalatably complicated to liquidate. Some were held in his name, some jointly. Some wine, the price of which collapsed about one month after he'd bought it. That had been his personal stake in a larger money laundering play too. Some low value art with a resale value approaching zero. That was about it. Yet the only justification for the delay he could muster was to say how time consuming it was to sell these illiquid items. The house represented what was left of their fortune, and whereas Penny thought that it was theirs fifty-fifty, the reality was that it was almost entirely hers, and represented the only means by which she could recoup her part of their lost fortune. And here, in France, they didn't sell like they did in England, particularly those that displayed ostentation. People in France tended to be more discreet about announcing their fortunes than they were in England. It might be on the market for three or four years.

On he drove, switching the radio on and off, as it variously reminded him too poignantly of all that was gone, or served to distract him from unwanted reminiscences.

EIGHT

Sticking out from his buttoned-up body-warmer, Robert Hamley-Flower's florid face wore an ear-to-ear grin as he stood waiting for Freddie. He had been alerted to his arrival about half a mile earlier when Freddie's car skirted the back of the house as it first turned into the long lane.

'That's it, that's it; bring her in here, straight up to me. Perfect. That's grand,' said Robert guiding the car into place. 'Come on in, come on in. It's fresh this morning, isn't it?' He smiled, almost laughed as he talked, not so much because he was amused by anything, but because his great joy and enthusiasm for life could not be kept from constantly bubbling up to the surface.

Freddie was ushered in across the gravel to what looked like the good end of an ancient building, going from the yard straight into the stone flagged kitchen where the raised fire was burning fiercely, and the table already set for a country feast.

'Jules is upstairs, she'll be down now. Now sit down and tell me all about Newmarket.'

There wasn't an awful lot to tell, Freddie lived up the road.

'Well, why had they never met,' asked Robert?

Freddie thought he recognised Robert from the sales. Robert definitely hadn't seen Freddie before. He'd have remembered. Thinks he can remember his name from when he was an amateur jockey though. He was one himself, but he was point to points and that side of life. Very amateur he said, not like you flat boys with your Epsom and your champagne.

Whereas Robert was a well-worn forty-nine, Jules was an extremely well preserved forty-five. She spoke with the merest hint of a lisp and had the manners of someone who'd received an expensive education. She greeted Freddie with one firm kiss on the cheek, which he found strangely intimate after the cheeks-brushed-together style of greetings favoured by the French. To Freddie's keen eye she was very attractive but certain aspects of her appearance put her in a different generation to his. Chief among these was her smell, rich and spicy, but one he associated more with an elderly relative than he did with the girls he knew. And she had one particular feature that was all her own, it was neither attractive nor unattractive: she was *flat*, very thin sure, but there was something wide about her frame, which meant that her slimness only worked in one dimension. Freddie felt that he had been caught staring at her when he heard Robert summon him outside again.

'We'll eat shortly, come and have a quick tour of the yard first,' he'd been saying, and he stood now, beckoning him out again towards the door to the yard.

A series of stone-built barns stretched from the main house making something of a courtyard, revealing that the property was, and would always be, a charming, ramshackle, Normandy dairy farm. His were not the classic style of horse boxes preferred by equestrians the world over, and the Normandy studs in particular; his were better looked at as adapted cow sheds.

Inside each of them he had taken away the wooden dividers of the original cattle stalls and replaced them, for the most part, with four-foot-high breeze block walls that he'd built himself. Where he hadn't done that, he'd used what was essentially post and rail fencing to separate the animals from each other. Some of the barns looked like work in progress, others like they'd undergone temporary enhancements for some particular purpose or other and had just stayed like that.

'Let's start with the star of the show,' he said, swinging open the large doors of the small barn facing the house. It was only about six metres deep and contained about five stalls, all but one of which was empty; and that occupied stall had been roughly adapted to enlarge it into a foaling box. In the corner, facing the wall stood the saddest looking specimen of horse flesh that Freddie had ever seen; her poor foal lying away from her in the straw neglected through sheer want of energy to do anything better. She hung her head as if she had given up on life and the skin hung from her bones like the rest of her body was not far behind in giving up too. A sorry sight if ever there was one. Robert simply beamed and said, 'May I introduce you to Miss Standard.'

Freddie was lost for words and in the intervening silence Robert added, 'She's a little tired after her last foal, the poor love,' then moving towards the mare herself he continued, 'Aren't you my babby? Just worn out, aren't you? We'll make you better won't we my babby?'

Then he turned back to his guest as if he had not witnessed this moment with his prize broodmare and picked up the conversation again.

'Everything she has produced has won, every son, every daughter all won.'

'How many foals has she had Robert?' asked Freddie.

'That's her seventh she's just dropped, by Steamship he is, no yearling, she didn't take last year, there's a two-year-old not raced yet and five on the racecourse. All won. All of them. *Evening Standard,* that's one of hers you know, he's running in the French Champion Hurdle that boy, Group III placed. And that two-year-old, he'll be a bloody champion that boy, bloody little champion, by Fastenuf. We got ninety thousand for him last year you know'

'Congratulations,' said Freddie. Perhaps he'd been a little hasty in his judgement after all.

'Ninety grand,' he said and started laughing. 'Fantastic mare she is. Fantastic.'

He declared the last *fantastic* with great relish, pronouncing every letter and spitting it out at the earth as if he was trying to convince someone, somewhere far away, of a truth that was only yet evident to him.

'Now, come with me next door, I'll show you the coming star of the show.'

They closed the doors behind them and went out round the back of the largest barn whose entrance did not face into the courtyard. This was the worst of the lot in many ways; it was made of the same hotch-potch collection of cattle stalls, but this one was to all intents and purposes open on one side. In other parts of the world, they would have called it a Dutch barn. It contained two mares with foals, and two solitary horses. Robert took him straight to one of the mares.

'This is her, Alpine Sunrise,' he said, and he pulled on her head collar to straighten her up so that Freddie could get a better view of her. This time he revealed a much better-looking horse; she was fleshy and healthy.

'Nice, isn't she?' he prompted his visitor, who felt forced to agree. 'Rated in the nineties on the flat.'

Freddie thought he was going to be introduced to Air Hostess. That was a good sign. 'Was she yours when she raced Robert?' he asked.

'No, no, no, God no,' he said and laughed. 'She came from the Newmarket breeding stock.'

'Do you mind if I ask what you gave for her?'

'Are you ready?' He waited for him to nod his consent. 'Two hundred grand. To be fair, only half of her is mine. I bought her fifty-fifty with Alan Halliday have you met him?

'Just the once, I think,' said Freddie.

'Alan? Where've you been? Are you sure you're in the same game as me?'

'Was,' said Freddie. Robert looked at him as if to double take. It meant, 'What are you doing here then?' He wondered whether he should qualify the statement – say something about preferring to concentrate on the racing side? Describe himself as an assistant trainer perhaps? 'Er…'

'Alan and his schemes,' said Robert. 'You've missed an experience there all right. Are you sure you don't know him? He's got his fingers into nearly everything.' He gestured with his thumb back towards the house.

'Does he have a stud over here too?' he asked.

'Stud? Alan? You're bloody joking, you're standing in it. This is *our stud in Normandy* or whatever he says on his website. Not that he's here when there's any work to be done. I think he's got me down as the manager of his stud. Me working for him! Here! I'll tell you what, I haven't seen many salary cheques while I've been working for him. Come on in to lunch I'll tell you some more stories about him.'

'Can I take a quick look at Air Hostess first?' he asked, 'Would you mind?'

'No, sorry, that's why you're here, isn't it? Sorry I was doing the usual tour. On auto pilot. A lot of people have been around here lately trying to buy off me directly instead of waiting for the sales. Been fighting them off we have.'

'Oh…?'

But Robert didn't pick up the cue. They walked across the courtyard to the barn closest to the house. He slid back the enormous doors and the sight struck Freddie as one of those scenes you see on the News when a wagon load of refugees is suddenly flooded in sunlight as their hiding place is revealed.

'Don't you turn them out?' he asked.

'Yes, they'll get a couple of hours, but these poor loves are all recovering from giving birth. We're just letting you recover nice and slowly aren't we ladies? All late foalers these girls, like Miss Standard,' he said.

'They all missed on the first two goes, and it's too late to cover them again for next year now. Expensive business keeping mares that don't have foals you know Freddie.'

Freddie nodded. He imagined it was.

'Have a look at her first,' said Robert, pointing to one of the mares, as he tried to manoeuvre through the stalls to locate Air Hostess. 'That's the mare with the three-year-old running in the Group III today, but before then – you will be staying to watch the race with us, won't you? – I'll tell you a story about her; she's a very good Alan Halliday story in her own right. Here she is, and that's her little chap. You've got the first son, haven't you?'

'Birkett has,' said Freddie, trying to downplay the link. 'She used to belong to one of his owners.'

'Did she?' said Robert, 'I bought her at the sales here, but it was from an English stud, I think. I'll have to check.'

'You might,' said Freddie. 'The original owner died, that was why she was let go. We think she's been through a couple of hands since.'

'That makes sense,' said Robert. 'She slipped in her second year, I guess they thought that they'd struggle to get her in foal. But we managed didn't we my babby? She gets in foal here all right.'

'But?' asked Freddie.

'No nothing like that. She's a corker, look at her. I mean, we don't know how good she is because she's hardly had a runner. Could be anything. Her yearling's out in the field and he's a little cracker.' But all the yearlings Robert owned were little crackers, and all the mares were unsurpassed in their beauty, even if they did look half dead in their desperate cattle stalls.

'Right, that's all, you've seen her now come on in.' Freddie nodded his thanks and followed Robert into the house.

NINE

There was something essentially English about the table set by Jules. It was that form of lunch so often given by English people that perfectly combines the best of a picnic and a buffet whilst taking full advantage of being indoors close to cooking facilities. There was a small ham which was served cold and a joint of beef already sliced and still steaming hot, there were large langoustines arranged in a Catherine Wheel around a garlic mayonnaise dip, a few plates of charcuterie, about three large bowls of salad, two made of leaves, one of rice, corn, and tuna; there were mustards, relishes, more mayonnaise and dips and there were baskets of chopped French bread wherever there was a space.

'This looks fabulous Jules,' said Freddie. 'I can't remember the last time I sat down to a table like this.' He noticed her glance at the wedding ring he still wore.

'Doesn't your wife like to cook?' she asked.

'Maybe for her new boyfriend,' he replied, and was struck by the thought that it sounded more callous than he'd intended, 'and only if he's taught her. She's more of a lady who lunches, than cooks.' Jules laughed, 'I'm sorry, I didn't mean…'

'Was it recent?' asked Robert.

Freddie nodded. 'I'm still not really used to it,' he said, holding up his wedding ring finger.

'You should have made friends with us,' said Robert. 'I can't believe you've only been living up the road all this time, and we've been down here. Honestly Jules, what a waste that's been. Sit down, sit down, start eating. You're at home now Freddie, just enjoy yourself with us.'

'An angel's passed,' said Jules to reference the sudden moment of total silence. The three of them had been heads down into their food, gorging and chomping since Robert set them at it. Freddie suddenly felt self-aware, as if he'd eaten as much as he could, as fast as he could, without showing the least courtesy to his hosts.

'Are you ready for a nice red?' asked Robert.

'A nice red? But this is…'

'Just you wait and see,' said Robert getting up from the table, tossing his napkin down onto his chair as he left.

He came back shortly afterwards brandishing a Chateau Petrus 1979, taking it straight to Freddie to show him the label. 'Have you been putting a cellar together Robert?' he said.

'Always had a cellar Freddie, always. We were in the hotel game before this you know.'

'Oh really,' said Freddie.

'This particular bottle was a gift from Bobby Danson, you know, the brewer. Fabulous man, fabulous. Wasn't he Jules? Lovely, lovely, man.'

'It's a nice gift,' said Freddie.

'Yes. This was probably the first gift he gave me like this. He gave us this when we bought the Pheasant from him in Gloucestershire, they were selling their little hotels at the time, and we were buying. Then we just became really firm friends more than business associates.'

'It was horse racing again, be honest, Robert,' Jules interjected.

'That's right. You see, that was when I was riding as an amateur and he was a big owner on the point-to-point scene. I didn't ride for him much; I did occasionally, but I looked after horses for him, sold good ones on to him, rode a lot of work for him. Great days,' he said and looked wistfully out of the window across the meadows.

'They were great days,' said Jules, 'and most of the work was done indoors,' she added and laughed.

'What made you change?' asked Freddie.

'The interest rate ruined us,' said Robert as if he were well practised with the question. 'We were going along quite nicely running about five hotels, small mind you, we owned four of them and rented the other, then the interest rate went to about fifteen percent do you remember it?'

'It was a while ago now,' said Jules as if she had been through the story before too.

'I know of it,' said Freddie, 'it seems ridiculous to think of that now. Do you think you would have ended up in France whatever happened?'

Jules was about to say "no" but was beaten to it by Robert who gave a very positive yes.

'I always wanted to go into breeding, and I don't think we could have set this up in England.'

'If we'd hung onto the hotels a bit longer perhaps,' said Jules.

'There's eighty acres here you know. Eighty.'

Freddie observed Jules as she held herself back from speaking again but this time it seemed to take a real effort, as if she'd trained hard to attain this level of restraint.

'Imagine that, where we were living in England; in that little triangle of countryside, the Cotswolds between Oxford and Cheltenham, you know it? Well, what are land prices there? They're not five thousand Euro a hectare, I'll tell you that.'

Jules tried to shoot a look to Robert but he didn't see it and so she made her point by clearing some of the things from the table.

'There'll be no new cutlery so hang on to what you've got,' she said as she got up from the table, trying to put a full stop to Robert's decline into melancholy.

For a while only the clink of cutlery on crockery could be heard until eventually Jules called over from the sink, 'Keep going back again until you've had enough, whatever's left will be thrown away.'

It felt like the right time to change the subject. 'So, Robert,' Freddie began, 'I hate to bring up business, but...'

'Oh yes, I promised to tell you about Alan Halliday, didn't I?

'Well, it was more...'

Jules shouted something else from the sink, which Freddie didn't catch. Perhaps they'd developed a code to try and control Robert's indiscretions. 'What?' he asked.

Freddie was unsure whether the question was directed at him, or Jules. 'Sorry Robert, do go on,' he said.

'Yes, well, where should I start? Oh yeah, the mare I showed you, Newmarket a few years ago, that's as good a place as any. Alan and I were there looking for broodmares. We'd bought one; that's right, we'd bought Kasbah the Kharefree mare, and we'd paid a lot less than we expected. We didn't really have a budget but we both felt that we could afford to go a bit more. Anyway, there was this lovely mare we'd both seen. Bloody lovely, a Twist mare, carrying a Fernando foal. Well, we'd forgotten about her, hadn't we?'

'Yes, it was on the News,' said Freddie.

'So, we're stood in the ring…' Freddie looked up, wondering whether he was supposed to laugh. 'We just happened to be there; you know – Alan was talking to someone with his back to the ring. And I was watching this mare walking round and the bidding was going up slowly and I'm watching and watching, so in the end I just went and grabbed Alan and said, "Come on are we going to buy this bloody mare or not?" And finally, I got him to wake up and take an interest in what was going on.'

'Go on,' said Freddie.

'Well, we bought her. She was knocked down to us at fifty thousand guineas.'

'Which looks cheap now,' said Freddie anticipating his point.

'Which looks very cheap indeed now. The trouble was, at the end of the sale when it came to doing the business I said to Alan, "Are we going to go halves, or should we each take one of them?" And he said he would prefer to take the Twist mare carrying the Fernando.'

'And were you happy with that?'

'Well, I'd have preferred to have shared both, but to be fair I couldn't really afford the more expensive mare on my own at that moment; I mean I didn't really want to pay that much at the time. So that was it. He owned Fearless, the Twist mare and I owned Kasbah, the other one.' Then he shrugged his shoulders as if the rest of the story was well known to everyone.

'I take it that Alan's mare has done well?' said Freddie, trying to coax him into finishing the story.

'Done well? She's done well alright but that isn't the half it. My mare didn't take that first year and since we've had her she's given us one foal and he didn't sell; he's still out there in the paddock.'

'And Alan's did?'

'Listen to this. That first foal, the Fernando, him running today in the Group III, that colt was born here, I pulled him out, didn't I Jules? Remember that night? That's another story that is; I'll save that for another time. That colt, we took him to Deauville for the August sales two years ago and he fetched a hundred.'

'Twice the price of the mare?'

'Twice the price of the mare, exact, but that wasn't good enough for Alan.'

'No?'

'He was pleased with the price but as soon as we sold the horse Alan took François – you know thingamajig, the trainer who'd bought him, off for a bottle of champagne with the new owners and he kept calling me on the mobile to go and join them. Well, I was really busy with the other horses so I said I'd join them when I could, but he kept ringing me, I couldn't get any peace from him. Anyway, eventually I gave in and went up to have a glass of champagne with them. When I got there, there was none left so I called for another bottle, had a drink with them and buggered off.'

'Yes?'

'Blow me, the next week I received an invoice from him for a bottle of champagne.'

'What? Had you split the money for the colt?'

'Did we buggery, I didn't get a penny, he was the official breeder not me. I got my three percent for presenting him some time later but no, all the money was his.'

'And he invoiced you for a bottle of champagne? Is he really as tight-fisted as that?'

'Yes, he is. He doesn't have the shame gene like the rest of us.'

'Think how close you came to sharing the two mares.'

'It's so typical of Alan that, if there's a fifty-fifty chance he'll come out on the right side, always.'

'At least it puts you on the map as a breeder.'

'No Freddie, no, it does nothing for us, except for us to say that the colt was born here on the farm but it's him who's the official breeder – it's his name in the foals' passports. You own the mare, you're the breeder. That one horse has made Alan Halliday more famous as a breeder than us. He's probably made another twenty odd grand out of his breeders' premiums.' With that recollection, Robert fell once again from garrulous host to silent contemplation.

Freddie was silent for a moment too, not sure whether he should try and take Robert in a new direction or let him work himself out of his current story on his own. Eventually Robert continued, 'He's his own worst enemy, he's too mean to be a proper success.'

'But he seems to be doing OK.'

'Take the mare for example; she's obviously a good mare, isn't she? She gets a good cover, and the foals sell, don't they?'

Freddie nodded.

'So, who does he put her in foal to?'

'Don't tell me he tried to introduce a new species?'

'What?' he shook his head. He wasn't sure whether he just didn't get Freddie's sense of humour, or whether Freddie wasn't really as interested in horses as he made out. 'Some stallion that he won a nomination to in a raffle.'

'A raffle?' said Freddie. 'How do you mean a raffle?' He started to laugh.

'You know these things they have at the Breeders' Society dinners. He would win one, though, wouldn't he?' He laughed himself. 'But he had to put that poor mare to whatever it was he drew, *Pear Tree* I think, instead of keeping that cover for a cheap mare. He can't help it you see; he's always got to be so penny pinching about everything. God if you could only own a mare like that, you'd treat her like gold dust, wouldn't you? And he's going to spoil her. He's even talking about selling her now. That's how short sighted he is.'

Jules was about to pick up the conversation, but Robert wasn't about to give way. 'In fact, he did try to sell her. He did, he tried to sell her at the last sale at Deauville. And guess what? He wanted so much money for her, nobody would give it and we ended up bringing her home again.'

'So, there is some justice after all?' Freddie tried.

'Not at all. Now, with this colt, this one this afternoon, running in Group races with the full season in front of him, he'll sell her next December for more than even he expected. He's chuffed as a pig, the bastard. He's talking about taking her to sell in Newmarket now.'

'Well,' said Freddie, 'at least you're partners with a lucky man. Some of it must rub off. Who is he sending the mare to next?'

Robert picked up the original story as if there hadn't been a break: 'There again, you see, I've told him I'll go halves with him on an expensive cover and share the foal, but he's not bloody interested.'

'And it does feel like you work for him,' added Jules. 'I didn't mind putting lunches on for him and Mrs Halliday, as he calls her,' and she laughed too, 'but he would ring up and say that he was bringing clients down for the weekend and would we be able to do something to make them feel at home,'

'Do you send him an invoice for that?' Freddie asked. Robert and Jules exchanged glances.

'He isn't horrible exactly,' Jules said. 'He wasn't at least. At first, we used to get on famously as a four... it's just that he can't differentiate between friends and business contacts. Once you understand that, I suppose...'

'He's what my dad used to call a *commission agent*,' said Robert. 'He'd do anything and betray anyone for five percent. Did he not seek you out to let him sign for the horses you bought?' Freddie shook his head. 'Look out for him if he does. He says it's just to help him out with his marketing, you know, getting his name out there – and he claims that it'll save the VAT for you, but the main things is, here in France, the auctioneers give back five percent out of the six percent their customers pay, to the agents who act for them. He's made a lot of income that way. He doesn't tell his new clients that though.'

'That's what he used to do,' said Jules, 'he worked in marketing for one of those City firms. He claims he's got a thousand clients.' She and Robert smiled at each other.

'Though to be fair, he got us in with Anglo-French bank in Jersey and we'd be lost without them.'

And so, Freddie came to be regaled by anecdotes about mean-minded, lucky Alan Halliday and what he'd put the Hamley-Flowers through during their time together. Eventually Robert brought it all to a halt by saying, 'Come, come now, enough, this race is off in a moment, let's go through and get ready for it.'

'I'll follow you through,' said Jules. 'Shall I bring coffee?'

There was a general murmured yes as the men got up and made their way to the living room. They went from the rustic but homely and lived-in kitchen, into a hallway that should have been the feature of the ground floor but was instead left largely derelict and in much the same state as they'd found it when Robert and Jules had first moved in. Then they passed through a formal dining room, an oasis of sophistication and quite out of keeping with the rest of the house. It had a solid parquet floor, a polished mahogany dining table, formal sideboards and works of art hanging on the wall. There were cigarette cases, candelabras, dinner services, silver coffee sets, boxes of cigars and a cocktail table containing every conceivable spirit. It was completely incongruous in that tumbled down old farmhouse and looked more like a newly constructed film set than it did part of the house.

They continued through it, up three stone steps and on into the living room, which was more in keeping with the rest of the house. Not quite shabby chic, too shabby for that, but for all that, loved and lived in. Copies of racing and breeding magazines were liberally strewn about the place and as Robert turned on the television, so close were they to Jersey that a UK channel came up first.

'Bloody lifeline that, you know,' said Robert. 'We'd be lost without that and English Racing. Don't know what we'd do without that. Are here we are.' He found the French racing channel.

Jules arrived with the coffees, and as they waited for the race to begin Robert told them again how he had pulled the foal out of the mare. It would have been true to say in the moments before the race began that it was not clear whether Robert wanted the horse to win for the kudos it would bring his farm and the love he had for the horse itself, or whether he wanted it to lose to prevent any more unearned reputation and prize money going in Alan's direction. But all that changed when the gates flew open, and the race started.

After the first six hundred metres of the two thousand metre race, he shouted out, 'Go on my babby,' and tears welled up in his eyes. Then as they came into the long straight, and Her Fearless Boy took up a position amongst the leaders, he shouted out, 'Whip the fucking thing!' at the top of his voice, after which there was silence, until, as they knuckled down to race in earnest with four hundred metres to go, and Her Fearless Boy came clear neck and neck with only two other rivals he was shouting unformed words, jumping up and down on the spot and making whipping movements with his right hand. Her Fearless Boy finally finished a close third and he'd run well. He'd also earned another few thousand Euro for his breeder, lucky Alan Halliday, but none of it was of any consequence to Robert who had completely broken down and was crying freely.

Jules was used to it and ignored him. Freddie was slightly shocked to see such a level of emotion and didn't know what to say. In time Robert dried his eyes and told them both he was OK. He laughed and said he always did that, and they should just ignore him. When he finally felt ready to speak again, he said, 'He's absolutely brilliant isn't he?' But he dried half way through and barely got the words out.

'I hate to do this,' said Freddie, 'but I really should get back on the road.'

'Are you sure?' asked Jules, 'it's not a problem to stay over.'

'Thank you,' he said, 'but I've got a rendezvous at Saint Cloud tomorrow, and I need to be prepared.'

'So have we,' said Robert, back with them now. 'We could have travelled up together. I wish we'd talked properly before you came down. Are you buying or selling?'

'Neither. I'm negotiating, with Penny – my ex. Horse-wise, I'm just going to watch a horse that I used to own get re-sold, and I don't really want to see how that ends up. By the way, you've never heard of a bloodstock agent called Edward Hamilton, have you?'

'No, never heard of him. Another Alan, is he?'

'You might say that,' said Freddie. 'I'll spare you the stories for another day. Er, before I go, I really do have to go back to that other matter, do you mind?'

'No, of course not son, fire away,' said Robert.

'Well, if you'd be prepared to sell, my boss, Birkett Coward, would like to buy the mare. He used to train her. And her foals too, if that's interesting to you.'

Robert creased his face. 'Her yearling's already in the August sale, I'm not sure about that.'

'It's her he's after mainly. He just asked me to mention the idea of a package in case it worked for you.'

He thought he noticed a quick exchange of glances between them again.

'You haven't got the money on you?' asked Robert, then laughed, in case it was taken the wrong way.

'Er no, that's the thing: we'll transfer the funds one month from today's date. What sort of money would make you interested?' It was a funny negotiation, because Freddie knew that Birkett would only go through with it if he pulled off the gamble with Milksheikh. 'You send over the horses, or have us collect them, any date after that.'

'We could bring them when we go to Ascot,' said Jules.

Robert raised his hand ever so slightly, to suppress her instincts. 'Freddie, thank you for your interest. There's nothing in principle to say no to at this stage, but as I said, we do have a lot of people sniffing round the farm at the moment. Would you mind if we slept on it for a night and let you know tomorrow at Saint Cloud?'

'Of course not,' said Freddie.

'Good, good, good. Well, it has been a delight to meet you my friend,' said Robert, slapping Freddie on his back. He then held out both of his hands and said, 'A demain.' He seemed to wait for a response, smiling in readiness. 'A demain,' he repeated, and continued with the double handed handshake.

Jules shook her head. 'It's his joke,' she said, holding out both her own hands, 'A deux mains. You may laugh now.'

Freddie gave Robert the best laugh he could drag up, and squeezed Jules, breathing in her heady aroma for the final time that day, and thanked them both so much for their exquisite hospitality.

'A deux mains,' he shouted from the courtyard, waving both of his hands above his head.

TEN

Saint Cloud racecourse always arrives before you're ready for it, up there in the nice suburbs just as you begin the descent towards Longchamp and the western edges of Paris, where it should be. It's at a healthy distance from all that, something kind of detached about it all. You'd go to the races there and wonder whether you'd got the dates wrong; and when the course hosts the breeze-up sales in the spring, that sense of turning up on the wrong day is stronger still. The horses for sale are behind the scenes in the racecourse stables, where you'll find most of the buyers too, and on the main concourse of the racecourse itself, there is scarcely a soul to be seen. One bar serves the entire crowd and only has a few scattered tables and chairs outside to double its capacity; and where normally there's an empty hall with betting terminals, it is now a sales ring, taken over for the day by auctioneers. No doubt there is always something of a crowd in there, but as you arrive, you see only a few of them as they linger outside its large doors. Besides those few people, it is just the other-worldly muted noise from a distant PA speaker that tells you that an auction was underway somewhere abouts.

Still, Freddie was in no mood for any unplanned meetings. He pulled down his sunglasses and put his stare to the ground until he found a safe place to wait. Pursued and pursuer; as much as he prayed for a fortunate sighting of Hamilton, who wouldn't be expecting him, he feared for being followed by his ex-clients. He'd made a last-minute decision not stay at his own home and had travelled in from a countryside auberge just outside Pont L'Eveque. He was here for what he expected to be just two perfunctory meetings. Robert's, hopefully of no matter at all, just a shake on a price; then Penny: a meeting that really could go either way, but no less short, because there was so little to say.

He was alone, in public, in France. It made him nervous, and in his anxious state, he decided to take himself as far away as possible from everyone and parked himself on one of empty benches on an empty lawn by the racecourse.

She'd been kinder since the news of Felix had broken. She knew he needed time to wind up the company and tie up his affairs, but since communication had resumed it was pretty clear that the amnesty was over.

It was still a while until the planned rendezvous, so once more, sat on his bench, he indulged himself in one more round of back of fag-packet Micawberism:

- Value of house, agreed at not less than three point five million (making her share one point seven five million, or if he preferred not to sell, to arrange a mortgage on the property for the same amount).
- One point four million representing her share of free cash and realisable assets. As yet, still unpaid.
- Her estimated share of illiquid assets, two hundred and fifty-k, in anticipation of a clean break. Otherwise, a re-evaluation would take place, at his cost, likely to be revised upwards.
- Total owed to Penny, not less than three point four million. A sum that was considerably higher than could be raised in a fire-sale of their house.
- Shortfall on client's account, seven hundred-k.
- Stake for bet with Birkett, twenty-k.
- Living expenses until a new source of funds was found: who knows? Twenty-five-k.
- Money pledged to Ced, twenty-k.
- Actual cash money at his disposal fifty-three thousand, five hundred and nine pounds. In total.

On the credit side of the equation, Edward Hamilton was presently holding, give or take, six million that once belonged to him and Felix corporately, and a further one point five million that once belonged to him (and Penny) personally.

A shadow fell across him and he turned to see a large figure, rendered monochrome by the strong sun. It was Jonny. Was that his idea of a joke, or was it a warning? He seemed to be smiling but it was so hard to tell with him.

'Just learning my lines for a new play,' said Freddie, 'how are you?'

'We are very well,' said Jonny, 'hope there's no hard feelings?'

'No hard feelings?' What a ridiculous thing to say, of course there were hard feelings – especially when you say 'we' instead of 'I'.

'No, of course not,' Freddie replied, and started to walk alongside Jonny back towards the stands.

'Penny wondered if you would be ready to meet in an hour from now?'

'Oh, I thought that's where we were going. Sure,' he replied.

'Good, I'll tell her. Back at that bench, OK? It will be quiet.'

'For a while it will be,' he said, as he found himself committed to walking with Jonny, who was presumably on his way back to Penny.

Should I just shake hands and take my leave? Perhaps that would look odd? Like competing lovers in a Jane Austen novel. I take my leave Herr Müller.

They went on a few steps more in silence.

'I didn't know you acted?' said Jonny.

'I'm a dancer. I've just got a few lines to deliver this time. That's all.'

Jonny looked at him for a moment, waiting for a further explanation of the joke, but Freddie gave none. Just a reflection of his insincere smile. He spun on his heal, clicked his fingers, and left Jonny Antoine Müller with a 'Ciao'.

'Oh, by the way, have you seen Edward Hamilton lately?' he called back.

Jonny said he hadn't.

'If you do, call me first. Don't let him know I'm here.'

'But Gordon's here,' he called out after him. 'He's working for Haras de Bonneville.'

Freddie registered the comment without reacting to it and continued on his way to the office with a view to paging Robert, but halfway there, amongst the sparse crowd standing outside the entrance to the lobby and sales ring, he saw him in conversation with a couple of others.

He went straight to them and waited his turn. The group comprised Alan Halliday who seemed to have no interest whatsoever in the conversation, Robert, and a small French man who was talking in a very animated way at great speed. His words were directed at Robert who himself took no real part in the exchange other than to nod occasionally. His greater interest seemed to be in keeping his eye on the crowd as it popped in and out of the sales ring, trying to spot anyone he might know. The little man started to draw to something of a close, pausing every now and then to make a concluding statement which began, 'Eh bien.' Freddie had noticed about three 'Eh biens' already as he shuffled his way forward into their circle. Robert too picked up on the fact that the end was coming, and began to look more earnestly at the man, trying to convey something of his understanding and agreement, which he did in his usual fashion, by using one of the few French words with which he had any real confidence in its meaning and which he often used because it was similar to its English equivalent. The word was 'exact', and he bowed most solemnly as he said it.

The little Frenchman took it as a sign that his point had landed, and offered one more 'Eh bien,' and followed it with a 'On est d'accord,' and nodding first to the tall gentleman, then Freddie, took his leave of the group.

'Trouble?' asked Alan.

'No more than usual,' said Robert. 'They sell a horse; we both get money. What's hard to understand about that?' Alan shrugged, and Robert added, 'It can't work any other way.'

It was enough to indicate to Freddie, in the few snatches he'd overhead, that neither of them had understood a single word the Frenchman had said.

Robert turned to him and put an arm out to embrace him. 'Thank God you turned up. They do like the sound of their own voice this lot, don't they? Now, can you honestly say that you don't know this man?'

Alan and Freddie shook hands. 'Alan Halliday,' he said, 'I don't think we were this formal last time.'

'Freddie Lyons,' replied Freddie.

'So, are you buying or selling?' asked Alan. Freddie glanced briefly at Robert and noticed an almost imperceptible shake of his head as he looked at the ground, then at Alan.

'Neither Alan, I'm here for a meeting with my ex-wife…'

'Ah,' said Alan.

'…who besides meeting me is also selling a horse that I sold to her new boyfriend last year,' added Freddie.

'So, some interest then?' Alan concluded.

'Er… Who knows? She might go a bit easier on me if it sells well.' Neither of them laughed, so he continued, 'But I'll be annoyed if it does, so I'd rather she didn't. I've already banked my losses.'

'Who's consigning the horse?' he asked.

'Jonny, Jam Roly-Poly, Müller, that creep over there with the seventies' haircut,' he said. It was supposed to be funny, but it sounded nastier than he'd intended, and only Robert gave him a conciliatory smile.

As he pointed out Jonny he saw Penny for the first time, laughing in that way she did. It was one of the first properly warm days of the year, but she alone seemed prepared for it. She wore a short starched pink cotton dress, which flared widely at the hem. Her exposed arms, legs and shoulders revealed a deep tan, as if she'd spent the time since she last saw him in the tropical sun. In the not very distant past, he'd have run over and whisked her up into his arms to make her giggle as he flung her up into the air, but that right had been surrendered now. He stayed with the scene for a moment, barely capable of rationalising it, before he came back to Alan and Robert. How readily she'd adapted to a new social group – as if they'd always been friends. Perhaps they had? Perhaps he'd missed all the signs. Perhaps he'd been so wrapped up in his work that he didn't notice?

'We've bought a lot of nice horses from Jonny over the years,' said Alan as he started to thumb through his sales catalogue.

'Well now you know where he gets them from,' Freddie replied.

'Only consigned one this time,' said Alan, looking down to examine the catalogue at the open page. 'Nice page. Fetched eighty grand.'

Freddie swallowed. His horse? Eighty grand? The one he'd sold for ten in last year's fire sale?

'What did he fetch as a yearling?' asked Alan.

'I sold him out of the ring,' Freddie replied.

He wasn't going to tell him that the horse was led out unsold because market confidence had collapsed in his consignment, and that he was forced to accept Jonny's derisory offer because he had no other bid and needed to raise as much money as he could at the time. Alan and Freddie exchanged looks.

Robert had looked up the same page in his catalogue, and began to say, 'That's the family that…' when Alan spoke across him.

'Well, better luck next time. They often flip in value once you've proved they can gallop,' he said, and turned to go, gesturing with his head to Robert that they should be heading to their next meeting. Freddie intercepted the move and grabbed Robert, turning him away from Alan in a conspiratorial hug.

'Do we have a deal?' he whispered.

Robert spoke more softly still, and replied, 'Let me shake him off and I'll come find you later, and we'll get it all sorted out then.'

Then, out loud, as he left his clutches so that Alan might hear said, 'We really don't want to take any more horses at the moment, you saw how full we were yesterday. I'll have a think about it.'

'Eighty thousand Euro,' he said to himself, he could make some good use of cash like that right now. Never mind, he'd have to make do with chasing down Gordon Melville, that might yield more in the end.

He found him tidying up a box, in the corner of the main yard, pitchfork in hand. Gordon, Sancho Panza, a little sneaky, greasy, yes-man. Gay-Gordon to Penny. Gordon was swinging the fork with the regular rhythm that only a time-served stable lad can master. Freddie watched his to and fro for a while, then grabbed it as Gordon swung it backwards.

'You?' he said.

'Me,' said Freddie. 'You didn't even try to hide?'

'I'm in the same position as you, you wee prick,' said Gordon. 'The arseholes have run off with my money too.'

'Have?' he thought, 'that's interesting.'

'Who are they?' he asked, and Gordon shrugged to say he didn't know. Freddie bent down and picked up the pitchfork and put a tine under Gordon's left eye. 'Who were you working for?'

Suddenly terrified, Gordon tried to shake his head.

'Give me your phone,' he demanded, and Gordon, backing away from the fork, felt in his breast pocket for his phone and handed it to Freddie.

'Anything you own, I'm taking. That way, you'll become as motivated as me to get to the bottom of this.'

'Do you think I'd be mucking boxes if I had any money?' he asked.

'In that case, perhaps I should put you out of work,' said Freddie, 'that way you might get motivated.'

Gordon backed towards the corner and as he did, Freddie felt the pitchfork disappear from his grip. He turned round to see two six foot something bodyguards. It didn't compute, Gordon, reduced to a stable lad, obviously close to the edge, and expensive close protection guards coming to his rescue?

One of them said, 'Leave this man.' The accent was eastern European. Then the pair of them stood aside to allow Freddie to leave the box.

'My phone,' Gordon cried out, and one of the men pulled Freddie back by his shoulder, holding out his hand for Gordon's phone, which he duly gave.

'Better than being forced to,' he reasoned, and left without another word.

He retreated to the safety of his bench. Who were they? If they were there to do him harm, why hadn't they? It was as discreet as a hotel lobby; they could have left him lying in an empty box. For a moment a sense of absolute security washed over him – that they could take him out whenever they chose to but couldn't for the attention it would draw on them. Then as quickly it disappeared, and he saw it instead as a warning, that they would be a constant presence in his life until the debt was settled or wasn't. Then a mad idea struck him – what if they were in league with Edward? That together they'd constructed a coup to get paid twice.

The idea was preposterous. Stuff like that was chicken feed for them. Felix's situation and all that flowed from that was about principle and management.

He stood up to take a short walk to the running rails and back, to distil his thoughts, but as soon as he did, Penny arrived, interpreting his suddenly getting up from his seat as a last-minute decision to avoid her.

'You've abused my good will – as usual. Speak.'

So, they were getting straight into it. He took a breath. 'They're asking things I can't give,' he said. 'I can't make the house sell any faster. All I can do is make it present well.'

'I know,' she said, 'but you need to top the paddocks and spray the weeds. And your cottage is a tip.'

'How did…? Yeah, I will,' he said. 'I'm going to live in England for a while. I'll get it tidied up before I go.'

'Oh yeah, you're booked for a run at the London Palladium, I hear.' He couldn't help but laugh out loud. Penny bit her lip.

'So?'

'I don't know what to say Penny.'

'Freddie. I no longer have any money to live on. My cards don't work.'

'I'm not hiding it,' he tried.

'What are you doing then? For Christ's sake, you're making me live off Jonny, it's humiliating. And it ends today.'

'Use the eighty grand you've just made off me.'

Penny slapped the air, 'Do not…' she was too furious to finish the sentence. 'I'm not here to negotiate,' she said, 'I'm here to tell you how it is. Read this – it's an uncontested judgment – you know, one of those documents you ignored. It says that you will transfer fifty thousand to me at the start of every month until the full debt is satisfied, and that you'll give a clear response to my lawyers about every asset we own jointly. If you fail in either of these we're coming after you, and if that means I take the house and every other last asset that has your name on it, I will.'

He recalled the inspiration he'd had on the A13 just before Evreux, it was as he'd driven past the Land Rover 4x4 centre, and one of the old familiar ballads had come on *Nostalgie*, 'On s'est aimé comme on se quitte', it was about a couple going through a break up. He'd realised then, with the moment of reckoning imminent, that if she was to offer him anything like a palatable deal, there was nothing to be gained by showing her how relieved he was. The best way forward had to be to tell her how unfair it was; to push for even more time however unreasonable it sounded. And eventually to agree to something that he had no chance or intention of honouring, so that perhaps, he'd buy a chance of one more default, and that might, if it all went well, get him two more months before he reached the actual dead-end.

'It's bad enough having to give half my money to an effete halfwit like him, don't make it any worse Penny. When I was married to you, I provided. Why can't he? Doesn't he like that part of the deal?'

'What's happened to you Freddie? I remember marrying someone who could outwit anyone he met, who possessed grace. Your losing spell has turned you into an oaf. And I'm not frightened of you. I know who you really are and what you do. I don't care if you ruin yourself by your own stupidity but do not dare ruin me too.'

'So, you chose Jonny instead?'

'What? The man who sold your ten-grand write-off for eighty? He could teach you a bit about being shrewder – he does not fall for the same sort of bullshit that you do. He makes me feel safe Freddie.'

'I bet he does,' he thought, and he imagined for a moment, Jonny negotiating with Russian gangsters, then shaking Edward Hamilton 'til every penny dropped out of him. He swallowed a smile. 'Put it in writing, and if you stop shouting at me in public, I'll take a look at your proposal.'

'For fuck's sake!' she shouted, 'it is in writing, we're past that stage now. The next stage is a court order for you to surrender every asset you own to me forever.'

He nodded an appeasing nod and resisted the temptation to say anything more to provoke her. 'If I get fifty-k to you this month, will you please call off getting the order? Then at the end of June, I'll pay you your share of the cash. You might have to wait for your share of the house, but if it doesn't sell this year, I'll mortgage half of it and pay you then. Please Penny, if you do it that way, you won't be disappointed again. Please – it's the only way I can do it.'

'You've got a short stay of execution. But one more lie, and the guillotine falls Freddie.'

Jonny arrived and they were about to leave just as Robert bounded across the lawns beaming from ear to ear. 'I thought this was you,' he said, 'Jonny, how are you?'

Jonny was 'impec' as usual and asked whether Alan was still on the racecourse.

'Gone already,' Robert told him, which made Jonny sigh

'You have a horse on your farm, I think,' he said. 'Could I ask you about it for a moment?'

'Bien sûr,' replied Robert, and the two of them stood apart for a moment to discuss the matter, Jonny talking, Robert nodding sagely, occasionally proffering a 'oui' or 'exact' as seemed appropriate at the time.

In the calm Freddie turned to Penny with a neutral question to show her that the animosity was over, 'Going anywhere good?' he asked.

'Eventually to the opera,' she replied, 'Manon.'

He paused for a moment, before saying, 'I've always seen you more as an oysters, champagne and getting touched up under the table type, myself.'

She almost laughed and said, 'I do both these days.'

They politely exchanged half-smiles to settle the detente then switched their attention back to Robert and Jonny. Robert still nodding, slipping in the odd word of French where he felt obliged to – at one point finding the courage to attempt a version of 'precise' in a French accent on the basis that a certain set of adverbs like that were transmutable between both languages. Finally, as Jonny finished his piece, he fell silent and waited for Robert's response. None came.

'So, what do you think?' Jonny prompted.

'They're a pack of absolute bastards,' Robert replied.

'Who are?' he asked, confused now by his own story.

And to prove that he hadn't comprehended any of the subtleties Jonny had conveyed in its telling, Robert replied,

'All of them.'

Jonny laughed, then tried again. 'Would you be interested though, if I had a buyer?'

Robert finally gave him a reply that made sense. 'If they come to the farm before the end of next week, they might have a deal, but we're very busy at the moment,' he said. He rolled his eyes at Freddie, as Penny and Jonny went on their way, as if all the hard work had been his.

'Thank God that's over. I'll tell you what, for a language without many words in it, they can't half make it stretch,' he said.

There was something about this man that Freddie adored already, and he hung out his arm for Robert to come closer.

'Now Robert, I haven't got any time left, I've got a ferry to catch,' he said. 'Tell me, do we have a deal that I can take home to Birkett?'

Robert fixed him with a hard stare. 'You do,' he said, 'but I can't sell you the yearling. I, er, he, look, he just has to go to the sales, there's nothing I can do about that. You can have the mare and foal for one-twenty, but I'd like a down payment to secure them.'

'How much?' asked Freddie.

'Fifty percent.'

'We can't do it. I'm sorry Robert,' he answered. Robert looked pleadingly at Freddie, waiting for the counteroffer, but none came.

'Then,' replied Robert, 'if we still have them when it's time to come to Ascot, they're yours, but there's been a lot of activity round the farm, now that we're not selling through the sales so much, and you'll have to take potluck that they're still there in a month.'

'How about if he raised the one-twenty to one-forty. Will you at least give him exclusivity for the month? Take no other offers?'

'If that's the case, you've got a deal my friend,' said Robert, and shook Freddie's hand with great sincerity. The two men looked each other in the eye, and for a moment Freddie thought he saw the formation of a small tear in Robert's.

Freddie walked away from the scene, skirting through the shadows cast by the large grandstand, until he arrived back at the security of his car. He locked all the doors once he was in and shrunk down into the seat so that his head was not visible through the driver's window. He'd just received an anonymous text. If those heavies were who he thought they were, did it mean that their employers, his clients, were close by too? Were they always close by? He looked at his phone and opened the message which read, 'No more trouble. Forget Hamilton.'

He texted back, 'OK. Are we settled on 3.3?' but when ten minutes later, no reply had been received, he knew that he wasn't going to get one.

ELEVEN

Freddie returned to the seldom seen sight of the yard going full tilt on Sunday. There was no sign of Birkett in the house, so he changed quickly into his work clothes and joined the effort. He passed Alison on the way to the yard, and she told him that Birkett had switched the rotas to make Sunday 'a normal day'. And to his puzzled look she replied, 'He wants to work the Ascot horses tomorrow.'

'A Monday gallop?' he said, and went to look at the board to see if they were working four lots, as they would on a normal workday.

He was trying to make sense of the handwritten notes which replaced the normal typed versions as Liam arrived. 'The only thing you'll be riding this morning is the barrow,' he said. He picked a pitchfork up from the barrow and threw it towards Freddie.

Freddie snatched it out of the air, swung it round and pointed the tynes towards Liam's head. Resting one on his cheek just below his eye, he said, 'Do you know Liam, if you had any brains, you'd be dangerous.'

Liam began to speak, 'And you'll find out how dangerous I am...' when Birkett appeared. He called over:

'Get in here will you Freddie, I want to hear about France.'

Freddie settled for sympathetic smile at Liam, let the fork drop to the floor and left him to it.

Halfway through the first packet of Ginger Snaps, Freddie had completed his debrief.

'What's the matter?' he asked, 'you look put out. You're not unhappy that I didn't bring the mare back, are you?'

'No. No, not really. I just got my hopes up that's all.'

'It's probably great timing, I think he'll be bust soon.'

'I know. You said. Poor fucker. But I can't afford to wait for that. I need her now.'

'She's starting to sound like more than just a little present to yourself Birdie.'

Birkett smiled wryly. 'Dear me Ferdy, what am I going to do with you?' He picked up the cups and saucers. 'We're going nowhere until we pull that bet off, so you can start by showing me how that stock exchange betting thing works.'

'Oh God,' said Freddie.

'What?'

'I've been dreading this. You promise you'll be patient?'

Birkett laughed, busying himself with a fresh pot of tea.

'Do you know anything about computers?' Freddie shouted over to him.

'I do the entries on them don't I? And the lot lists. You having another?'

'Bring us a glass of your nice scotch and I'll show you,' he said.

'Bloody hell, Ferdy!'

'What?'

'We could have had twenty odd years of fun like this if you hadn't been such a precious prick.'

They sat down in front of the computer, Freddie at the controls, Birkett alongside.

'No don't switch the tele off,' said Freddie, 'it'll help in a minute. Right,' he continued, 'tell me if I'm going too fast. This is the site. See the address. I've logged in now, OK? Right, we'll click on Horseracing, and now see that there's a list of race meetings. See that?' Birkett nodded. 'You're not having me on, are you? Do you know how to do this already?'

'Just get on with it,' said Birkett.

'So, I'll click on a race coming up soon, OK? Right, we're in the market for the race now. There are two columns in the middle, a blue one to the left, a pink one to the right. The blue column is the price at which you can currently bet any horse. See that one there? It says seven point eight right? That means that it's six point eight to one – like on the Tote, you knock a point off for your stake. If you wanted to have ten quid on that horse, you'd click on it. Look I'll do it and show you. See, I put ten in that box, and see there, it says profit sixty-eight pounds, liability ten pounds. I click confirm, and I have struck a bet on that horse to win at six point eight to one. Get it?'

Birkett nodded again.

'Now see how the prices are moving all the time? That's because people are putting up new bets to be backed or laid; some people won't like the price and they'll put a higher one in to see if someone's prepared to take it – it's like seeing the whole of the betting market in one place. Just watch the screen for a moment. Got it? The system always shows you the best possible price to back a horse in the blue column.'

'So what's the pink column?'

'Well, if the blue column is back, the pink column is lay. You don't want to be a bookie and lay bets, do you?'

'Not at all,' said Birkett, 'it's illegal for trainers anyhow, isn't it?'

'Yeah, I think so. But it's there for people to lay bets, as well as put them on. Like I was saying, anybody, not just bookmakers. But ignore that side of it for now, just use it for betting.'

'What if they can't afford it?' asked Birkett.

'It's not an issue. They must have the funds in their account to be able to put the transaction up. If they can't then the system won't let.'

'OK,' Birkett said cautiously.

'Look, I'll prove it. I'll try to *lay* the same bet for ten thousand. That means I'll have to have sixty-eight thousand pounds in my account. I try to do it, and look, there's a message that says, *insufficient funds in your account*. Right? So, you can be certain that it takes the money out of your account as soon as you put up the bet, or as soon as you lay the bet – whoever you are, you've got to have the funds there to do whatever it is you're trying to do.'

'OK,' said Birkett glancing out of the window at the work in the yard, 'that's good. I was worried about that.'

'Just try it for small stakes. You can't do any damage,' said Freddie, and left him at the computer to walk over to the window and look at the same scene outside. He smiled to himself as he observed the ordered chaos, everyone busying about like worker ants, scarcely speaking yet seeming to intuit how their little bits of industry interacted with everyone else's. Horses went on and off the walker, slices of hay and pails of water left outside boxes yet to be mucked, placed inside those with freshly made beds. It was like one of those street scenes from a musical just before it all becomes coordinated into a dance routine. He watched Milksheikh as he was returned to his box, that particular complex three-way tango that got him home again. The horse himself, imperious, observing it all with a sort of detached enjoyment.

'That's why I could never be a trainer.' He said to Birkett, returning to the room.

Birkett, still fixed on the screen, distracted, said 'Why?'

'Because after a while, the job becomes about achieving the morning's work and returning everything to order. It's easy to lose sight of the big picture.'

'Your problem is that you don't realise how clever you are Ferdy. Hey! What's that!' said Birkett, pointing at the computer. 'That *suspended* thing?'

'That happens when a race is off. Look up there now at the tele. The race is running, and as it's in progress the prices of the horses are changing – even faster now than before.'

'Why's it still going?' asked Birkett, 'the race is off.'

'It's a thing. People back horses during the race these days.' They watched for a while, Birkett moving his head up to the look at the TV screen then down to the computer, trying to distil a sort of correlation between what he was seeing on the two devices.

'Now lots of them have gone to a thousand to one.'

'That's because the race is coming to an end, and they've got no chance of winning.'

'And now they're all a thousand to one apart from one of them.'

'That's because the race is over.'

'It isn't, they're still running, look.'

Freddie explained. 'The TV pictures will be a few seconds behind the live event, because it's coming through a satellite. There'll be people at the track, or with fast TV systems that are determining those prices. The actual event will be finished, but our pictures show that there's three or four seconds to go.'

'That's half a furlong!' said Birkett. 'You mean there's some poor sods out there still betting horses that they think might get up, and it's already lost?'

'I do,' said Freddie.

'What's the point?' asked Birkett.

- 86 -

'Well, for the person who puts the bet on, none at all, but presumably they don't know that they're betting against something that's already happened. For the person laying the bets and taking their money, there's plenty of point in mopping up all the fivers and tenners with absolutely no risk at all.'

'Can't they see that everything's a thousand to one bar one, and there's no point?'

'Yeah, I see what you mean, but presumably they're looking at their TV pictures and still think that their horse has got a chance – or maybe they back their horses just before they go a thousand to one but it's too late to take them down again. I don't know. I don't think many people do things like that.'

'But on that screen, you could bet on a thousand to one for ages.'

'I don't know,' said Freddie, 'they probably keep the market open 'til four or five have past the post, just in case anything odd happens. It's not important Birdie. Just concentrate on the bit that matters.'

'Jesus, as if it wasn't complicated enough,' he said, 'they have to add all that in.'

Freddie swigged off his drink. He shrugged. 'Will that do for starters?'

'Yeah, that's enough for me, for now,' said Birkett, 'will you have another?'

'I'd better not,' said, Freddie, 'I've got a session to finish out there first.'

'What time did you get to bed?' asked Birkett.

'I didn't,' said Freddie.

'Well in that case, fill your glass and bugger off upstairs. We've got a big day tomorrow. Go and get a good night's sleep.'

As he climbed the stairs his phone pinged again, and his stomach turned a somersault. He dared to look at the message and was slightly relieved to see that it was from Penny, forwarding a message from her solicitors which put in formal terms the agreement they'd made at Saint Cloud.

He put his glass down onto the nightstand, switched on the radio, then sighed and sat on the edge of the bed. It had been a long time since he'd said his prayers. Had he ever as an adult? He dropped down onto his knees, facing the bed, and clasped his hands. 'Please God,' he said, 'if you can't spare me, spare Felix.'

He got up, drained the glass, turned off the radio, then spent the next two hours trying to sleep.

TWELVE

Monday morning at five o'clock, as the day begins. Silently closing the bedroom door. Leaving the note that says first lot to Racecourse Side, with the exceptions of Milksheikh, Bugbear and Slipshod, who are to be taken to Long Hill. Milksheikh to be ridden by Alison; Bugbear, Freddie; Liam, Slipshod.

Alison came in to Milksheikh's box to find Birkett already there, tacking him up. Once done, he left her with the horse to hot walk him round the four sides of the yard while the others got themselves ready. He went back towards the office, then stood at the corner of the yard and watched it come to life. First to meet him was Liam, at the board where the lots were pinned up.

'Long Hill, boss?'

Birkett nodded. 'Y'up.'

Freddie arrived.

'You're still here, are you?' asked Liam.

Freddie and Birkett exchanged a puzzled look.

'Well, when he walked off the job yesterday, we wondered.'

Birkett said nothing, Freddie looked at the floor.

'Did you ride the three of them all right?' asked Birkett.

'We rode Slipshod and Milksheikh,' he said. 'I thought you wanted him to ride Bugbear?'

'I did,' said Birkett.

'Well ask him then, I don't know.'

Freddie seemed to stutter over a response.

'You mean the horse hasn't been out?' asked Birkett. 'On the most important day of the year? Get him out and get him warmed up.'

Freddie set off to tack up Bugbear, leaving Liam with Birkett.

'Most important day of the year?' asked Liam. 'So, why's a leg iron like him riding the lead horse?'

'Him? He's ridden over thirty winners you know…'

'Where were they? In the Donkey Derby on Blackpool sands?'

'…and I can trust him.'

'You couldn't trust him to ride one side of the cunt,' Liam said and set off to tack up his own favourite horse.

'Just keep him walking Freddie lad,' shouted Birkett. 'Stick on him. Not you Alison, you keep walking.'

Eventually the entire first lot string were circling the fountain and Birkett promptly sent the majority of them to the Racecourse Side, leaving him with the three horses that represented all his thoughts and hopes and plans.

'We're going to Long Hill. Freddie leads on Bugbear, Liam next. Walk to *The Severals* and trot as many circuits as you can until I arrive. I want them warmed up. No fucking nonsense.' He fixed Liam with a stare that meant that he directed the comment at him.

As soon as they were out of sight, Birkett took out his mobile phone. Normally he'd get in the car behind the horses, and if he got lucky with the traffic, he might pull in to the four-berth car park just off the main road as the string arrived. Today, as he waited for a confirming call back, he made another cup of tea, and checked the confirmation dates for next week's races one more time. Ten minutes later as he pulled in, he saw Tolley with a young apprentice jockey waiting for him as arranged.

'Good lad Tolley, morning. Thank you,' he said. 'Follow me.'

The three of them walked to the centre of the small grass square, which has been used since time immemorial as the place to warm up your horses before they set off up the Warren Hill, and Long Hill gallops. He watched the horses trotting, saying nothing as they continued to trot around the all-weather perimeter, then signalled to the riders to join him in the middle.

'It's not kicking up much dust yet,' he said to Tolley, who agreed.

'There's never been a week without rain yet,' he replied.

He asked Alison to get down from her horse and to hold it while he legged Tolley up into the saddle, then asked Freddie to do the same, so that he could swap positions with the boy jockey. It produced a winning smile in Liam, not least for the surprise that was difficult to disguise in Freddie's face when he was given the order to get down.

'Right young fellow,' said Birkett, 'set a good swinging canter, then start to wind it up before you turn the corner. Make it hard for them to get by you. Go right to the end.' Turning to Liam, he said, 'Give him five lengths, and ride out your gallop to beat him.' Then he said, 'Tolley,' and the two exchanged nods. 'Do another two laps walking to give us a chance to get up there. Look for Alison at the top and circle by her when you pull up.'

Then the three of them set off to Birkett's old 4x4 and left them walking their horses quietly round the grass square.

They pulled in onto the large grassy lay-by on the public side of the Long Hill gallop, and walked briskly together to the best place to look back down on them. Looking through his binoculars Birkett saw that they hadn't yet left *The Severals* and hurried to put his charges in the right place to observe the work.

'Alison, stand there and call them when they've finished. Watch the end of the gallop. Take it all in. Tell me how soon Slipshod's back in his wind. Right?' he said and left her at the top of the gallop.

He walked on with Freddie, to position him about a hundred and fifty yards further back. 'Was he trouble. The Irishman?'

'No, not really,' said Freddie. 'He was just giving out to you for coming up Long Hill.'

'You know why we're here?' he asked. 'You've ridden all the Newmarket gallops in your time, what's different about Long Hill?' 'It's the longest. And the toughest I suppose. It feels like it will never end when you're riding it.'

'Wrong,' said Birkett, 'it's the only away-gallop in Newmarket. All the rest face into town, and you can always get a false piece of work when a horse is running home. No one ever told you that before? This is where you'll see a proper piece of work. Now then, keep your eyes on Milksheikh and never take them off. And start counting when they pull up and tell me exactly how long he takes to come back in his wind. To the second Freddie, don't let anything else distract you.'

He went on to take up position further along the dog leg, then watched as the three horses came over the road and gathered themselves at the foot of the long slog. No other string was in sight.

In an hour's time, it'd be like Piccadilly Circus, but now, before it all got going, Birkett had it just as he wanted. He'd see it all as it should be.

And he was rewarded by a gallop that on the face of it went well. Bugbear, to his instructions bowled along in front and put up the fight of his life to cling on to the lead. Slipshod, with honest endeavour behind, kept tabs on his lead horse, and though looking like the task was beyond him halfway up the hill, stayed on and slid past Bugbear as the ground began to level out. Milksheikh seemed to run to a different agenda, without pulling hard he travelled for the first half mile putting his head first left, then right, as if they weren't going fast enough for him, then as the first two battled to the top of the hill, he quietly closed, and came upsides Bugbear just before as the young jockey dropped his hands and called the work over. They circled, no jockey speaking until spoken to, and then only giving a 'Yes, fine, guvnor' to the question 'All OK?' The riders were swapped again, and Birkett drove the jockeys back to Tolley's car at the bottom of the hill while his employees rode the horses quietly back to the yard.

Freddie had just finished showering down his horse as Birkett drove back in.

'Come and see me in the office when you've finished with him,' he said, then went to talk to Liam, who was walking the yard with Slipshod, drying him off.

A mug of strong, lukewarm tea, with three ginger snaps alongside in the saucer was waiting for Freddie as he went into the office.

'Did the Irishman tell you anything worth knowing on the way back?' asked Birkett. He sat behind his computer on the other side of the desk to Freddie.

'Nothing? You?'

'He's like a dog with two dicks,' he said.

'Look, Birdie, I'm sorry I didn't take Bugbear out yesterday, I didn't know. I know he doesn't like me, but why he'd let that spoil his own interests, I don't know.'

'Nasty just seems to go alongside thick in people like him,' said Birkett dismissing the problem as old news. 'Some horse though, isn't he?'

'Who is?' asked Freddie.

'Bugbear. Jesus, I wish I had a yard full like him. Did you see him? He had no right to stay with them that long. What an attitude.'

'So, you weren't so happy with the work? For the other two?' Birkett stood up from behind the desk, trying to disguise the wry smile on his face, 'What did you think?' he asked.

'It was a hard piece of work,' said Freddie, 'and they all did it honestly enough…'

'Slipshod?' asked Birkett.

'Workmanlike. No that's unfair. He did it well. It's difficult for me because I don't know how good Bugbear is, but he picked him up well, and he seemed to have a bit left. Good without being amazing, I'd say.'

'I think you've underestimated him,' said Birkett. 'Bugbear did that gallop carrying seven and half stones. I don't think Slipshod's a true Group I horse. He's entitled to run in the race next week. I mean, he's good enough to take part, but can he win races like that? I'm not sure. He won't beat the French horse, and there's probably one that will beat him from Ballydoyle, but he's earned his place.' He took a long draw on his mug of tea. 'Milksheikh?'

'Did it nicely. It was a very good trial for a handicap.' He laughed nervously, suddenly unsure of his snap judgment.

'How long before he was back in his wind?'

'Forty-five seconds I made it. What did Tolley make of the work?'

'Just pass me his saddle over, will you?' asked Birkett, collecting Freddie's mug.

Freddie leaned over the low wall of document boxes to pick up the saddle indicated by Birkett. 'My God!' he said, 'What have you got in here?'

'One and a half stones more than Slipshod carried,' Birkett answered.

'What?' A cold shiver ran down Freddie's back.

Birkett turned back to face him, smiling ear to ear. 'You better believe it son. Tolley told me that he'd only just got him going when the gallop finished. He told me he could have beaten both of them without switching leads. That, Ferdy *is* a Group I horse. A true Group I horse. Slipshod's good, but that lad is different apples.'

'Birdie?' he said, slowly shaking his head. 'What have you done?'

'Listen, I'm going to put Tolley on both, then no one will read anything into it. I've got my money ready for you. And there's... oh yeah. I just want you to show me that stock exchange thing one more time.'

Freddie smiled warmly at the old rogue. 'You haven't emptied my account trying to work it all out, have you? I need every penny I can hang on to at the moment.'

'Nah,' said Birkett. 'Just the odd tenner. One of them won – I think. I just can't get my head round that thing where you can back a horse at a thousand to one in the race. It doesn't make sense to me.' He sighed. 'Forget about that Birdie, it doesn't matter – just leave that to the traders and pros who work the system.'

'But that's what I mean Ferdy, why would anyone do it? What's the point?'

'I've told you. They don't risk anything. The result's already known. They're just mopping up the bits and pieces from losers who don't know any better.'

'And nobody does anything about it?'

'No. If someone's stupid enough to back a horse that can't win, why should they care?'

'What if the one that should win, doesn't. What if the horse breaks down, or the jockey falls off?'

Freddie sighed impatiently. 'Well, in that case, no one would care if the sharks who exploit all those small punters got a bloody nose every now and again. It's all correct and above board you know.'

It didn't compute to Birkett. He shook his head and turned to go to the sink with the mugs. 'Something seems wrong about it to me,' he said returning. 'I worry that it'd make them do something to one of our horses.'

'Birdie, don't worry. They can't. All of that happens far too close to the finish and is far too unpredictable for anyone to profit by it. Leave all that stuff to me. I promise you. They won't even know that we've backed the horse. It'll be fine.'

'If you're sure,' he said, still far from convinced. He went back to his desk. 'There's my share, in the briefcase over there,' he said, pointing to far the corner of the room.

'Cash?'

'Yeah, what else is there? I told you I had a job for you.'

'Do you know how hard it is to deal in cash these days? Even to pay it into a bank?'

'No. Can't you do it then?'

Freddie made a beckoning sign. 'Give it to me. I'll make a start this afternoon.'

Birkett went to the corner, then handed him the briefcase containing twenty thousand pounds in cash. Freddie made a weighing gesture as he did, and thinking that it felt light for such a large amount of money, opened it, and looked inside.

'Don't you trust me?' Birkett asked.

'It's not that,' said Freddie, 'I'm just not used to cash anymore.' He closed the case again, wished Birkett goodnight and went upstairs to his bedroom.

He'd have to take an unwanted trip in and out of London to deal with the cash, which he didn't relish. He imagined meeting Penny, who'd have it off him as soon as she knew what was in the case, Ced too. He laughed to himself. His clients too, probably, just to make the point. He stopped laughing at that thought.

He threw the briefcase down onto his bed and sighed. Thoughts danced across his brain. What was the mantra Felix adopted at times like this? 'Seek perfection in the present.'

He looked straight ahead at the blank wall and forced himself to think and do nothing at all until he'd measured two minutes on his phone. He wasn't one for praying, but as the two minutes expired, he imagined himself channelled into Felix's own thought-waves, as if they were bound in a secure two-way communication. 'Stay with me,' he said, 'You get better for us, and I will get it all back.'

As soon as second lot break was over and third lot out on the gallops stood down from riding duties, Freddie took a quick tour of the yard before setting out for London.

There he saw Davey Flint, alone in the place, like the White Rabbit, scurrying from job to job, constantly stopping to check the time on the yard clock.

'Don't run away,' Freddie said. 'I've got five minutes to give you a hand.'

'Oh no, sir. We work to a particular system here, by the time I set it all out for you, I'd have finished the job anyway.'

'OK,' said Freddie, 'if you're sure.' He turned to go

'How did the work go this morning?' Davey asked, 'I thought Liam seemed happy but you can't really tell with him.'

'It was all right,' said Freddie.

'Is that all? I thought we were going to have a winner at Ascot. Aren't we? Isn't the boss happy? I thought we were going for those Group I's.'

'I don't think we'll be winning any Group I's Davey. A handicap maybe.'

'Oh dear,' he said, 'Liam won't be very happy to hear that.'

'Well, his horse is in the right race,' said Freddie, 'if it's good enough, it'll win.' He didn't want to leave him with the idea that they were planning to win a handicap.

'Oh good, that's a relief to hear,' said Davey. 'You get going sir, before he's back and starts getting all angry.'

Freddie thought that the very best thing he could do would be to wait for Liam to return and he stayed put. 'Who's your favourite horse?' he asked Davey.

Davey's answer surprised him, 'I think Milk's sister is going to be OK,' and he indicated the dark grey filly with a splodge of white on her muzzle just a box or two away from them, 'Sugar, we call her. She hasn't got her own name yet.'

Freddie asked whether Liam liked her too. He remained silent until he coaxed a reply out of Davey, who eventually, reluctantly, replied that he did. Freddie smiled, and decided that he would keep chatting with Davey until their angry little colleague returned.

THIRTEEN

Birkett parked his old Japanese 4x4 in the car park between the lad's hostel and the racecourse stables, where it would stay until they left for home on Wednesday evening. It no longer locked, and the torn canvas-plastic hood couldn't be relied upon to keep thieves and the weather out. They went from the car without taking any of their belongings to check on their horses before they did anything else. Alison confirmed that both had settled in well and had taken a drink.

'He loves it here,' she said of Milksheikh, 'being amongst other horses, next door to his pal. I think it's 'cos it's such a change from his lonely old box at home.' Birkett nodded to agree and smiled at his favourite horse, as he went to rub his muzzle with its strange off-centre splodge of white.

'Happy to be with your pal, are you? Maybe we should start running you in the same races,' he said, and caught Freddie's eye as he turned back to face them.

'Liam's giving Slippy a shower,' Alison offered unprompted. 'It's roasting here today. He keeps breaking out.'

Milksheikh, she said, was not as bad. 'He's just too cool for school, but I give him a nice walk when I start to think it's getting a bit too hot. There's a lovely breeze round the back.'

'Good lass,' said Birkett, 'Keep it going like that. Tell Liam I was here, and I'll come back and walk up with him for the race.'

They left the stables and headed to the hostel, picking up their clothes and travel kit on the way. Freddie was used to staying at different places to this, but Birkett would not contemplate staying anywhere else – especially since it got its makeover when the racecourse was upgraded ten or so years ago. It now resembled a budget hotel. There were still dorms, but single rooms could be booked too, even doubles for couples – and there was a passable canteen, open from early 'til late, a lounge, a bar, a large TV. For some lads, here for the week, they'd get as much fun out of their *holiday* as their owners would in the five-star hotels up the road.

They showered, put on their morning suits, locked their valuable possessions into their rooms, and left for the long slow slog up to the racecourse now shimmering in the heat haze in the near distance. They collected the hand-written paddock badges from the office on the main road, then crossed towards the entrance to stand in-line behind the already growing queue waiting to pass through the airport security scanners and into the course.

'Let's go in the old way instead,' said Birkett, leaving the queue. 'It reminds me of the old place.'

'Why would they ever change this place?' he continued, as they passed through the old car park and into the course proper. 'I think whoever redesigned the place must have done his apprenticeship in Butlins…'

'Remember the old paddock, just here?' asked Freddie.

Birkett shook his head, as if the forces of progress were determined to destroy everything that was once good. 'Do you know Ferdy, I've been coming here for over forty years, and it has never not been boiling hot on the opening day?'

'I was going to say that too,' said Freddie, 'or is that just the way that all childhood summers were hot and sunny?'

'Aye. Always been the best day of the year,' he sighed. 'It'll need to be mind you, it rained every day last week. They were given it good yesterday; it'll probably be good to firm by the time they run the first. Not that I'm complaining.' He was doing that thing again where he talked as if in conversation, but they were no more than his own thoughts spoken to the air. Then he went back to whistling the 'Ascot Gavotte' from *My Fair Lady*. He broke off and said, 'Oh, what did Robert say when you rang him?'

'Nothing. He wasn't picking up, remember? I'll give him another ring now in fact,' said Freddie. 'I guess they're travelling.'

As he put his phone to his ear, he recognised his name being called, and a man on the other side of a small picket fence, about twenty yards or so away was waving at him. He left another message, and putting away his phone, he squinted to see that Ced was trying to get his attention. Four cars had backed towards each other to make exclusive a faraway corner of the grassy car park, and already dozens of people had flooded to this little gathering which was made all the more their own by the erection of the little fence and the placing of a guard at the access point. As they approached, the guests became distinct as individuals, and the closer they got, the smarter the party seemed to be. It was all the more incongruous for the car park itself not being full, the neighbouring picnics barely underway, but still, this happy throng went at the festivities as if this were the very height of the high season.

'Come inside and talk to me,' demanded Ced from the other side of the fence.

Having nothing better to do for an hour or so, and being unable to think of a better excuse Freddie said, 'Ced, I thought it was you. I'd love to.' Instinctively, he looked quickly left and right, before he went ahead, and crossed into Ced's party.

Birkett begged a more pressing engagement with the owners of Slipshod and went on his way towards the grandstand to meet them, telling Freddie to be at the saddling boxes by one-thirty latest.

'Get the saddle early and bags us a good box,' he shouted as he went on his way.

'He's looking well,' said Ced as he greeted Freddie, transferring his glass to his cigarette hand, 'they'll come round in a minute with a glass for you.'

'You wouldn't say that if you were getting him out of his incontinence pants this morning,' Freddie replied.

'No?' he said. 'Does that mean you're in charge there now? I didn't know you'd started with him when we were up in Newmarket.'

'I don't know whether I'd finally committed then. But there's a lot of us and he's quite good most of the time. Look at him. He thinks he's at the seaside, but he looks happy.'

Ced took an admiring look at his sometimes friend. 'Look at you,' he said, 'how you can just turn your hand to things like this. Turning up on the first day of Royal Ascot with a live runner in the Queen Anne. It's amazing the things you can do. Look at me, same old stuff, getting all these lot drunk. Painted-on face...'

'I thought you loved all this,' said Freddie, 'I can't imagine anyone else doing it the same way.'

'I hate it,' Ced confided.

Freddie thought that perhaps he'd started a bit earlier than usual and probably didn't mean any of it.

'All this,' Ced said, and waved towards the marquis under construction just beyond the little cordoned off party they stood in presently, 'lunchtimes here, evenings spent in that tent, afternoons in Conrad's box, five days, no relenting, rubbing shoulders with every person it's worth knowing. I won't see any racing you know... How is Felix? Sorry, I was forgetting myself.'

'It looks bad, Ced. He's still in an induced coma but each time I call, hoping for a little sign of improvement, expecting a response that says he's just the same. I... well, I just pick up on this vibe that he's not pleasing them, you know, getting a little bit worse by degrees. They never say it like that, but they constantly remind me about the terrible trauma his body has suffered. And they always ring off by saying that they'll ring as soon as there's a change. Which they never do.'

'I'm so sorry,' he said.

'Do you know Ced, finally I get what it means to be partners with someone. I'll never take him for granted again.'

The sudden presence of a made-over teenage hostess with a tray of champagne flutes made him jump. He took one, and Ced swapped his two-thirds consumed glass for a fresh one, then, as if drilled as a pair in the ways of serving such a party, a replica teenager came behind her with a tray of interesting canapés on Chinese soup spoons. She waited a moment, as if attending Freddie, waiting for a compliment, was it? Or just a polite wait to get her spoon back?

'Would you like another sir?'

'I can't I'm riding in the first,' he said.

Ced laughed, and the young girl made a noise like a dog and moved on.

'Do come by, it's such a treat for me to see proper people like you,' said Ced. Then as if he'd suddenly remembered something important, he added, 'Oh yeah, you've got to drop in, especially in the tent in the evenings, we really have got a stellar line up this year. There'll be some great people for you to meet, especially if you're thinking of setting up in training on your own. There's so much new money in town these days,' he whispered behind his hand.

It seemed something of a volte face from the maudlin nonsense he was spouting just a moment earlier. 'Perhaps it's the way drunks go,' thought Freddie. 'Perhaps his liver is so shot that the alcohol bypasses that and goes straight to his brain, and he's incapable of holding a rational line of thought?'

'I've got loads I want to catch up with you about, and people I want you to meet. I could really do with you casting an eye over someone we've got in this scheme,' Ced was saying.

Ah, the scheme: that which he planned not to mention; that which he had no intention of being part of; that which was completely beyond his financial wherewithal to contemplate; that which was for the big swinging dicks who worked in investment banks, and not for a shrewd time-served horseman like Freddie.

'Yeah, sure. How's it all going?'

'Generally, very well,' he replied. 'We're over-subscribed – but don't worry, I've stood over your share. We've got one of the horses in the trial scheme running this week – in the three-year-old handicap. And,' he stressed, 'I will be taking time out to watch that, *whoever* I'm with. We fancy him a bit. Do you know that the winner of that race – you know, *The Britannia?* – most years the winner gets sold on to Hong Kong for a mill. There'll be bids down to about the sixth.'

'What?' said Freddie. 'What did you pay for him?'

'Fifty thousand. We've turned down two hundred and fifty for him already. Honestly Freddie, this scheme could be anything. You'll wish you'd taken more; I already do.'

'Look Ced, I'm sorry I haven't paid yet. I've had a lot of stuff to sort out with Penny. I should be able to settle up with you at the end of the week. As soon as I've finished with her lawyers anyway.'

'Don't worry, I know you're good for it,' he replied.

'He might be a piss artist, but he's a really good salesman,' thought Freddie.

'Does that mean you're anticipating a winner?'

A new teenage waitress came by with an even more complicated canapé - it seemed to require an extra hand. He declined, leaving himself free to take whatever it was that was coming on her heels: mini-Yorkshire pudding, fine slice of filet steak, slice of gherkin, knob of horseradish, unseasonable, but such a nice change from cornflakes and ginger snaps.

He pointed at Ced, as if to make the remark more earnestly than the words conveyed, pausing as the horseradish smarted his eyes. 'We're not,' he said, 'our horse in the Queen Anne is the best we've got. He can't win, but he'll run well. And he's a bit of a guide to see where we're at with the others.'

Ced smiled, Freddie was going to turn into such a great asset for him to parade about. He pointed out Warren and Conrad in the distance. 'I really want you to talk to the boys for a moment. Conrad wants to ask you about a stud farm in France. He's been getting it valued for a client, do you mind?'

A thought crossed his mind: 'I've got one they can have.' The boys were in conversation with a couple of hefty looking new-money types, the sight of whom filled him with cold dread.

'Look Ced, I absolutely promise to come back and see you all, but I've got to get the saddle out early so that we're ready for the first race. I don't want to mess up on my first big meeting.'

Ced acknowledged the better call on his time, and allowed him to go, but not before he'd extracted a solemn undertaking to see him several times during the week coming, and at least one evening session all the way through, whatever that meant. He consoled himself with the thought that if the worst came to the worst and he found himself in one of Ced's parties in the early hours of the morning, he could at least slip off unnoticed back to the lads' hostel.

They shook hands solemnly, turned it into a shake with a grip on the elbow by the spare hand, met eyes, then seguéd into a manly embrace before finally meeting eyes properly and each telling the other how much they missed each other, and that they were going to spend a fabulous week together.

Freddie still had a lot of time to kill but the experience with Ced had unnerved him slightly. He'd been wrong – being in a crowd did not bring a sense of greater security, being hidden in a Suffolk backwater brought that. This swelling crowd, the Ascot opening day, did not feel safe at all.

He skirted round the bars and enclaves and corrals and other private parties that were just getting underway and reflected on the democratisation of Royal Ascot from what it had been just a few years earlier, when it was difficult to find the little seafood bars tucked away in the perimeter buildings, and harder still to get a table if you did. In those days most people stayed at their car park picnics until it was time to come over the racecourse, knowing that once there, eating and drinking had effectively finished until after the last race. And back then, if you weren't invited to the Royal Enclosure, you travelled between the grandstand and the parade ring by means of a congested underground tunnel, sacrificing either watching the race or betting on it, if you were to take that chance. Now it had all been rendered a sort of Club-Med experience with a barely detectable boundary between the Hoi-Polloi and the Royal Enclosure. He walked through it all and winced slightly at the memory of youthful indiscretions in the car park in those far off days. Too much drunk, snogging girls from the office; once going home without a single penny left in his pockets and walking back to his flat from the dropping off point, afraid to say that he'd insufficient funds remaining to hire even a minicab. At least he'd never had to walk home without his shoes, and it's not everyone that could say that.

He arrived at the far end of the grandstand, then taking a glance behind him, turned quickly to the left to set off to walk the course. It had rained the entire week previously and been hot and dry since. In the old days when it went hot, the most used part of the course on the far rail was always fastest on the straight course, and the grandstand draw a disadvantage. When wet, the opposite was true. All instincts told you that the ground sloped down towards the grandstand, but the estate generally fell away down to Swinley Bottom, near the mile start on the Round Course. Was there not a small lake in there somewhere in the middle of it all? He wished now that he'd done this in a professional way and brought a stick with him that he could push into the turf and take a meaningful report back to Birkett. Slipshod had been drawn in the middle of a field of thirteen, which shouldn't make much difference at all but Milksheikh, running tomorrow, was drawn two of thirty. Right over on the far side. That might make a difference. It probably wouldn't in these conditions, everyone said that the draw had been neutralised since the course had been redesigned and the track relayed.

He decided to walk to beyond the start of the mile course down the grandstand rail, then back up the other, detouring into part of the round course as he did. As long as he was ahead of the Queen, he'd be OK. Out there alone, he felt safe.

One hour later he crossed the course at the winning post, went back along the horse walk under the grandstand, past the giant fans blowing out chilled moist air, already in action on this stifling day, and made his way to the weighing room to collect the saddle. He walked the horse walk that linked the pre-parade to the paddock the public hanging off the other side of the white rails that separated their space from his. They examined him as he walked by, trying to guess whether he might be a celebrity they should know. He tried to do the same, looking at them out of the corner of his eye, ever vigilant for unhappy ex-clients, and anything that resembled Edward Hamilton. He thought that he noticed Penny walking with Jonny in the near distance and just suppressed the instinct to wave, then turned his gaze to the ground as he left the walkway and shuffled through the little crowd of people congregating outside the weighing room.

Inside the air-conditioned safety of the lobby, he was surprised to find several empty seats available despite the frantic bustle of preparations for the first race. He chose one closest to the steward's room and waited.

FOURTEEN

Slipshod came into the pre-parade ring between his two handlers and immediately stopped. Ears pricked, he looked all about the place to drink it in, then, understanding all: competition, facilities, audience, he consented to move again. The two men either side of him laughed independently at his antics, then resumed their swift pace to keep up with his long raking stride. After two laps of the pre-parade, Birkett peeled off to leave him with Liam and greet Freddie. He dumped the kit bag with brushes, sponges, and a carton of water alongside the tiny saddle Freddie had placed at the corner of the box to mark it as their territory, then picked up the saddle to unwind the surcingle and hang it round his neck. He seemed to draw a deep breath as he too surveyed the ring to take in the competition.

'Not a drop on him.' He spoke to the air in front of him but aimed his remarks at Freddie. 'It's stifling, isn't it?'

'He's coping with it a lot better than some of them,' said Freddie. 'Better than you,' he thought. What would he be like tomorrow afternoon? They watched together in silence as the horse completed several more laps with Liam who wore an expression of dead disinterest. The whole world was his enemy right now, and he was the best possible partner a horse about to race could have.

'OK Liam lad, bring him in,' said Birkett. Liam led the horse to the back of the open-fronted saddling box and turned him so that they'd saddle him facing outwards. Birkett went without reflecting to the near side of the horse with the number cloth tucked under his arm, prising apart the jelly, which would provide the immovable foundation for the saddle and kit as he did. Liam reluctantly handed the lead reign to Freddie, looking at him as if to say, 'You'll have to do,' and commenced his mirror image support of Birkett opposite him on the horse's offside. As Birkett secured the kit on the top of Slipshod with a firm hand, Liam worked away below, pulling the elasticated fastenings as tight as they'd go, then he would replace Birkett's hand as did the same. When all was done, Birkett came to the front of the horse and pulled his legs forward to make sure no skin nipped in their pulling and fastening, knocking Freddie to the side in his single-minded attention to the job. Still saying nothing, he reached into the bag to find a sponge, soaked it in water and rinsed the horse's mouth, then said, 'Go on son,' and stood out of the way for Liam to lead him off into the history that awaited him.

'Right, I suppose we'd better go too,' he said, and the two of them began the hard slog with the other trainers, owners, and hangers-on towards the parade ring. Freddie swallowed hard as he entered the throng, acutely aware that he was prey for anyone who desired to make him a target. He shook his head as the thought struck and told himself he was being ridiculous.

'Poor buggers,' said Birkett, watching the horses parade. 'I bet they'd rather be anywhere else than here, and they get that smell of fresh cut grass too. Do you think he's feeling the heat?'

Freddie reassured him. 'No Birdie, he's all right. Let's go to the far end we'll see more of him up there.' The two of them wandered up to the far end of the paddock under the large TV screen where the crowd was thinner.

'I don't think I can stand much more of this,' said Birkett. 'God knows what it'll be like tomorrow.'

The bell rang, as suddenly the bright phalanx of riders became visible, already in the paddock.

'Where did all that time go?' Birkett asked. He looked genuinely alarmed at the prospect of having to send his horse into a race. Tolley first went into the thickest part of the crowd to find them, but emerged eventually, looking around concerned, until he spotted him in his far away corner. Freddie raised his hand to tell him to stay where he was.

The gossip in the weighing room was that the French horse was 'A good thing', he told them.

'I know, he is,' said Birkett, then looking to the owners to check that they'd heard too, said, 'right, you know how he goes. Drop him in and ride him to finish.'

Tolley nodded to tell him that all was understood.

'Well let's not mess about,' said Birkett, 'we'll go and find him over in the corner and get on him quietly.'

As the stalls flew back, and the racecourse commentator announced, 'And they're off,' a muted roar began in the main grandstand, but it had fizzled out by the time it reached the Royal

Enclosure, where Birkett and Freddie stood together on the lawn about fifty yards from the running rail, half a furlong back from the line. The spot afforded a decent view back down the straight course and of the enormous TV screen opposite. They got a clear view of him when the camera angle went to side on, and it showed their horse anchored in last place, detached from the main field by a few lengths.

The pacemaker for the Irish horse was similarly detached by about four or five lengths in front and the race had reached that stage, just after half-way, when some people in the crowd started to believe that he wouldn't come back to the field, the commentator was becoming slightly sceptical about the chances of that happening, and the jockeys absolutely convinced that it would.

> And still the pacemaker travels well in front, there's a break of about five lengths to the horses vying for second, and the main pack sits about two lengths further adrift of them, Slipshod still content to sit in rear. But this pacemaker goes on, I call him that, but his jockey looks very comfortable as they move on towards the two-furlong marker. Lord Nelson in a hack canter in front, Machin et Truc, still happy to spot him a four-length lead, and the pack sits waiting. Now, for the first time Lord Nelson's jockey gets down behind his horse and pushes him to maintain his lead, Machin et Truc, and Buckingham Place finally start to close, and now we've got a race on. And in a matter of strides, the favourite is upsides, and all of a sudden, Lord Nelson folds, and it's all too much for Buckingham Place too. It's Machin et Truc and he's off and away, Yellow Jersey comes out of the pack to try and throw down a challenge, but this winner's flown. It's Machin et Truc, who surely can't be caught now, Yellow Jersey chasing him in vain in second, and only Slipshod from the pack has enough left to mount a challenge. Machin et Truc, it's all about him, as he's eased down to win by a comfortable looking three or four lengths, and it's going to be an interesting race for second as Slipshod throws down a real challenge to Yellow Jersey, who... just holds on for second. It'll be a photo for the minors, but it

looks pretty clear to me, Machin et Truc is a very easy
winner, from Yellow Jersey, just, in front of Slipshod a
fast finishing third. Those front three a long way clear of
the fourth horse.

Freddie turned to look at Birkett. He wore an expression that
said, *you know what this means don't you?*

Birkett seemed to understand. 'I know,' he said.

As one they set off towards the walkway under the stands that
brings the horses back from the course into the unsaddling
enclosures. Slipshod was ahead of them and was already being
spoiled by his surprised and delighted owners as they arrived. Tolley
waited for them, saddle in hand, obliging the owners and their friends
with photographs, then took a pace away to confer with Birkett as he
arrived.

'I was very pleased with him,' he said. 'The first horse is
obviously a bit special, but he's as good as the rest. He can win a
Group I for you if you avoid the winner, and he'll get further too. He
wasn't stopping.'

'How did he like the ground?' asked Birkett. 'Loved it. Keep
him on it. But keep away from that Machine thing. It is a machine.'

'He must be good Birdie,' said Freddie.

'Why's that?'

'Because he's even made Liam smile.'

'Jesus son, he's got divine powers that fella. Come on,' he said.
'Let's go and enjoy it now before we start planning tomorrow.'

Birkett linked arms with Freddie and set off with him to find
the Pimm's' tent.

FIFTEEN

The first bolt of lightning woke him when it struck at four o'clock. Freddie rolled out of bed without thinking and went straight to look at the computer screen. The glow from that, and a million different things on his mind meant that he hadn't really slept since he last looked at it. Some more of the money he'd fed into the machine to back Milksheikh had been taken. More than he'd expected, and he made a quick calculation, like he did when he was in the bank on early starts like this, to think about how many new countries had woken up since he was last here. Twenty thousand was on now. That figure, twenty-k, made him first think of Ced, then from there, Penny and her lawyers, then as soon as he'd dismissed the thought, his ex-clients. His stomach turned over. 'Stop. We'll think about it all afterwards,' he said to himself.

He went back to the screen. If he could get the remaining stake down closer to ten-k in what was left of night, he'd get that on easily amongst the UK bookies when they opened in the morning. He was going to disobey Birkett and direct a part of the stake into the place market. If the worst happened, it would provide some insurance. He wouldn't split the stakes, half to win, half to place; he'd have just enough on to get their money back if the horse ran to a place only. Currently showing six and a half to one, that meant about six thousand of the forty to be diverted in that direction. That though, could not be put into the market in one go, and if he tried, it would alert the layers to action on their horse that would spoil what remained of the win part of the bet. He knew what Birkett would say, but he was in charge of this side of the enterprise.

He dripped some more money into the market and set his phone for one hour's time and tried again to grab another morsel of sleep. As if to tell him that it wasn't going to happen, another bolt of lightning flashed, and this time with it, the heavens opened, and tropical rain began to beat hard against his window.

Whether it was the satisfaction of having a job almost done, or the regular rhythm of the storm against his window, his body finally gave way to sleep. He missed his alarm, then woke with a start at six, as the thunder rumbled again. All the money he'd put up to be matched had gone, so he hurriedly re-staked a large chunk of what remained. The price had dropped from averaging somewhere between forty and sixty, down to the low thirties but there was no cause for alarm, there was lots of money available at the prices, and had he chosen to, he could have finished off the bet in one go. Instead, he put most of it in above the market, and went to shower and change. When he returned it had all been taken. He finished off the bet, and left his room, noticing for the first time the intensity of the rain on the Velux windows that ran the length of the corridor.

He made a quick tour of the breakfast room, and finding no sign of Birkett, pulled his cap out of his pocket and set off towards the stables. He passed through the TV lounge on the way out; that had been the bar lounge last night, and he wondered how and when it was transformed back into an acceptable condition. They'd finished there, him, Birkett, Liam, and Alison, all in their cups, delighted, fraternal, slightly enriched by their betting, all full of Slipshod and his brilliance, sometimes talking about whether their luck might hold, and if they might win a handicap the next day. No one particularly confident, all of them hopeful. Even Liam, who knew now that his horse was the Group I racehorse, and that Milksheikh was the handicapper, had allowed them their moment. He'd have a few quid on each-way himself at twenty-fives or thirty-threes, if the bookies were stupid enough to offer that sort of price. After all, Milksheikh had got within hailing distance of Slipshod on their last piece of work.

Some of the lads were looking up at the television which was showing rolling news. 'Here it is,' said one of them. 'Look at this.'

It was the News, and the weather forecaster was saying, 'And as for sports, if you're heading to the cricket, don't. And if you're heading to Ascot, these are the scenes right now.' The picture cut to the empty grandstands covered in great pools of water, then panned round to show the course itself in a similar state.

'That rain will stop, I promise you,' said the presenter. 'But not until about midday. They are confident that they will be able to race, but whatever happens you can expect very wet conditions underfoot for racegoers and horses alike.'

Freddie found Birkett in Milksheikh's box. The horse was tied up as he mucked out around him. He looked up to the door as Freddie arrived, wearing all his woes on his face.

'Cheer up Birdie, it hasn't happened yet.'

Birkett continued with his work.

'Do you want me to wrap him up and take him out for a minute?' he asked. Again, Birkett didn't answer, just shook his head, and kept to his work.

Freddie left him to it for a moment and took a brief walk under the shelter of the overhang. Alison and Liam had already left with Slipshod. Another empty horsebox was on its way with a lad to lead up Milksheikh. He looked for someone to talk to who might provide an insight into the weather, someone who'd been up to the course perhaps and could provide some hope that it wasn't as bad as everyone said, that the hot weather meant that the rain had been much needed and was being soaked up into thirsty ground, that everything would be all right by the start of racing. But there was no one around. Anyone with work to do had been out, done it and got themselves back in the dry as soon as possible. They'd left their horses safe and dry, the best they could do for them at that instant, and they'd gone back to get ready and hope that what they had to deal with later in the morning would be better than that which faced them now.

He tried Birkett again. He'd finished mucking the box now and had let the horse down. Freddie took the wheelbarrow from him and went out into the rain to dispose of its contents, leaving Birkett under the dry of the overhang.

'So, he'll handle soft ground you said?' he tried, as he returned.

'Aye, but he can't fucking swim, can he?' Birkett took a brief turn along the stable block, then made a great effort to get out a few words. 'How much have you got on?'

'All of it, just about. Thirty-three at an average of just under fifties, seven at about sixes for the place.'

'Jesus,' he said. 'Can we get out of it? Get our money back?'

'Yes,' said Freddie. 'If you're happy to write off about two thirds of it, I could undo all the bets.'

Birkett sighed heavily, unable to pick up his gaze from the ground.

'I think we'll have to withdraw him, especially from that draw,' he said, then lapsed back into ruminative silence once more.

'But we've told the world about him now, we'll never get that price again. And if we don't go here, where are we going to go? The whole timetable's fucked up.' He withdrew into his thoughts once more, then after an age, just as Freddie had decided that there was no more to come from him, he said, 'Jesus, let him run, we'll still probably win.'

'I'll tell you what we'll do,' said Freddie. 'We'll have an early lunch, walk the course, then watch the first race – that's a big field on the straight course. Then we'll make a final decision after that. Birkett agreed, and they arranged to meet next at the racecourse at midday.

Neither man could eat. Freddie spent most of the lunch looking at his phone, trying to find out when the rain might stop, while Birkett looked out of the window thinking the same thoughts. 'What do you make of the first race then,' he asked Freddie.

Freddie, who had done his homework as a means of distracting himself from other thoughts, replied, 'All the good horses are drawn on the stand side, we're not going to find much out. In fact, we might become even more despondent after we've watched it.'

Birkett shoved his uneaten lunch away from him and said, 'Come on, let's walk the course and see how soft it is.'

That walk, and the fillies' race, only confirmed what they already knew: that their exceptional and underestimated horse would have to be every bit as good as they believed him to be to win the race. They decided immediately that the chance of crossing over from the bad draw on the far side to get amongst the horses heading over to the stand side was out of the question. The ground they'd have to surrender would reduce their chances to zero, especially in ground so soft. No, they'd take their medicine and go up the far rail with the few other horses who, like theirs, had been dealt the rough end of the draw. There was some encouragement in that very few of the fillies were likely to stay far side, and there wasn't much chance of the ground getting chewed up before they ran on it.

'Look at it this way,' he told Freddie as they returned from the course. 'It's that bad, none of them will like it, and we know that he's better than all of them. Come on son, let's have a go and give it our best shot.'

Tolley Woolf didn't provide much more encouragement when he came into the paddock. 'It's sloppy not sticky, but it's very deep,' he told them as he joined them to make a three. 'But he's a strong horse, he should go through it, and all the horses drawn well are dogs,' he added.

Birkett merely said, 'Good luck lad,' as he put him on the horse, and picking up Freddie again on the way out of the parade ring, trudged disconsolately with him to the almost empty, treacherously muddy lawns of the Royal Enclosure.

As the last horse was led up to the stalls, Birkett turned to Freddie and held out his hand to shake.

'Good luck son. Let's hope it's our turn,' he said.

Freddie nodded and they turned to look at the screen together.

And they're off for the Royal Hunt Cup,' said the disembodied voice at the top of the stands. 'And immediately two thirds of the field make their way over to the stands side. More than that actually, as only six runners are left over on the far rail. And as they settle down, the old boy Railway Line leads the near side group, Mack Hill Roy leads those just away from them in the centre, and Sprake takes them along on the far side. They're going steady in the conditions, and already at this early stage some of them are putting up the white flag. Still it's Railway Line on what we think is the favoured stand's side, as the horses there close to form one group, but they're not going fast enough for Milksheikh on the far side and he takes over from Sprake to lead that group. As they run down to halfway what will the cameras tell us as we look at them from side on? And yes, it says that the stand's side group have about ten lengths advantage. More maybe. The backmarker nearside is Roberty Bob, and there's a clear gap between him and the far side group. On they plod, no one is doing too much too soon apart from Milksheikh who's quickly gone six or seven lengths clear of the nearest horse behind him and he seems determined to put himself into the race.

Birkett and Freddie stole a glance at each other. He couldn't, could he?

And as they head towards the two marker, still no one wants to commit, in these desperate conditions – it looks more like a national hunt race only Milksheikh catches the eye, he must be fully twenty lengths in front of the horses on the far side, but how close is he to those on the stand's rail? Looking across as the leaders pass the furlong marker and he's… a long way back. The race seems to involve this side, as Railway Line eventually surrenders to Barrington Womble, who's finally asked to go and win his race, suddenly it all looks very difficult for everyone in behind. They're running on fumes most of them, Capriccioso comes out of the pack with Clever Clogs and Barty to try and throw down a challenge, and Glorious Gaynor who suddenly looks like she's the only one relishing the conditions. She has come from miles behind and she's making relentless progress. Milksheikh on the far side still improves but can he get involved? The line is surely coming too quickly for him as the old boy Barty starts to overhaul the leaders on this side; he's getting closer with every stride, Barrington Womble hangs on, Glorious Gaynor and Capriccioso fight it out for the minors, and poor Milksheikh, he's going to finish out of the money in fifth. Can Barrington Womble hang on? It's desperate out there, Barty's coming, Barrington Womble won't say no, Barty's… and Barty gets up to win the Hunt Cup beating Barrington Womble into second, Glorious Gaynor ran on for third in front of Capriccioso but the story of the race has got to be Milksheikh. You've got to say he's been beaten by the draw and would surely have taken all the beating on this side. He may just have got his head up for a gallant fourth, and by goodness he deserves it. But we'll leave that decision to the judge.

Then before they'd had time to digest the result, the commentator came back on again and announced:

The judge has called the result of the photograph, and it's Glorious Gaynor third, Capriccioso fourth, and

Milksheikh finishes an unlucky fifth and out of the money.

Without speaking, the two men went to wait for Tolley in the unsaddling area. They'd been reconciled to losing, yet somehow knew that they'd had to run. The rest of the world knew what they knew now. This was what horse racing did to people. They'd been right about everything and still lost.

Tolley confirmed what they knew already. 'He's miles better than that lot. Different league. You see what won it? They couldn't get placed in a normal Hunt Cup on good ground. That race was all about the ground. He hated it and still nearly won.'

'How far off them were you?' asked Freddie.

'Far enough,' he said. 'He could see them out of the corner of his eye all the way, and he was desperate to get them back, giving me everything he was. But this ground. He could have given them a start on the stand side and still beat them but on the far side it was like counting to ten before you set off. I've been on some unlucky losers in my career, but him Birdie...'

He shook his head, touched the peak of his cap, and left them to contemplate their losses.

SIXTEEN

Thoroughly sick of Ascot, its baubles, and the crowd, like a Hogarth painting so publicly drunk and wretched in their few hours of leisure together away from whatever it was they did every other day, Freddie and Birkett left the racecourse and installed themselves instead in an empty pub on the High Street.

Birkett, roaring with the conviction of a drunken man, only halfway down his first drink, banged his glass down on the table and said, 'We'd have still won on the wrong side if Slipshod was in the race. He'd have drawn him into the race for us. I'm never running him again unless Slipshod's there to set it up for him. That way, he's unbreakable.'

They sat in silence for a moment.

'What are we doing here Freddie? We can get the horse packed up and do all this at home. Come on drink up.'

Freddie got up from the table, grabbing Birkett's nearly empty glass as he did, and went to the bar to order the same again. 'So,' he said, putting the full glass down in front of him, 'you've given up on the idea of buying the broodmare?'

'Jesus, the mare! Two dreams go up in smoke in one fucking thunderstorm.'

'The thing is,' said Freddie, 'I'm going to have to talk to Robert… I think I saw him earlier. I guess the deal's off? It's the least we owe him, I can't leave him in limbo.'

'We're not gambling Milk again. Can't. He runs on merits from now on,' said Birkett.

'I know Birdie. That bird has flown.'

'Or Slipshod. There are no gambles left him in either.'

'Yes, I know that too. In fact, *we* won't be gambling on anything.'

'I'll tell you… what?' Birkett said, suddenly drawn back into the room again.

'I won't be gambling on anything for a while Birdie,' said Freddie, 'I owe Penny fifty-k at the end of the month, and I've just spent twenty of the fifty-five I had left.'

Birkett continued to murmur to himself for a moment longer, never quite tuned in to the detail of what Freddie was saying.

'I'm going to have to say something to Robert,' he repeated, 'And I'm going to ring him before we leave here.'

'I know, yes, I hear. I'm listening,' said Birkett, still staring at the floor between them. 'We've got horses, one or two. You know – the two-year-old, and Slipshod *will* win for us. We will get the chance to raise a little stake if we play it canny,' he said.

Freddie reached out and braced Birkett's thigh. 'Birdie. Listen to me. What are you talking about, playing it canny? We've just played and lost. Big. That's it. All we can do is take it on the chin and move on.'

Still Birkett hung his head, and Freddie began to wonder whether perhaps more had been lost on this frolic than just their money. Eventually Birkett swung his head round to look up at him. Freddie couldn't say for certain that he hadn't been crying.

'Where are you going to move onto then?' he asked. It sounded aggressive, and Freddie took a moment to take the sting out of the remark before he answered.

'Well, I'm going to start by running away from Penny and her lawyers, then I'm going to run away from my clients.'

Birkett didn't laugh.

'And when I get my breath back, I'm going to gather whatever money I've got left and go and in search of the people that ripped me off, until I get what was once mine back again. That should keep me busy.'

'Is that what you are then?' asked Birkett. 'Is that what your banking turned you into? That. Is that the way you want to live your life?'

It had been leading somewhere, and this was it. Here it came. Birkett in his mad, deranged, panic-stricken state, had hatched a plan for Freddie to arrange a line of credit for another crazy idea.

'No, but… I'm limited as to choice slightly Birdie. There are only so many options left…'

'Are there?' he asked, and Freddie's heart sank again. He sighed, all he wanted to do was get home and take the first step towards facing the future.

'Birdie,' he said. 'First I'm going to ring Robert…'

But before he'd got any further, Birkett interrupted him and said, 'Tell him we'll pick her and her foal up in late August, maybe the bank holiday, depending on how the dates fall.'

It was going to be another long night.

It wasn't meant to sound like a plea, but before long Freddie heard himself doing just that. He told Birkett that he was still in shock from the events that had just happened, that now was not the right time to be hatching new plans, that right now they were at their weakest and most vulnerable to idiotic notions that could take their ruination a step further away from being recoverable. 'The only sensible thing to do,' he said, 'is to go home and take stock.'

But Birkett simply replied, 'No.'

Robert needed an answer now, today, and they weren't going home until they'd talked to him.

'Tell me this,' he asked Freddie, 'did I get it wrong today?'

Freddie hesitated, searching for the right thing to say.

'Well? Did I? Look me in the face and tell me I got it wrong.' 'It's gambling,' Freddie tried. 'It's horseracing. We're going home forty thousand lighter. You've got to acknowledge the truth of that statement.'

'What are you now, a fucking lawyer, to add to your banking?'

'What?'

'You sound like one. I got fuck all wrong. Didn't you listen to the racecourse commentator? Didn't you listen to Tolley? Look on your phone or wherever it is you get these things. Tell me anyone out there that says I got it wrong.'

'I know what you're saying,' he said. 'But…'

'No,' he slapped his open hand down on the table. 'No, you don't Freddie,' he said. 'A freak of weather spoilt what was an absolute stone-cold certainty, that we had backed at fifty to one.'

'Yes,' said Freddie, 'one where all the cards fell right. Something that happens once or twice in a career as long as yours.'

Birkett nodded. He was smiling.

'And we still lost. What? Suddenly you're going to do it twice in the same year are you?'

'No,' he said, shaking his head, 'No, not again. Not in the same way. Today was different, I'll never get that chance again, you're right. This is more of a workaday thing. The sort of thing I'd pull off once every year or two.' He laughed.

It didn't matter what the plan was, Freddie wasn't going to play. How often had he heard people speak like this over the years? Racing and banking both. You're persuaded that there is nothing better than this plan, this horse. What could go wrong? Can you not see? You are in on this, and we cannot lose. Then *we* do lose, and then you are told to be a good sport and to summon up the same enthusiasm for the next project. Sure, he didn't have Birkett down as that type, but gambling, and losing big at gambling, did strange things to people.

'I've told you about it already,' said Birkett.

'What?'

'Bugbear,' he said. He was changed now. The sorrows of the afternoon were behind him.

'Bugbear?'

'Yeah, Bugbear. I've always been going to win the Monkey Puzzle Seller with him. I told you that. It just hasn't been at the forefront of my mind because of Milksheikh, but now it is. It's the next project. I was always moving on to that next after today. We just have to win a little bit more now than I'd originally planned, but we can do that. You can do that bit. The horse will still win.'

'Birdie, Birdie, please. Please don't do this. Not now. I mean, do it for yourself, of course. But don't ask me. I can't. This is the sort of thing that proper recidivist gamblers do, the things that bankrupts do.'

'Resi-what? Honestly, you need to come down to the level of us ordinary men Freddie, you'd get much more out of life I promise you.'

'Yeah, maybe I would,' he said.

Birkett shrugged at Freddie; arms wide open. 'But you're a banker. That's how you people swing isn't it?' he said.

'Once, maybe,' said Freddie. 'But these are different times. I'm hard against it, I owe more to Penny than I've got and she's my easiest creditor. That puts me in a different place. My risk profile has changed Birdie.'

Birkett got up from the table with the almost empty glasses to go to the bar again, and this time left Freddie alone with his thoughts. He came back with the drinks and seemed to drop them as a pair onto the table.

'Forget it then,' he said. 'Just tell me this though.'

Freddie nodded; they'd already drunk too much. He took another deep draught from his pint and leaned back into the corner of the bench.

'If you scrape up the money to pay your Mrs, what are you going to do then? What are you going to live on? How are you even going to fund yourself while you search down those fraudsters? Eh? How will you ever keep ahead of those other wrong-uns you owe money too? Well? How are you?'

Freddie had no answers, other than he would because he had to.

'I'll find a way,' he said, 'we've got our house. That'll sell one day.'

'The one where you've got a ten percent stake? That one?'

'I could get a job.'

'I've given you a job. Or do you want to work for that slippery cunt Ced back there, selling shares for him, working on commission?'

'No, I'm not saying...'

'Well have you got anything better?'

'No... bu'...'

'Do me a favour,' said Birkett. 'Ring that bloke Robert now and get things straight. I'm doing this whether you're in or not. Then don't come to work tomorrow. Just go somewhere and think about your options.

Freddie looked at him.

'Even if it goes tits, so what? You lose another two months of your life, and a bit more money. It's not going to make things a whole lot worse for you, is it?'

He had him cornered. There was something that felt so wrong about it all – like the bad boy at school who had ruined his exams for him, and to make amends, had taught him how to smoke.

Freddie raised his hand, asking for a moment's silence, then eventually he said, 'You want me to help you with this?'

Birkett nodded.

'Well, it's time to tell me the story.'

'What story?' asked Birkett.

'The real story. The one that pulling off these gambles is only half of. That one. The one you've been keeping to yourself – the way you kept this horse to yourself in the yard at home. Come on Birdie – you want a partner in crime? You want to make more than a million dollars – because this is what it's all about isn't it? Yeah? Well, it's time to come clean.'

'What are you on about?' said Birkett. 'I've already told you; you ignore what's under your nose.' He took another swig of his beer, then seemed to think better of it, and sat looking forwards towards the bar, unprepared to offer any further explanation. Freddie did the same, and for a while the two men sat in silence alongside each other staring forward. If he'd smoked, he'd have left the pub for a moment's quiet contemplation. So instead, he got up with his almost empty drink, and went up to the bar. Halfway there, he decided that another drink was the worst thing he could do and stopped. Birkett quietly examined him, the barmaid too, a grin spreading across her face. It would be mayhem in about two hours' time. Until then, you took your fun where you found it.

'I can smell bacon,' she said and looked over to Birkett to cash her joke, but he looked straight ahead still. 'I'm here all week, you know' she tried.

Freddie turned and smiled at Birkett.

'There's no three-year-old, is there?

'Three-year-old what?' he answered.

'Milksheikh's dam, Air Hostess. You've got Milksheikh, the oldest, there's no three-year-old, you've got the two-year-old. She's not just sentimental, is she?'

Birkett didn't exactly grin, but his facial features relaxed a little.

'You were really put out when I didn't bring her back from France. You're quietly buying up the whole family, aren't you? You think she's going to be the next Urban Sea?'

'Who?'

'The filly that won the Arc, then bred the best stallion in the history of racing, and all his half-brothers who also won the Derby and turned into good stallions too. You're going all in on the mare, aren't you?'

Birkett said nothing. She was only a barmaid, but she might know someone and remember to say the wrong thing to the wrong person. His silence drew Freddie back to his seat.

'What's with all the cloak and dagger, and pulling off gambles? Why don't you just buy her? Why didn't you keep her when she retired?'

'Because I'm like three quarters of the rest of them in Newmarket; I'm one bad debt and a funeral away from bankruptcy, and I own at least a leg in every horse I've got in the yard. I haven't got a pot to piss in, and no bugger in his right mind would lend me anything. That's why.'

'So, Birkett's launched a plan to buy the goose that lays the golden eggs. You old rogue.'

Birkett re-adopted his sullen stare into the distance.

'I thought you told me that Air Hostess didn't even get black type?'

He'd been goaded too far now. 'I did. But she should have. Would have. I know now – and I see it in her foals. I've trained a Group I winner before, and this season I've got Slipshod, and I'm telling you this – that horse today and his sister are different class.' Freddie smiled. 'You haven't told me why you didn't keep her when she retired yet.'

'She wasn't mine to keep, she was my owner's. He's dead now. Then she washed up in France. And I didn't know then what I know now. It was only when Milksheikh came in the yard that the penny started to drop.'

'If you're right…'

'I am right…'

'If you're right, she's worth, what? Millions? More – what would anyone pay for the mare of Galileo now? What would they pay for one of her sons? If you think about it like that, fifty million is cheap for the family.'

Birkett shrugged.

'What do you want all that money for? What are you going to do with it?'

'Nothing,' he said. 'I'm going to do nothing forever, and stop living on my wits, keeping this ship afloat.'

'What's my share for helping?' Freddie asked. He was grinning. He had the old man cornered now.

'It's my idea. I'll do without you. I've come this far.'

'No, no, Birdie. I've paid twenty large to have a look. I'm in.'

Birkett took a long, considered draught on his pint, and didn't begin speaking 'til he'd carefully placed it back on its beermat, then looked Freddie squarely in the eye. 'You'd better get weaving then because I've got to get on with this horse. At the end of the season, I'm going to make sure that I've at least got a Group I winner to sell on as a stallion and at the moment, your stake amounts to fuck all.'

That word, 'stake', stung Freddie into sobriety; he didn't even have a stake to punt on Bugbear, let alone anything else. But Birkett, more conciliatory now that it was all out in the open, told him it would be tough, that they'd fight and scrap, and turn every little opportunity they came across to eke out a little more, until, before long, they had just enough to make the punt on Bugbear worth having.

'One way or another we'll only be doing it with someone else's money,' he said, and finally he drew a comradely smile from Freddie.

'Have I just been played?' Freddie asked.

Birkett said nothing, but he seemed to smile as he raised his glass to his lips.

'What's there to lose?' he'd said, *two months of your life, and a tiny bit more money*, put like that it sounded like the only option. Especially when the prize could be counted in millions.

'What's the matter with you now?' Birkett asked. 'You've got to try and enjoy this. It matters. Especially when you get beat.'

'I'm in, I'm in,' said Freddie, 'you've got no choice in that.'

'If you're still thinking about paying off your wife, don't,' said Birkett.

'Don't?'

'She's a clever girl. She's got a well-off boyfriend. She wants for nothing. So what if you owe her it for a few months? Tell her, if it makes you feel better, but she'll survive whatever you do.'

But that wasn't what was on his mind. What concerned him most was the small matter of seven hundred thousand owed to his clients, now that the Milksheikh gamble had gone down.

The roar of the crowd billowing over from the stand told them that the fifth race had ended.

'Come on,' said Birkett. 'Let's get after him.'

'I'll tell you what I'm going to Birdie,' Freddie told him. 'I'm going to make him leave the horses here. For one, possession being nine tenths of the law and all that, they're better in our care; and two, if the worst comes to the worst, and we don't make our money again – don't interrupt, it's just happened, it might again – we can open the deal up to him and put him in.'

Birkett began to object but Freddie wouldn't let him.

'   I'd rather have one third of plenty, than half of nothing. And I know Robert, he's struggling. He'd love a deal like that. It might be our last throw of the dice, but at least we'd get a go.'

Birkett mused for a moment, then said, 'Ferdy, I knew you'd start paying your way before long. Fire away lad.'

Freddie had been right. Robert wasn't doing very well. He hadn't yet reached that part of the phone call where he told him he'd have to wait a little longer for his money when Robert put him out of his misery, 'The mare's not mine anymore, the bank has foreclosed.'

'What?' He should have sympathised, but his instinct was only to shout out questions. 'When? Why didn't you tell us? Where is she?'

'She's at home still,' said Robert.

'Can we meet, Robert? I don't quite follow the details. Are you here? Are you free for a few minutes?'

Robert sighed and consented to the meeting, as if to say, 'Why not? What else is there to do?' Implying somehow that Freddie was one of those who'd conspired against him. And within five minutes they were together at the back of the bandstand.

'I'm sorry Robert,' said Freddie, 'I had no idea. When did it all happen?' Robert's version of the story was that it came without notice a week or so ago, that there was a manager installed at their farm, and that he and Jules were allowed to stay on as tenants for another three months.

'They were all planning and scheming all the time Freddie. I just didn't see it until it was too late. Too trusting you see. I love people. Always have. And now I'm paying rent to live in my own house.'

'I'm really sorry Robert,' he said again.

'So am I,' said Robert, 'I had you down as one of them for a while, when it all happened. You know, all these faces buzzing around the farm, taking an interest in everything all of a sudden.'

'I can assure you of that,' said Freddie, 'we wanted the mare. We still do. I don't suppose...' He trailed off, it seemed inappropriate to ask.

It didn't to Birkett though. 'What will they do, put it up for auction?' he asked.

'No,' said Robert laughing. 'All that's done. It's already sold. At a distressed price, whatever they call it. All the bank wanted was enough to cover the loans, they didn't care about leaving us with anything.'

'So, who owns it now?' asked Birkett.

'Tara Fitzsimmons. You know, the woman who owns all those jumps horses. That's who I pay my rent to. Do you know her?'

'I don't,' said Freddie, 'but I know a man who does.'

He begged a moment from his new friend and called Ced, then reported straight back. 'The tent up there is too wet, they're in Conrad's box,' he told them. 'We're invited up. Fancy it?'

'Hold on, hold on,' said Birkett. 'Is she up there with them?'

Freddie glanced briefly at Robert before replying. 'She may still be there,' he said, 'she was there earlier. It's pretty crowded. He's asking Conrad now. I've told him to find out whether she's having a dispersal sale or not. Come on, at least we'll find that out. Or would you rather not Robert?'

'Hold on I said,' said Birkett again, before Robert had replied, then continued, 'don't just go jumping in asking about the mare, not with someone like that.'

Freddie assured him that he wouldn't, but wondered whether Robert as previous owner, was prepared to meet with Tara, and perhaps ask her about her plans for the farm, and the stock?

He was, not least because he'd been forbidden from talking to her to date, and if he did, you never knew, any little morsels that were to be cast aside, might come back at a fair price. And he knew their real value all right. 'You should never count such things out,' he told the others, and so they set off as a three, to find out just how unsalvageable all their various plans really were.

Ced, standing sentry duty just behind the half-opened door to the box, weaving slightly, seemed surprised to see that they'd turned up.

He greeted them with a hiccough, 'Boys, lovely to see you,' he said. He started to say, 'How's your day been?' but just pulled himself up in time, and righted it to, 'God, what awful luck you boys had today. Yours was the best horse in the race.' They silently nodded their agreement, and swallowing as he rebalanced himself, he said, 'Let me call Connie over for you.' He beckoned Conrad from the distance to come and join him. 'He's been with clients all afternoon, but he should be OK now. Connie!' he shouted above the din, and at the opposite end of the box, in the opening of the French windows letting out onto the balcony, Conrad lifted up his head and signalled that he'd make his way over. 'He's coming now,' said Ced. 'Let me go and find you boys a drink.' He staggered off in the direction of the mini bar set up on the far wall, which now had just a couple of empty champagne buckets, half a dozen dirty glasses, and a carton of orange juice left on it.

'Hya, fellas,' said Conrad, exhaling, as an athlete might at the end of a contest, as if to say, *that's been a tough day.*

'How are you all?' he said. 'Hey, what a run from your horse in the Hunt Cup. Nothing's won on that side all day. I was talking to one of my ratings boys and he says you can mark that performance up twenty pounds.'

Birkett and Freddie exchanged looks as if to say, *yeah, we were thinking something similar.*

'He didn't go unbacked either you know. They reckon he'd have taken a couple of *mill* out of the book. I'd say he had a few supporters now.'

Both men looked at the ground, they had nothing more to say on the subject. 'Is Tara here?' tried Freddie, 'Ced was saying that she was still around?'

Conrad confirmed that she was, but would be leaving any minute. 'I can try and introduce you, but perhaps not all three at once, you know, she's trying to have a day off.'

'Has she said anything about what she's doing with the farm?' asked Freddie.

Conrad replied that he'd asked her, and she'd said they hadn't looked through the stock properly yet.

Birkett decided that he'd make himself useful by leaving the party to search out any auctioneers that still might be about, to see if Tara had made any special arrangements with any of them. Conrad shrugged at him, saying, 'Be my guest, if you think that will help.' He gestured to Freddie with his head to have him follow him, then started back towards Tara. Robert, uninvited, followed too.

They set off to shuffle sideways through the still dense crowd, and Conrad turned to Freddie and said, 'Did you hear? Our colt runs in the Britannia tomorrow. Not a bad draw either.'

'Yes,' said Freddie, 'Ced was saying.'

'You know that this year's scheme has filled up fast too?'

'Yes,' he shouted in his wake.

'We're closing it July thirty-first. It all has to be paid up by then.' Then he added, 'Sorry, it's just that Ced doesn't always deal with the specifics.'

'No, that's fine,' said Freddie. 'I was talking to Ced about doing something by the end of this week.'

'I'm so glad that we've got people like you in,' he said. They arrived at the space occupied by Tara. She was perhaps the only woman in Ascot wearing a man's suit - the tailored lightweight cashmere, discreet heels, and mock trilby, accentuating her tall, slender frame, and lending the impression that she towered over the small men standing to each side of her. Freddie was drawn to her severe bob. It looked like an artistic statement, as if she was parodying the 1920s flapper. About his age, he wondered if he'd met her before, when she was on her way up. When she was less striking perhaps?

She was talking quietly to one of the small men at her side, her racing manager, Freddie assumed.

Conrad made the deftest of movements of his head to try and catch her attention, which she acknowledged in the same way back, then, whilst continuing with her conversation, held out her left hand, which also held a wine glass, and raised her little finger to say that she'd registered the request and they were next up.

Robert, following behind them, was disgorged a moment later from the jungle of bodies into the peaceful glade around Tara, and brushed himself down as he came to stand alongside Freddie. 'Well, I'm glad they never gave me a bloody drink, I'd have never made it through that lot,' he said, 'is this her then?'

Freddie nodded to say it was, and as he did, three other men arrived from the balcony. They too stood in Tara's midst, and something about the way they settled, waiting, indicated that they were part of her entourage. The last of the group was Alan Halliday, and, towering over everyone else in the room, he scanned it constantly for faces he might know. As his gaze spiralled in decreasing circles it finally came to rest on Robert, who returned it with venomous reproach.

Truthfully, the never-bested Alan Halliday recoiled at the sight of Robert, and seemed, for the moment at least, in want of an explanation for his being there at all. But it was not just the sight of Alan that made Robert's lip curl, it was the other two men that stood between him and Tara – the manager, and his account manager from the Anglo-French Bank; their coincidence together as a four pushed him from merely angry into a seething rage. 'You fucking dirty bastards,' he shouted.

Tara and Conrad looked round sharply as one, as David Spencer, his account manager from the bank, broke ranks, and politely, but firmly, whispering placatory words throughout the manoeuvre, led Robert away by the elbow.

A be-suited, heavy-set ape like the ones who intervened in Freddie's confrontation with Gordon Melville at Saint Cloud, came from the shadows and followed Robert and David back through the crowd.

'Is there any trouble?' asked Tara.

Conrad jumped in to say, 'No, I was just going to introduce you to Freddie Lyons, the assistant trainer of Milksheikh. He wanted to say hello before he left.'

Tara swapped the wine to her other hand, and lazily held her free hand out for Freddie to touch gently.

'Frederick T. Lyons. I remember the name.'

It was how it used to appear in race cards when he was riding, Mr. Frederick T. Lyons. He was impressed. Whatever she did for a living, her racing knowledge was vast and deep if she could recall things like that.

'So, this is the club that had its fingers burned today?' she said. 'The fate of all great each way bets, eh? Me too. You're not going to try and sell him to me after that are you?' And all her advisers laughed at a rare joke.

'He doesn't mind the winter ground, but he wouldn't like the eight fences,' replied Freddie, trying to insinuate an equally poor attempt at a joke in return.

'Is Birkett here?' she asked, 'I've been promising to send him a horse for a while.'

'No, he's gone out to do some marketing in the Pimm's Tent,' said Freddie, adding, 'why haven't you – sent him a horse I mean?'

'Because he's a loner who can't be trusted, I suppose. But now that he's surrounding himself with smart PR types, I might have to have a re-think.' She took a sip from her glass, 'provided you stick at it. Did you have anything specific you wanted to bring up?'

He did, but not now, not in the aftermath of... no it would better wait. 'Nothing that's appropriate for here,' he said, 'perhaps I could contact you through Conrad again sometime?'

'Perhaps you could,' said Tara.

He smiled at Conrad to say thanks then turned to leave the party in search of Robert, pushing his way through the sois-disant turfistes, who for one day in June, and another in March, at Cheltenham, presented themselves as devotees of the game.

At the door he met Penny, talking with Ced, 'Aha! You can avoid me no longer,' she said.

'I haven't been avoiding you. In fact...' He was about to reel off a list of compliant actions he'd taken since they'd last met. All fictitious of course, but still.

'I mean earlier, you oaf,' she said, 'before the first race, I saw you and you saw me, but you put your head down and pretended you hadn't.'

'Oh that,' said Freddie. 'I thought you were taking your monkey for a walk.'

Ced laughed out loud, and it brought the attention of the butt of their joke, standing with his back to Ced, who turned round to ask what the laughing was about.

'Nothing,' said Penny, 'just Freddie trying to deflect attention so that he can avoid talking about his responsibilities again.'

Freddie said nothing, then after making everyone endure an excruciating silence, shook Ced by the hand and said, 'Thank you Ced, you're a dear friend, I really appreciate it.' Then without looking at his ex-wife and her new man, left the box in search of Robert.

But Robert had gone.

Freddie searched in vain for Robert after he left the party, but he refused to answer his phone and there was no obvious place to seek him out. So, he went back to the hostel where found a note pinned on his door from Birkett, written in his usual mix of lower case and capitals, which said, 'I'vE goNE. No NeWs. GONe iN bOx. YOu bRiNg caR.' The keys were left under the driver's seat as usual, and he jumped into it without calling - hands-free was something that belonged to the future when Birkett's car was made. He set off for home, glad of the silence and time to himself and his thoughts. He plodded home by the back routes and A roads and arrived back just in time to go straight to bed. Birkett was already asleep.

He kneeled against his bed, more weary than in supplication, and said to Felix, 'Sorry mate. Don't give up on me yet.'

EIGHTEEN

At second lot break, Freddie and Birkett met, ostensibly to have look at Milksheikh to see how he'd taken the race. He was stiff and lame and could barely hobble from his box into the yard. He told Davey to take him for a pick of grass and said that he'd come by and have another look at him later.

'We'll get those shoes off him and let him right down for a couple of weeks,' he said, 'then I'll swim him.' It wasn't a conversation, just the usual internal thoughts spoken out loud.

Smiling, Liam Williamson came by them on his way out of the yard on the last horse in the string, and said, 'Never mind lads, I hear they're putting on a three-legged race here next week.'

Birkett spun on his heel and shouted, 'He pays your fucking wages you, insolent prick,' then turned back, refusing to look at him in the eye, putting the matter of a reply out of the question.

'Get in the car and tell me about it all,' he said to Freddie, 'He's been three days in charge here, and it needs putting right.'

'Why don't you sack him?' Freddie asked.

'Do you know how much that costs? Or where I'd find a new one if I did?' said Birkett.

'Oh yeah, you said.' said Freddie.

They got into the car and headed out onto the Cambridge Road heading towards the not-quite car park by the July Course to watch the string work. The truth was there wasn't an awful lot for Freddie to tell Birkett, nor Birkett, Freddie, just that shared sense of a life changing event having slipped through their fingers.

'So, you didn't specifically ask her?'

'No,' Freddie replied. He couldn't quite make Birkett understand how inappropriate it had seemed to ask after Robert's outburst.

'We might get another chance with her,' he said, 'and I wanted to keep my ammo dry so that when we do, we do it properly. I don't want her to associate us with an embittered prick like him.'

Something still rankled with Birkett, but he fell short of articulating it.

'What was I going to do Birdie? We've got no money. All I could do was antagonise her. At least this way, if there's any chance that the deal's still alive, it still is.'

'I know son. You're right. I'm just so…' He banged the steering wheel. 'What a prick. If that Robert bloke had just phoned us to say that they were trying to close him down. He could have got the horses away to us – it wouldn't have made any difference to the price she paid for it all.'

'Maybe it wouldn't,' said Freddie, 'but he wouldn't have seen it like that. He'd have been demanding cash now to try and save his business, and we wouldn't have had it to give him.'

'Aye, happen,' said Birkett.

They drove on in a new silence to the car parking area at the top of the July Course, both in their different ways feeling that they were close to having done the right thing, and yet not quite able to grasp what they could have done better. They each tried to say or think of that thing that would have been the right thing to do, or to come up with some stroke of genius to resurrect it all.

'Don't you think…' said Birkett, 'no forget it.'

'What?' said Freddie, 'Say anything. It's only us here, we might accidentally say the right thing.'

'No,' he replied. 'It's only hindsight. I was thinking that we should have been bold and cut Robert into the deal from the off – like you were saying. Given the poor bastard the chance of a payday like we're after. It's too late though, isn't it?'

'Look. The bloke's an emotional prick. If we'd have cut him into it from the start, he'd have already given it away by now. We didn't do anything wrong. We were just unlucky.'

'Hindsight,' said Birkett, 'the gift by which all losers judge themselves.'

'Just forget Robert,' said Freddie. 'It's nothing to do with him anymore. He can only fuck it up.'

'So, what are we going to do then? Keep at it? How exactly?'

'Birdie. Let's face it, we're hanging by a thread. We've got no money; all we've got is a minor "in" with that Tara woman. Let's explore that, see where it takes us, and if it gives us a chance, it gives us a chance. If there's a dispersal sale, we might have to persuade a couple of owners to finance it and get what we can that way.'

'Yeah, but I can't keep holding back on Milksheikh, I've got to start... and when she sees how good he is...'

Freddie's phone rang. He threw a look at Birkett, then answered.

'Yeah. So, where are you? No. Not really. Er... I just thought you'd be more... Yeah. OK. Yeah, OK. Did he? I hope you haven't given the game away. Sure? I don't... Yeah, I will. I will. Course I will. See you there. Bye Robert. Don't dare say anything until I arrive.'

Birkett was halfway out of the car. 'What was that?'

'You might want to get back in for a moment,' said Freddie. 'Robert's had an idea.'

Birkett improvised an archly curious expression and pulled the door shut behind him.

'Right,' Freddie said, 'don't take this the wrong way. He's still very angry, and maybe he's still too much of a loose cannon for us to trust... but it seems that his contact at the bank – you know, the one I told you about who took him out when he started kicking off? It seems that he trusts him. I don't know whether the bloke – David Spencer he's called – I don't know whether he talked him down, whether he's on Robert's side or theirs; and I don't know whether this comes from Robert or him – we'll find all that out. He wants me to meet him back at Ascot tomorrow. But what he just said to me then is this – these are Robert's words not mine: why don't we say that the deal was done before the bank sold his farm to Tarara or whatever she's called?'

They looked at each other in silence for a moment.

'Nah. That can't work,' said Birkett.

'It can't, can it?' said Freddie.

'What's in it for him?'

'That's the thing. Nothing. I mean, even if we made the case, the money would still have to be paid to the bank, not him, I think – I'll find out. I guess he's looking for a kick back, and of course, he's spoiling the deal for the people who ruined him, so there's a bit of revenge in it. Well, a lot really. That's his main motivation I think.'

'It can't be. We're being set up.'

'Not by Robert, we're not. I'm sure of that. Maybe he's looking for more than he said on the phone – but I don't think he's smart enough to think that way.'

'I don't know. It smells fishy. It's all too soon. And what can he do? He's lost it all. That woman owns it. I mean, what the fuck? We should be concentrating on her.'

'He tells me this David Spencer is worth listening to. I've got to give it a spin Birdie. It's worth another trip to Ascot and back, isn't it?'

'Aye, it probably is,' said Birkett, without communicating any hope with his words.

Freddie felt the same. He had to try, but going back to that place again, full of unknown people? It was bad enough chancing an encounter with someone pursuing you for their ounce of flesh when a million-pound prize was within your grasp. It was quite another to return empty handed, clueless and desperate.

NINETEEN

Passing through the imposing wrought iron gates at the main entrance of Ascot racecourse felt to Freddie a little like returning to school for the end of term after you'd sat your exams knowing you'd made a mess of them. It was early, and he had that sense of being alone with just the staff; they somehow having transformed the scene of debauchery and decay from around about seven o'clock the previous evening into something as fresh as paint, ready to welcome the new revellers, today. It was remarkable, especially considering how wet and muddy it had been two days ago.

Robert had sent him the name of a restaurant, and an accompanying name of the particular section of the behind-grandstand hinterland that it sat in, but none of it meant anything to Freddie. Still, he was early enough to walk round it all. He didn't find it on the first pass and wondered for a moment whether it was going to be one of those places hidden away inside the grandstand – that great concourse that fell somewhere between an airport on the day that all the flights had been cancelled, and an edge of city shopping mall on the lead up to Christmas. If it was in there, there were just too many angles to cover from unwelcome interlopers, and for a moment he gave up, and set off back towards the exit. Then he persuaded himself to try again, this time more methodically still, starting over from the far end of the pre-parade ring, and making his way from the farthest point east, to the farthest point west. For some reason it mattered that he didn't phone Robert to ask where he was. Why did they add to the complication by doling out names like that, *The Bustino Courtyard*? What did that mean? It really was like the way they named things in holiday camps. His phone rang, he answered, then simultaneously saw Robert waving at him in the distance. 'It's me you bloody fool,' he was shouting.

The restaurant was tucked away beyond the walkway that took horses to and from the course, in a little forgotten island of calm and isolation. Neighbouring bars and restaurants had hardly got round to cleaning down their tables, yet this one was set up and ready to go. Already a liveried waiter stood at the lectern of the open plan terrace, as if expecting him. As it came into full view, he saw that

Robert and David were sharing their first glass, sat on the terrace too, with a three-sixty degree perspective on everything around them. 'Well scouted,' he said to himself, and laughed as he pictured Robert as a reconnaissance marine leading the company.

Robert got up to greet him, embracing him like an old friend, somehow returned to the person Freddie knew him to be from Wednesday's version.

'Come in, come in,' he said, giving anyone who cared to look the impression that it could have only been his restaurant. 'Now, I get to sound like a stuck record with this boy, but I can't believe that you two haven't met. You haven't, have you?'

David and Freddie shook heads then took each other's hand, briefly exchanging that non-committal half-smile that was part of the protocol for men like them.

It seemed remarkable to Robert that Freddie, all those years in France, had not thought to use the services of Anglo-French, David's bank. 'We all did,' he said.

'Yeah, and look where it got you,' thought Freddie. For all that, David Spencer did not seem to Freddie a banking type, especially one at the retail end of the spectrum. He looked quite normal – someone else who'd ended up on the wrong path in life. He had this thing that looked like a duelling scar under his left eye.

'You must have gone in through the back door if we didn't even get to pitch you,' said David.

Freddie forgave him the crap joke. Awkward business meetings always needed lubricating. 'Our networks maybe aren't as good as we think they are,' he continued, 'you're not still based there are you?'

'Oh that.' Freddie told him that he wasn't, then corrected himself to say that his principal home was in fact still there. They chatted briefly about the difficulty of selling houses of prestige, as David put it, quickly in France, and Freddie resisted the desire to tell him that it mostly belonged to his wife now. It was perhaps a mark of the man that he then proceeded to extract the asking price from him without sounding like he was prying. Perhaps he was a little like a banker after all, thought Freddie. 'Three point five,' he told him, and noticed it register with him, and not a little with Robert too.

'If we can ever help you with that, please just get in touch,' said David. Freddie nodded that he would, sliding David's card towards him under his middle finger from where it had been left between them. He glanced at it briefly then transferred it to his inside pocket.

'Oh yeah, they've got loads of people to sell your house to Freddie, but don't expect to get anything out of it yourself,' said Robert. In doing so he cast a sheepish glance at David who returned it with an admonitory shake of the head, as if to say, 'We've been through all this Robert, haven't we?'

Freddie smiled, picking up the menu to pretend to read it. Then sensing that he was being drawn into one of those so familiar events that were somehow labelled business meetings – where an hour or two was spent dancing around a subject which, by the time it is finally addressed, is dealt with in two or three brief sentences, said, 'How come you two are friends again?'

'We're not,' said Robert.

David smiled.

'He's part of the lynch mob and he knows it. This is my account manager.' He pointed with his thumb whilst looking at Freddie. 'And he watches while they throw me to the wolves.'

'It's not like that…'

'And,' interrupted Robert, 'they just so happen to have found a great little asset for one of their mates for a fraction of its real value. See where their loyalties lie Freddie? See who they're working for?'

An awkward silence descended. Freddie contemplated asking the obvious question but David, making that placatory peace gesture with his hands before he took up the point again said, 'Robert will come out of this horrible situation far better by working with us, than working against. And…'

'He says it wasn't his idea. That's his saving grace as far as I'm concerned,' added Robert.

David was becoming slightly irritated with his client, and said, more forcibly than was proper, 'It wasn't. My job was to see the sale through once the decision was made. The decision had been made at a higher pay grade than mine to, er… foreclose.'

A waiter hovered at Freddie's shoulder. 'We should order,' he said.

'He sold it quickly enough,' said Robert, as the waiter disappeared, then turning back to David continued, 'If you'd worked with me, told me I had to sell up, showed a bit of patience – like we're entitled to expect with a managed account, I could have got out of it better than this. Then you wouldn't be having to work with me now to *make the best of it* or whatever it is you say you're doing. We could have all gone our separate ways…'

'Robert,' said David, 'we've been through this.' He looked up at Freddie, he didn't want to repeat confidential matters in front of a stranger.

'Don't mind Freddie,' said Robert. 'Speak away. I've done nothing to be ashamed of.'

'Let's just eat,' said David, 'we've got other things to talk about. We'll get more out of looking forward than looking behind us.'

'Exact,' said Robert, and for a while silence fell as they each took a piece of bread and waited for their starters to arrive. A sort of dry, staccato conversation stuttered into life between David and Freddie, without really taking hold, while the resentment continued to bubble and build in Robert. Out it came through his little white lips framed in dry spittle, out through the top of his bald head, pulsing through the prominent veins on his little red face, out through his ears and his eyes, never quite settled between an apoplectic fit, a heart attack, and a nervous breakdown. As much as he acknowledged that there was nothing to be gained by it, it was beyond him to put a halt to the tide of emotion that rushed up from his guts.

He choked back his words, unable to join the small talk, grinding his teeth with increasing ferocity, until eventually he could not hold back. 'Yeah, everybody got a good deal out of it, apart from the bloke who broke his back building up the business.' He dropped his knife and fork onto the table, barely able to hold back the tears and anger.

'Robert that's not…'

'I thought Tara was your client?'

'She is. In a way. I deal with her people.'

'And you don't get your finder's fee, or your little brown envelope?'

'If finder's fees were handed out, they've overlooked me again,' said David.

'Well, it's all in there – all the commissions and add-ons that make the whole shebang twice as bad as it need be.'

'Robert, Robert, please,' he said. 'If Tara Fitzsimmons was charged a finder's fee that's perfectly legitimate but it wouldn't have been added to your liabilities. We are entitled to make charges like that, it's how banks work. But I'm telling you, if we did, and perhaps we did, none of it came to me.'

'You see this, Freddie? Still, he won't admit it. They were in a bigger rush getting a cheap asset to their most valued customer than they were in helping a good loyal one get back on his feet.'

David Spencer had had enough, and wanted this unseemly row put to bed, not least because there was something more constructive they could be talking about.

A new waiter cleared their starters, Robert's hardly touched, while the original waiter hovered behind with their main courses. They watched him place the plates in front of them, determinedly mute, until they had withdrawn again.

'Robert. The bank had decided that your liabilities were too far in excess of your assets and had to make a decision. They could throw more money at what they thought was a lost cause, or they could redeem what they could while there was still a chance. I'm sorry. I count you as a friend as well as a client. But it really is how it works. It's horrible but it's true.'

It was. Freddie knew that. You didn't join a bank to make friends, as he'd been told countless times himself during his career, especially when it came time to deliver some ice-cold compassionless ultimatum to an unsuspecting client. He'd never liked it, and it didn't get any better when you were sitting next to the victim witnessing it all as a neutral.

It was odd the way that businesses like that worked, he thought. All or nothing. No party ever interested in seeking out the middle way. Sure, it was probably time to call Robert in, but why did they suddenly switch from consoling confidante to callous executioner? Couldn't they have found a way some time ago to see the problem coming and say, 'Times up, sell your horses and put the property on the market'? That would have reaped far more than an instant fire-sale to an acknowledged unscrupulous dealer. Despite his maddening obstinacy and inability to put his points properly Freddie felt a great surge of sympathy for Robert railing against the unbending might of the Anglo-French Bank.

The waiter came and did that thing, where they make you stop enjoying yourself, to ask if you're enjoying yourself. Freddie took a sip from his glass. Chilled white wine. Chilled! What a fabulous novelty in a place like this.

'Can someone please explain what I'm doing here?' he asked.

'Well, we had a deal,' said Robert.

Freddie and David exchanged glances.

'Yes,' said Freddie cautiously, 'we had a deal, but I'm guessing...'

Robert jumped in again. Yes, they had agreed that Robert would sell one of his mares with her foal; the price had been agreed, the date and point of delivery had been agreed. There was a record of it somewhere he was sure, but what he was saying was correct and the Anglo-French Bank's usurping actions had cut a swathe across their intentions, and denied the deal that they'd legitimately made before ever the bank had started with its intervention.

Had these assets had been bought and paid for? David wanted to know, because he was quite sure that he hadn't seen a transaction for, what was it? One hundred and forty thousand? He would want to speak first with the bank's lawyers before he committed himself, and given that the bank was Robert's primary creditor, they would be quite keen to see that any such funds had been transferred to them.

'Oh no. You've had yours,' said Robert, 'that'd be mine.'

David turned to gesture to the waiter for another bottle of wine and as he did Freddie looked briefly at Robert who, looking straight ahead towards David's half turned body, gave a trademark almost imperceptible shake of his head.

'That's not really how it works,' David continued. 'And Tara, now having bought the farm for value, would be unlikely to accept that it was worth the same minus two valuable assets.'

Robert cut across him. 'She'd have given the same whether they were there or not, and you know it.'

'Erm,' David pleaded to go on, free from his interventions.

Freddie held out a hand towards Robert saying, 'Let him finish.' He wanted to say, 'Let him say his piece, before we decide what we have to say.'

And David did finish, and as he brought it to an end he said, 'I promise I'll look into it with the lawyers, but I'm not too hopeful. What's the mare called by the way?'

Freddie jumped in next. If this desperate throw of the dice led to nothing, as he believed it would, what was to be gained by alerting Tara to the horses they were after? If David didn't mind, Freddie would rather keep that information under wraps for a moment.

'You're going to have to say the names out loud at some point,' said David.

Instead of answering him on the point, Freddie asked, 'We've heard that she intends a dispersal sale of the stock, can you tell us anything about that?'

David laughed, he said he couldn't. She'd send everything to the sales that was left once she'd had her team pick through it all. But he hadn't quite finished his point – had he understood them correctly? Had Freddie paid for the horses?

Finally, he says it, thought Freddie. We were almost home and dry. 'Er...'

But before he could reply Robert interrupted again and said, 'What if he had? What difference would it make?'

David did not jump all over the remark, as a banker might, as Freddie had expected him to. When you got to know him a little better, he seemed to have something of a fondness for Robert, with his old-fashioned amateurish way of looking at things, at least a high degree of tolerance of his ways – that was perhaps the better way of putting it. 'Robert,' he said, 'if you're telling me that you've squirreled away some money that we should have known about that could have repercussions, because you should have declared that before now, and well, if we've missed it, we're both in trouble. If the money hasn't been transferred yet, that's different. Your deal is easier to prove, but your case is weaker for doing it that way.'

'I've been telling you this all the way through,' said Robert, though whatever that was, he offered no further details.

'You do know,' said David, 'that the money can't benefit you, Robert?'

'Yes, it can,' he said, 'for one, I'd fight tooth and nail for it, and if that fails, one hundred and forty grand paid into my insolvency fund or whatever you call it, can do nothing but benefit me. It's better than it going anywhere else. No, David, me and Freddie made a deal and I intend to stick by it.'

David set his lips in a sanguine expression and cocked his head, as if to say, 'Why not? Fight for everything, if it means that much to you.'

'The bank's happy with what they've raised,' said Robert, 'maybe this payment's just hanging around in an unknown account waiting to be claimed.'

It was an embarrassing thing to say, and it fell to Freddie to change the subject. 'It's a pity, isn't it? – I used to work in a bank myself, as you probably know,' he said, waving away the offer of a menu, '...that there are all these people out there, all doing something good for the economy, all bringing their little bit of genius to make a small thing that's part of the big thing work a bit better. Whether it's their talent for bringing other people together; whether it's the little bit of magic they weave that wouldn't be missed if it wasn't there, but when it is there, it makes everything better; then as soon as...' he paused, placing his hand palm upwards in front of David, '...a bank such as yours,' he nodded deferentially, 'brings down the guillotine, that's it. It's not just Robert's business ended without a chance of redemption but all of those little enterprises that react with it, mine in this case, poof! They're taken out in the same crass, insensitive overreaction.'

He thought for a moment about whether he should go on, then decided to go for it.

'You see, the transaction we proposed to Robert was something we've worked on for a very long time. In our hands the deal could be worth a fortune. In others not so much. We hold all the cards, David. And the actions of your bank have snuffed out the prospects of an enterprise that would make the sum you've gained in the margins in putting Robert out of business, look like very trifling figures indeed.'

It was David's turn: 'I'm sorry if I've come over as too much of a banker here today. I've just been fighting my corner against

Robert. He'll forgive me one day. But let me say it now in front of two witnesses, you have all my sympathies; more than you realise. When the big boys start shouting, we just jump on our steamrollers and squash everything in sight.'

They sat to consider his words for a moment. Each somehow feeling bound by the openness that they had begun to share.

'While we're confessing,' said Freddie, 'I spoke too effusively. Please David, I am asking you to keep our confidences. Robert is still your client, and I may well be too if we get this scheme off the ground. Specifically, I'm asking you not to share any of this with Tara.'

David stretched out both hands in the direction of his dining companions. 'You have my absolute word, that this conversation is between us three alone and will never be repeated.'

So, they ended up dancing around the real subject after all, Freddie maintaining his own counsel throughout, unwilling to commit himself lest he contradict something that had been said before he arrived, nervous that Robert would misread the situation and blurt out something to spoil the finely balanced discussion. Slowly the chat wound itself up, and as David proposed a round of digestives, he changed the subject to something lighter: 'What do you fancy today?' he asked.

Freddie replied, 'Mexican Hat Dance.'

'Where's that?' asked Robert.

Freddie laughed. 'In one of the handicaps.'

David smiled back at him, acknowledging his reading of the situation.

As they got up to leave the lunch, David put his card away, waving away their thanks and said, 'If I were you, I'd just approach Tara directly, tell her what you had planned, and try to work the deal through her. She's not an ogre, she'll listen. If you do, leave me out of the loop. I don't want to complicate things, just approach her yourself – you said you had an in, didn't you?'

Freddie nodded that he did.

'Good, it would be wrong if I introduced you, it would compromise me, and it would make them look at it all in a different light. But I will have a discreet word with the lawyers, like I said, and

I will have another look for the money to see if we've done something stupid – Robert, if you think it's in an account we haven't seen, now would be the time to have a look. Until the next time. And I hope I might see you in France when you're next there, Freddie,' he said, and left them.

Robert shouted, 'A deux mains,' as he left the terrace but his voice didn't carry against the noise of the racecourse that had now sprung into life.

Robert and Freddie chatted on a little while longer once he'd gone. They talked about how they might approach Tara and how they were going to support their assertion of a deal with an actual payment. Robert assumed that they had the money, and Freddie decided that the time was not right to tell him that they were potless too.

'Look Robert,' he said, 'I'm not certain what it is you're after. All the way through lunch I held back from being specific in case it contradicted anything you'd already said to David, and the more it went on, the more certain I was that you had agreed something.'

'Why's that?' asked Robert. 'We've just got our deal, like we discussed.'

'Well, didn't you find it odd that David didn't go into any detail about whether we'd paid or not? It made me feel uncertain, and I didn't want to say anything.'

'Oh that,' said Robert laughing, 'he's fly isn't he? That's why I wanted you to meet him. All the others are rotten bastards, but he keeps both sides open.' Then he bent towards Freddie's ear, and said, 'I don't think he's on the best deal.'

'Oh, right. And what are you looking for out of this Robert?' he asked.

'Anything,' said Robert. 'Count on me for anything. I want revenge on everyone who did this to me – and I'll get to them through him. And you perhaps,' he added. 'And if I get any of my money or horses back, even better.'

Freddie debriefed Birkett, then next rang Ced. He didn't tell him how close he was to the racecourse for the good reason that Ced, drunk, would agree to grant the favour of facilitating a meeting with Tara, only in return for Freddie turning up at his party to be paraded around as a racing celebrity.

'It's important,' Freddie told him, 'I really need to get one on one with her for a few moments.' The urgency with which he pressed for the meeting contradicted the casual deal he'd described, but Ced went with it.

'I get it,' he told him, 'But Tara is Conrad's property, not mine. I will ask him, and he'll do it if I ask hard enough, but he'll want something in return. It's not my style as you know Freddie, but it is his.'

'I know, I know, I know,' said Freddie, 'I am in the scheme, committed. I will take at least one share, and I'll get the money to you in the next couple of days – in fact, send me the bank details by text and I'll do it now. Please assure him of that Ced. I need this. It will blow some hard work if I don't get to meet her – and,' to add some interest for Ced, he added 'yes it does involve horses. We've got a very good one that we can't run until we've secured this deal.'

A little while later, as Freddie finally hit the A14 on the way home, he received a text, which said, 'Ring me. She's meeting her art man in South London tomorrow. You are PROVISIONALLY invited. Compliance is requested.'

'Provisionally?' thought Freddie when he read the message. He must have a very good spell-checker if he can manage words like that by text at this stage in the afternoon.

He pulled in at the first service station to make the call and was told by Ced that she may consent to his seeing her between eleven o'clock and midday the next day at a venue in South London. 'Don't worry, it's on the river,' he said, 'but you're not getting the address unless she agrees to see you. You'll get a text tomorrow morning. It's Bermondsey or Rotherhithe or one of those sort of places I think,' he said.

Freddie called Birkett to bring him up to date then took the next turn to London.

TWENTY

He received the text message earlier than expected so he decided to walk to the location from the Double Tree hotel where he'd spent the night. Had he been here before? If he had, it had changed. Much of it was like the rest of London, gentrified, with streets full of expensive cars, but there were spaces, you could park here. Yes, that was it, there was something different about here, the air felt fresher somehow, and there was a suggestion of space, a strong hint that something resembling real wildlife was going on just behind these riverfront rows of houses; it was nothing like what he'd expected to find – that derelict, semi-industrial, decayed suburban space, full of metal and broken infrastructure from the past. As he walked on, he came to the old merchants' buildings, now renovated into luxury apartments, but amongst them real working buildings too. And the more he progressed westwards, the more the buildings improved, until suddenly he came across a little estate of council houses, once a dreadful place to be sent to, now favoured by their location, cleaned up and gentrified. A noisy moped suddenly came from nowhere – it almost clipped him as it came from behind, skirting him closely – the driver unapologetically focussed straight ahead down the road, as it sped off in front of him. He stopped and looked around anxiously. Was that a reminder? Had he been followed here? Perhaps he was under constant surveillance. Perhaps his function was to lead them to Edward?

He walked on, this time more vigilant for people than architecture, distrusting this no man's land between the groups of buildings, and had just decided to return to base and the security of his car, as the water-facing buildings began again. He changed his mind and stayed with the walk a moment longer, and within minutes he came to the address: the worst of all the buildings he'd seen – a sort of concrete 1970s attempt at a waterfront warehouse that somehow did not capture the essence of the originals it tried to copy.

There was a sort of council block feeling to the entrance – the heavy door with blistered yellow paint, the long vertical chrome handle which did not pull open as he expected it to, and the intercom entry system to its right long since gone out of repair. He first tried the number on which he'd been messaged but that went to an anonymous, non-attributed, answerphone message. He didn't want to have to call Ced again and begin that whole relay of phone calls back to the person who was standing within a few yards of him. He went back a few paces, looked up, and saw no sign of life. There was no waiting limo. He waited. He was early, but was he too early to be punctual? He returned to the door and gave it what seemed like a futile bang, then walked away again to look up at the six-storey building, this time from fifty yards away, straining to see onto the flat roof, when suddenly the door opened. A thick-set, suited man looked directly at him. 'Was that you?' he said.

Freddie confirmed it was.

'Name?' said the man.

'Er, Freddie, Freddie Lyons.'

The man brought a notebook from his pocket and turned it over to the last but one written on page. 'Got an initial?' he asked. Freddie smiled and said, 'Oh that, yeah, T. Would you like to see some proof?' he asked.

The man declined the offer, and said, 'Third floor,' and indicated with his head towards the concrete steps beyond the lift at the far end of the lobby.

Tara was standing with her adviser, he presumed, looking out of a window down towards the water as he arrived at their end of the third floor. They were in the largest still intact room in what had once been two or three flats on that level. The adviser kept his head outside the window as Tara responded to the noise of his footsteps and turned round to greet him.

'Mr Frederick T. Lyons,' the name clearly amused her. She came forward and thrust out a hand towards him. 'Who'd have thought? So soon.'

Freddie began to explain that Conrad's box at Royal Ascot was the wrong venue for what he had to say, but before he'd got much of it out, Tara said, 'That was a brave ride, your first Amateur Derby, coming up the inner like that.'

'Thank you,' he said.

'Who was it you beat?' she asked.

'Oliver Warner. Major Oliver Warner.' If she could remember his name, she'd remember Warner's – the nasty, uncompromising, most revered man of his day. Ridden Cheltenham winners too, a trainer now.

'That took some pluck, I'd say,' she said. 'What do you think?' and she made a gesture with her arms to indicate that she was talking about the building.

He thought about saying something about owning the worst house on a good street, but settled for, 'Great potential. Commands an impressive view.'

It was supposed to be a joke, but instead of taking it as a cute observation on the arch lexicon of the estate agent, Tara said, 'Oh Jesus you're not one of those are you?'

'No...'

'Hey Max, we've got one of those here.'

Max came into the room and shook his head to show his solidarity with Tara's perspective about whatever it was they'd been talking about.

'I suppose you consider the mortgage-backed upgrading of this area an improvement too?'

He didn't, the opposite in fact. Perhaps this was part of her technique? Jumping around constantly the way the police did, not giving you a chance to find your ground.

'Well... I don't, really. At all... .'

'Just be careful I don't get Max to give you one of his lectures on the ruination of Manhattan through the collaboration of banks and safety-first grinders.'

She looked round and saw that Max was busying himself looking out of the window again and, speaking conspiratorially to Freddie said, 'Just as well, there are times when I just want to say – *just stop talking for a minute*. Do you know that feeling?'

'Yes,' said Freddie, 'that's how men feel all the time.'

It was perhaps too early in the relationship for observations like that. 'But I know what you mean – about mortgages. I once worked in a bank myself.'

'I know. And then you did something that looked a bit like a looser form of banking, and now you seem to prefer horses.'

'Always did,' said Freddie.

She beckoned him to the window. 'Look down there,' she said.

The river. It lapped against the wall that held up the building. A large piece of metal stuck out horizontally over the water. 'Guess what that's going to be?' she said.

'Is it one of those things where you hang people as the tide goes out?'

She laughed. 'Only a bad boy would think of something like that. No, it's an abandoned project I'm thinking of picking up.'

He ignored her. 'A mooring?'

She snorted out a laugh. 'This is on its way to becoming a green-art building,' she told him. 'That, outside will be one of very few permitted developments.'

Ecological gentrification. How fucking worthy, thought Freddie. 'Should I say congratulations?' he asked.

'Do you know those wind-up radios that we send to poor parts of the world? You know, like you used to have on gramophones?'

He did.

'Well, that's what it's supposed to be – a water wheel. It goes one way on the incoming tide, and the other on the outgoing, on a ratchet, to store power. Clever, eh?'

'Honestly. Who thinks these things up?' he said, then realised for certain that she had a very different sense of humour to him.

The building was to be knocked down ten years or so ago, she told him, to make new flats, until someone decided that it would be better turned into a young artists' collective. 'This had been their business plan: for the price of shared equity in what they produced, the artists would live free of charge. They were to share one kitchen between them, and one shower block – you know,' she said, 'like the sort of places some of us went to on our holidays in the 1970s, when places like this were being built. And, get this,' she added, 'they are tapped into the National Grid, to deliver and receive power, but the deal they were to be given was, the moment the building ever became a net consumer of power everyone got evicted.'

Interesting, thought Freddie, *enthusiasm? Her soft underbelly?* He gave her one of his amused-but-pensive grins, like the way you did in meetings to undermine your opponent as a person of no consequence.

'What do you make of that as an idea?' she asked.

'It sounds like something Mao Zedong would think up,' he said, 'or Trump.' *Or you*, he thought. 'I hope they were going to keep enough electricity back to shock them out of bed in the morning.'

She nearly laughed but resisted. 'Yeah, a bit too zealous for the liberal arts. I was thinking that.'

'What's the point?' he asked.

She shared a few quiet words with Max before responding. 'I told you. Green art,' she said eventually.

'And?'

'And so that one day, should I choose to invest, that someone will buy it off me for ten times more than it cost me.'

'So not green then,' he said. 'More, one half red, one half green, like your racing colours.'

'Well, it wasn't my idea,' she said, and shrugged her shoulders, holding him all the time in her gaze. 'Do you know how close to impossible it is to produce ecologically sound art?'

He didn't. 'No,' he said.

'What is it you want?' she asked. She flashed a very quick false smile at him.

The volte face disconcerted him. Suddenly she had on her game-face; this was how she operated, constantly shifting direction to undermine you. This was a game. To win it, you didn't try to follow her through her dives and decoys, you ignored it all, and refused to be played. Some of the assholes you encountered in banking behaved like this, carried away with the idea that they were being smart and sharp. All you needed to defeat them was to stick to the point in issue. That, and to recognise that all the participants in a negotiation were essentially the same coarse animals, all possessed of the same basic desires to extract some fun from life – laughing, gorging, drinking, playing, having sex.

She went on, 'If you're planning to rip anyone else off, don't make it me.'

'What?'

'Your Russian clients. Feeling a bit short changed, weren't they?'

It was deliberate. It was all technique. Any response on point was a weakness.

'By the way, how is your partner?'

'He's still critical, thank you. Look, Tara, when you bought Robert Hamley-Flowers stud in Normandy recently, two of the horses you acquired had already been sold. To me.' He returned her hard stare.

'How are they getting on?' she asked.

He laughed. 'I'm not here to give you an update,' he said, 'it's to arrange to collect them.'

She laughed, 'You're not very good at this are you?'

'What?'

'Jesus Christ!' she shouted, 'Just because I'm wearing a suit don't confuse me with all those other pricks you used to work with.'

He returned her cold stare.

'If you really believed they were yours, you'd just send a box to the farm to pick them up. You wouldn't come and talk to me like this. This,' she pointed towards the ground, 'This Frederick, is what you call a negotiation.'

'Good,' he said. 'That's all I wanted to know. I'll get them picked up next week.' He turned and left the space, back towards the stairs by which he'd arrived.

He nodded to the security guard as he reached the ground floor, who then got to his feet to let him out. He'd played now, he could have twisted. He'd said stick. These negotiations weren't about who was right, they were about establishing a position and doing everything you could to support it.

Out on the street, he heard his name being called. Tara was leaning out of a third-floor window. 'Don't go straight to the farm,' she said, 'you're a prick but you're still too young to be shot.' She told him to wait for her in the street, and a few minutes later, she joined him there.

'And pretty,' he said.

She didn't smile but jolted her head backwards to say, 'explain?'

'Young *AND* pretty,' said Freddie.

Tara snorted, 'Oh yeah that. Look, let's just talk reasonably,' she added. 'By turning up here you've shown me that it isn't cut and dry. What's your case?'

He told her, implying more strongly than was the case that they'd paid for the horses.

'Audit trail? All there?' she asked, and he nodded.

'None of this came up in due diligence,' she said. 'Someone's going to lose a job over this, you do realise that don't you?' He nodded again. 'However it turns out. Who is it?' she asked.

He was on the point of saying *David Spencer* before he stopped himself, realising that she was asking a different question.

'The horse, the name of the horse that is subject of your alleged contract,' she asked.

He told her, and Tara hardly taking a moment to reflect said, 'The mare of your unlucky horse at Ascot?'

She was talented – one of those people that Felix would have placed in his top band of intellects. It didn't matter whether she was a hedge fund manager or a bloodstock expert or something else, she possessed the genuine talent that separated the people who achieved great things in life from those who were merely smart.

'…that's interesting,' she added.

So that it might be made less interesting, Freddie said, 'Yeah, Birkett trained her, and didn't want to let her go, but her owner's dead now, and he's been chasing her down for a while. There's him, and another chap who owned a bit of her, and they want her back.'

'Why would that be?' asked Tara.

'I think they thought that they'd never really got the best out of her, and this is a way of having another go. It's sentimental as much as anything else. We're all just a bit pissed off that the bank rode roughshod over a deal that had already been made.'

'I'm sure,' said Tara, who had never had a sentimental thought in her life, 'they get to you these horses.'

She held out her hand for him then turned back to the building, where Max Paton and her minder stood waiting for her.

'All that I can advise you to do is to contact the bank. I would be very surprised and upset if they'd made a mistake, but you'll understand – I need to hear it from them, not you.'

She waited for a response, but Freddie gave none, '…with respect,' she added.

He wanted to finish round one at least level on points, but he couldn't just walk away. 'Tara,' he called to her as she walked back to Max, 'do you know a bloodstock agent called Edward Hamilton?'

She shook her head. 'I don't deal with those shysters, I have my own,' she said, 'why, did he broker the deal?'

'No, something else,' said Freddie, 'it's not important.'

She pouted her lips as if to say, 'Why mention it then?'

Then for some reason, Freddie went on, 'He's like a sort of young fogey, Yorkshireman.'

She delayed before answering and said, 'No. I'd remember.' Freddie nodded to acknowledge her answer, and this time, he turned away, and did leave.

TWENTY-ONE

'So, the bank referred you to her, and she referred you back to the bank?' asked Birkett.

'That's about it,' said Freddie.

He was in the process of putting his phone back in his pocket.

'Who was that?' asked Birkett. 'One of them?'

Them? Freddie told him it was no one to worry about. It had been his estate agents in France, they had received an offer which they wanted to discuss with him, and they'd sounded a little put out that he was in England and wouldn't be coming over.

'Just a low-ball offer on my house in France, and another set of office bods who think they're working if they're sat in meetings.'

They were walking together during the second lot break to take a look at Milksheikh who had been turned out.

'What's Robert's opinion?' asked Birkett.

'He thinks we've got them in the crosshairs,' said Freddie.

They went on a few more yards and stopped at the corner post of the small turn-out paddock.

'But you don't.'

'Robert thinks that if you want something to happen badly enough, it will,' said Freddie. 'Tara on the other hand is a formidable opponent, the sort of person who'd fight you for a penny. And she knows we're bullshitting.'

Milksheikh heard them and trotted over to say hello.

'My God,' said Freddie. 'What have you given him?'

'Nothing,' said Birkett, 'he's a natural. Took him a day to shake it off.'

Freddie shook his head in wonder. 'Here, give me one of those carrots,' he said. 'There you are boy, what a champion you are.' He rubbed his itchy forehead, then as the horse responded, worked up and round to behind his ears.

'I think you've fallen for him as badly as me,' said Birkett. 'She's not having it then?'

'Making out that the deal was done is tough enough; getting that idea past the bank, very difficult, getting it past Tara – virtually impossible,' he said. 'Then, *if* we win that argument, which we probably won't, we've got to come up with a hundred and forty grand that we haven't got.'

'Why difficult?' asked Birkett, ignoring for the moment, the one hundred and forty grand part to explore the lesser challenge. 'What? They don't believe us, and we haven't got any evidence,' said Freddie.

'I've been thinking about this,' said Birkett. 'We have. What Robert said. We did have a deal. We're not making it up – it did happen.' Then as if to anticipate Freddie's next point, he said, 'And in how many deals do you pay before you receive the goods? Very few – never with horses – it's reasonable to have payment terms attached. They might not suit the bank, or Tara, but they're the terms we agreed with Robert – or we can say we did. He'll back us up, won't he? I mean, he was going to deliver, and we were going to pay, during Royal Ascot.'

'You mean that we invent a little bit of detail for the deal that wasn't actually there?'

'Why not? Who'd know? Only us.'

'I've been thinking something similar – and it's what Robert was alluding to,' said Freddie. 'But it's more the question of getting our hands on the one forty we haven't got, that bothers me.'

Birkett leaned on the fence and stroked his chin. He spoke in a considered way, as if he somehow wanted to convey to Freddie that he had spent the entire time during Freddie's absence doing nothing but thinking about this conundrum. 'The way things are going, none of it'll get done 'til after Bugbear runs in August anyway. I know that Tara's a different kettle of fish, but the bank will accept terms, that's what they're all about isn't it?'

Freddie's smile was returned by Birkett. 'Sounds like you don't need a banker on your team. What's left for me to do now?'

'You have to make it happen,' said Birkett. 'Which is an entirely different thing.'

'And if it doesn't work?'

'Then you can assist in carrying out Plan B.'

'Which is?'

'You sell the mare, her foals, and the yearling to my owners, set up a syndicate, all that sort of stuff, and we'll keep a leg. You'll get a few weeks.'

'You have been thinking about this a lot, haven't you?' said Freddie.

'I like plotting,' said Birkett.

There was a pause. Freddie turned to the horse again, stroking his muzzle as he contemplated things. He became lost in the moment, entirely absorbed in Milksheikh's kind, non-judgmental company. He began to confide in him, not entirely sure whether he was vocalising some of his thoughts out loud as Birkett did.

Birkett gave them their moment, then eventually interrupted. 'What is it Freddie lad?'

'Birdie,' said Freddie, 'it's impossible, isn't it?' But before Birkett could reply he said, 'everything we've got to do,' then edited his words, 'I've got to do – *God that's even worse.* Even if, by some miracle we find a way to pull it off, we then take the contribution of these lads for granted. We just assume that they'll turn up and deliver for us. And they'll expect nothing for it. Just a pick of grass, a scratch behind the ears, a manger of food...'

'Aye,' said Birkett.

Freddie knew that Birkett read him better than that: that he'd witnessed the moment that Freddie stepped outside the narrative that had sustained them both until this point. That he saw in him the realisation of a cold, hard truth arriving to stop him in his tracks.

Birkett said nothing more. He reached out his hand and put it on his shoulder while Freddie fell silent again.

God, they were in a hopelessness situation. The bank wouldn't give terms. The whole idea of conjuring a hundred forty thousand up out of nothing to which he had to add fifty for Penny, twenty for Ced, then the small matter of seven hundred for his clients. Sometimes miracles could be achieved by applying the right energy to the right idea. Other times, the task was so great and the starting point so weak, that it needed more than Tara's free electricity – it needed an alchemist.

Liam arrived. 'How's he doing today?' he asked. The concern seemed real, and for the first time ever there was no gratuitous dig at Freddie, not even a sideways scowl. Perhaps he had finally come to acknowledge what the horse had achieved and that he was a good, if not a great horse in the making.

'Ah, Doctor Grass, eh?' said Liam. 'Mind you, it's better getting them over soft ground tiredness than it is hard ground tiredness. You'll be off and running again soon, won't you son?'

He went on his way with his bucket, in search of the medicine cupboard in the office, and as he went, Birkett confided to Freddie, 'Oh yeah, haven't you heard? He loves him now, the little prick. And he's not the first person to ask me about him lately either.'

Freddie's phone rang. It spared him speaking. It was David Spencer. He looked up at Birkett as he answered to indicate *this might be interesting.*

'Tara's been in touch,' said David. There was a silence, which Freddie took to mean that David expected a reaction from him. He said nothing.

'Fortunately, well I don't know whether that's quite the right word, the boss was out, and I took the call. I imagine she's talked to him since – he might call you, I just wanted to give you a heads up about that.'

'Thanks David,' he said. 'I haven't heard anything yet. I get the idea that all's not well?'

He didn't know whether he detected a little laugh before David started to speak. 'At the moment,' he said, 'Tara's position, which would have to be supported by the bank, is to deny the deal.'

'Oh.'

'...that being based on the fact that it was not reported by Robert, or me, and so did not come up in due diligence. I haven't been asked to do this yet, but I suspect that before long I will be required to go into everything again to see what I can find.'

Freddie resisted speaking, but David still had more to say.

'Er... Look, when are you next in France?'

Freddie told him that he had a reasonable excuse to be there within the next few days.

'Well good, as soon as it's fixed tell me, and I'll come and see you.'

'I will, thanks,' said Freddie.

Then, expecting to hear him go through the wrapping up drill, David kept the conversation alive a little longer. 'Look, Freddie,' he said, 'I think you said that you might have something in writing with Robert – if you could put your hands on it, it might be a good moment to do that.'

He put the phone back into his pocket again and said to Birkett, 'I think I will go over to France for that meeting after all.'

'Will you be safe?' asked Birkett.

'If I can find a quiet way to get there, I'm as safe there as anywhere,' he replied.

'Come on,' he said, 'third lot,' as Freddie pulled the phone from his pocket again.

'I hear you,' said Freddie, 'I just want to call Robert while it's fresh, to get things moving.'

It felt cruel to ask a favour of Robert. He no longer had an office to call his own, and Freddie's request forced him to beg a favour from his landlords. One which they would certainly have declined to offer had they known what it concerned.

TWENTY-TWO

They met at the Brasserie de la Digue on the seafront at Villers-sur-Mer, a couple of villages westward along the coast from Deauville. Freddie had hitched a ride in a private plane from a friend of a friend of Birkett, Newmarket to Deauville direct. Under the radar.

At Freddie's instigation they had shared a dozen oysters and they were now both eating his suggested main course, turbot with pommes ecrassées. 'This,' he declared, 'is my absolutely favourite place in the world.'

David did not reply, but returned a puzzled look that said, 'Here? Really?'

This was David Spencer. At least six inches taller than Freddie, and yes, that did look like a duelling scar under his left eye. He was a type that Freddie knew from his days in banking, cold-hearted yet fair. He saw a sort of unambitious polymath in him; perhaps a difficult person to get to know well, but one who had at his core a willingness to bond for anyone who could work out how to get that far with him.

Felix would have called him a category I type. They met all sorts of people, as they travelled the world together, meeting different people, trying to find fledgling companies to turn into real clients for the bank. It stuck with him because it chimed with a lesson that his father had often tried to drum into him too. 'I don't mean merely clever,' Felix had said of whoever it was, 'I mean someone who has a certainty about his intellectual capabilities, as if he possesses a consciousness of his own intelligence. Well, that's a category I. Then there are others, category II, who come up slowly, come from within – learning, observing, growing in confidence as they do.' Freddie smiled, recalling that thing he used to say when they first met, 'in ninety-eight per cent of people, intellect does not match ambition.'

'You know,' said Freddie, 'gastronomy is such a massive thing in England now, isn't it? There are Michelin starred chefs everywhere, everyone is a foodie, we're all so informed through TV and radio and magazines and cookbooks, we go out to eat and we tell all our friends about it; then you come to France, and within half an hour of your first meal you realise that we are light years behind.'

He took a sip of still icily chilled white wine.

'I mean, we're all so book-learned, aren't we? Whereas it's just a way of life here. You could go to the next restaurant along, and the next, pick any at random, and no matter that they look as ordinary as this – a concrete floor, a plastic-Perspex windbreak, garish plastic awnings, plastic chairs, they're all extraordinary. Somewhere like this would be a burger joint in England. If you saw this from the outside you wouldn't go in – I was reluctant to come in here the first time I saw it.' He picked up his knife and fork again.

David smiled. At last, this man was revealing himself.

He'd drunk too much too quickly. 'Oh, you know, once, I went to a betting shop in Deauville, you know, a PMU bar, and I had the best gigot d'agneau I have *ever* had. And they apologised because it was the only thing they could rustle up on the day. Imagine that?'

David was laughing. 'Well, the other day I got a melted Kit Kat and tea in my own mug in the local bookies.'

If Penny had been with him, she'd have nudged him under the table, and it would have meant, 'You're starting to sound pretentious.'

'I'm starting to sound pissed,' he said to himself. Is that why he'd decided that he liked David already?

'So, you came over to sell your house?' David asked.

'Not really,' said Freddie. 'It was to meet you really. I need twice as much as they offered. I just went to make it look like I was trying. All this is off the record, you know that, David?'

David nodded sympathetically. 'Well, if we're speaking off the record, I don't know whether you picked up on it or not, but I was trying to reach out a little too.'

Freddie responded with an elongated, 'Yeah.' He didn't add, 'I was hoping that I'd interpreted your call correctly,' but took a moment and said, 'Do you have a proposal for us?'

'It was more of an idea,' he said, 'But…'

'But what?' asked Freddie.

'I get the idea that money's tight.'

'It's more non-existent than anything else,' said Freddie and laughed.

It wasn't reciprocated, and when David asked how he had planned to finance the deal, Freddie thought it was time to tell him the story of the gamble that got away. It was just another story about horses and gambling to David, until he got onto the bit about two million quid.

'So, what was your idea?' Freddie asked.

David spun the stem of the glass between his thumb and index figure. 'Between you and me, Tara was pretty rattled by your telling her that the deal was done.'

'Really?' asked Freddie. 'She didn't seem it.'

'Well, that's because she's good at things like that, but believe you me, she was. I got the first onslaught. And it was from her, not one of her lackies. If this goes against her, heads will roll, and unfortunately, I'm the only scapegoat within swinging distance.'

'Oh no, I'm sorry David.'

He batted away his apology. 'You probably realised – you worked in a bank, didn't you? – I did all the hard yards on this – this is way off the record too – you don't repeat this to Robert...'

Freddie agreed.

'...I crunched all the numbers on Robert's business. I was the only one with a handle on it, they had no clue, it had needed closing down for a while – it was an accident waiting to happen. It's my relationship with Alan Halliday that got it all up and running and eventually away to Tara. He had already decided to move his horses, and after that, the whole house of cards was going to fall in. Alan, as you know, doesn't do any actual work, so I made the running there. In short, I saved the bank from a very nasty accident and got them out in front, and I packaged up a superb little asset for Tara for peanuts – as I have done many times before now – and my reward for it all? No finder's fee – which my boss will take, no rewards when she turns the business to a profit, as she and her coterie of advisers will award to themselves, not a penny if it's sold on. No, my thanks will be a P45, for having "missed" a deal that was never there in the first place.'

Freddie made a sympathetic gesture. He sensed that the moment was close but suppressed the frisson of excitement that rose in his chest. Whatever was said next would reveal something about the speaker's willingness to step outside the bounds of what was considered permissible behaviour or put them firmly on the other side of the line.

'What's your deal David?' said Freddie.

David allowed Freddie to fill his glass before speaking. He looked briefly about him before he did, then said, 'It's not too late to find an audit trail to your transaction.'

Freddie's turn now. This was the moment.

'We do have a written *Heads of Agreement...*' he said, reaching into his inside pocket to bring out the very brief document that he and Robert had concocted the previous evening.

David dragged it over to his side of the table, looked at it, smiling as he did, noting their efforts to keep it authentically simple, then he put it into his inside pocket.

'...obviously, we didn't expect it to be seen in these circumstances,' said Freddie.

'Absolutely, why would you have thought that it would need to be any more formal than that?'

'Do you have terms?' asked Freddie.

He did. 'This is how it would have to be. You'll need to prove the transaction, which means paying one hundred and forty thousand sterling into one of Robert's non-Anglo-French accounts. I'll then do something with your agreement, and that payment. Then we will let the various parties come to realise that it has happened. For my role in bringing this about, I would like to receive my finder's fee. Not the one I should have received from Tara. All I want is fifteen percent of the one-forty. And then, I would like your undertaking to give me your future bloodstock business that I can take with me to my next employer.'

His forthright, uncompromising, honesty – yes honesty was the right word – took Freddie aback.

'OK. But didn't I just tell you that we didn't have any money?'

'Hold on,' said David, 'you've been pushing for this deal, and you're here today, how were you planning to pay for it? Not another gambling coup?'

There was something in the delay in responding that told David that he had hit on a pertinent issue.

'Tell me about your bloodstock business first. Let's see if it's worth it.'

'OK. It's this,' said Freddie, and he came clean about the Air Hostess project.

'Well, that's a very exciting upside for a very small outlay. But... how can I say this? I'd like to be involved, but I don't see what my role would be.'

Freddie winced slightly and spread his hands. 'It's not good David,' he said.

'You haven't even got the one forty?' He laughed.

Freddie laughed too. 'It sounds pathetic, I know. It's shaming David – you know the main reason, there's others, but I won't bore you with it all now. But yes, we're properly skint, in the old-fashioned sense. What do you say? No chance?'

'Whoa, whoa, whoa, step back,' said David. 'I've seen situations like this dozens of times. You've got options.'

'What are you thinking?'

'You told me earlier on. The reason you're here. Somebody has given you a firm offer of two point five for your house.'

'Yeah, and I told you that I can't afford to take it,' said Freddie.

'I know,' said David, 'but even at that low level, it being a real, and provable offer, someone like me could arrange a mortgage for you.'

'Oh no,' said Freddie, 'I'm in enough trouble as it is. That is a bridge too far.'

'Let's have another drink, and discuss this slowly,' said David. Freddie took a bathroom break and returned just as their drinks arrived.

'To get a mortgage to the value of five percent of a proven offer – is it cash?'

'It is,' said Freddie, 'you know – the French way. Two point five above the table, two hundred below.'

'Yeah, I know, and they think that we run the unscrupulous Anglo-Saxon business model. But with two point five above the table, honest, provable, in writing?'

Freddie nodded and went to his inside pocket again.

'It would be child's play for me to fix you with a mortgage of up to five percent of that value. Above that, it takes a bit longer and there's a few more fees to pay. But one hundred and twenty-five thousand can be turned round in an afternoon. Isn't that a sufficient war chest for you to get on with this deal?'

Freddie sat on the idea for a little while, then said, 'Thank you. It probably is.'

'Look,' said David, 'if you need more, we should perhaps look at other avenues. There are a couple of schemes I'm involved in, one at the bank, the other... more off-balance sheet. They have more money in them, probably looser from a regulatory point of view too, but there'd be no immediate turn around with either of them and they'd want points in your plan.'

'It's got to be now,' said Freddie. 'If you can organise all this, what do you want out of it?'

'I told you,' he said, 'I'll throw in the mortgage work, all I want is fifteen percent of one-forty, but I want all your future business wherever I am. Oh, and whatever it is,' he added.

'Is that it?' asked Freddie.

'I'm a phone call away and I'm at a stage in life when I need to look beyond a salary.'

Freddie reached over the table and shook his hand.

'So, what happens next?' he asked.

'Should we order a digestive?' said David.

TWENTY-THREE

Freddie arrived back in the yard just before Birkett returned from watching the second lot. They met at Milksheikh's paddock just as the string returned.

'He thinks he's getting one over on me,' Birkett said, gesturing with his head backwards towards the string.

'Who?' asked Freddie.

'Who do you think? Him, Nasty Knickers. He thinks I don't realise how good that cheap horse Pogg-thingy is.'

'Pogle?' said Freddie.

Freddie watched Liam throw the reins over his horse's head, then hand them to a young boy before stealing off to speak with Davey who was beckoning him from the door of the tack room.

'But I'm running him in that maiden,' said Birkett.

'What maiden, Birdie?'

'The one for cheap horses. It's always bad. He'll win that easy. Come in for a cup of tea and tell me about your trip. You look happier than when you went. I hope you were safe?'

'I was. I only risked one taxi ride up to the house and stayed low. But he hasn't heard of Edward Hamilton either. I'm beginning to think that he didn't give me his proper name.'

'And the other thing?' Birkett asked.

Freddie continued to look over his shoulder beyond him into the yard, drinking all the activity in. He yawned, 'Yeah, a little bit of hope, perhaps.'

Birkett smiled, 'it's not the despair that kills you, it's the hope.' But it didn't get a reaction. 'Go and tell your pal about it, then come and find me in the office,' he said, then slapped Freddie on the shoulder and left him at the paddock gate.

Freddie stood a moment then hopped over the fence into the paddock that contained just Milksheikh. True horseman that he was, he didn't approach the horse directly. How many times had he watched experienced people do that then spend the next half hour chasing the horse in circles and still not catch it. Freddie went to the centre of the paddock, stood still, and waited. He tried to empty his mind of everything, even of the horse himself. Then after ten minutes or so, Milsheikh arrived, telling Freddie he was there by a gentle nudge at his pockets, looking for treats. Freddie turned into him to stand shoulder to shoulder so that they faced in the same direction. He hooked his head with his right arm to cradle it backwards, and Milksheikh responded by lowering it to rest on his shoulder against his face.

'There's no mints today buddy, just me, looking for love.'

He brought him up to date with everything. From the untreated weeds and overgrown grass at his house, to being unable to see Felix who had been just a few miles down the road in a hospital bed. And his new friend. He really wanted to hear what Milksheikh thought of David.

Milksheikh thought that he had raised an important issue and promised to think it over very carefully, and suggested that Freddie do the same.

Freddie promised to come back with a carrot as soon as he could, then he gave his mate a final rub behind the ears before saying to him, 'us two, we've never met our equal yet – I wonder if we'll ever get the chance to prove it?'

He left the paddock as third lot was getting organised and ran into Liam, carrying a saddle.

'Ah, the horse-whisperer's back. Thank God, we might start having some winners.'

Freddie gave Liam an insincere smile and continued on his way. Behind him, he could hear Liam laughing at his own joke, something about feeding horses on bananas. He thought about turning around. Then didn't.

Birkett was on his way out of the house back into the far yar.

'I'll unpack that case then come and find you,' said Freddie, pointing towards the enormous suitcase on wheels he'd brought back from France. 'I've quadrupled my wardrobe,' he said.

'About time,' Birkett replied. 'I still haven't had any breakfast, I'm only here for a few minutes, meet me back in there,' he said.

Fifteen minutes later they were sat across from each other at Birkett's desk, Birkett eating a bowl of cornflakes so large that an entire pint of milk had disappeared beneath the cereal.

'I've been playing with your betting exchange thing,' he said.

'I hope you've left some money in it,' said Freddie, 'every penny counts now you know.'

'I know,' said Birkett, 'I tried something out. I had two quid on every horse in the race and set my price to a thousand to one,' he said.

Freddie smiled. 'And you lost the lot?'

'I did, you're right. All bar the winner was taken up, and one of them came right out of the pack at the end and nearly got up.'

'And so, you were encouraged to have another go, eh? It's heroin for mug punters Birdie, you need to stop your fixation with getting a thousand to one winner.'

Birkett smiled quietly to himself. 'It might have to come to that if you haven't brought good news back with you.'

Freddie gave him a rundown of the conversation with David.

'Are you mad?' asked Birkett.

'Yes, I am actually.'

'I'm sorry son,' he said. 'I just can't do it; the business won't take it. Unless I do that borrowing from future earnings thing you were talking about.'

'You don't have to,' he said. 'This way I earn my place in the deal with you. I'll pay it.'

'How much will it leave us with?' asked Birkett.

'One way or another,' said Freddie, 'we have to turn the one-two-five into a hundred and sixty-one. That means we have to scrape up thirty-six extra between us. Don't panic,' he said, looking at Birkett's face, 'I've got about thirty, but that's to live on, bet with, and everything else you can think of, and must include a contingency in case this goes wrong. Oh, and then pay my alimony.'

They fell about laughing.

Then, suddenly earnest, Birkett said, 'Are you just going to send a hundred and sixty-one thousand to that David bloke? Are you sure you know him well enough?'

Freddie laughed. Things like this seemed absurd to outsiders. To him, he'd done things like that hundreds of times. Of course, you trusted counterparties; of course, you transferred thousands of pounds to foreign banks without thinking about it.

And so, the two of them, with a short break for the third and fourth lots, spent the rest of the day working out how they might manage to find thirty-six thousand pounds between them to add to their new one hundred and twenty-five thousand pounds loan.

At about four o'clock, Birkett suddenly exclaimed, 'We need a stake for Bugbear too where are we going to get that from?' Then just as suddenly, he said, 'Oh no, we won't need to do that, now will we?'

Freddie stopped, and asked Birkett to do the same. 'Wrong,' he told him, 'the deal we're doing might start paying some time in the future, whereas the mortgage I've taken needs to be repaid as soon as humanly possible; we also need to buy the yearling, and currently, there's nothing in the pot for that; we need to make up the forty grand we lost on Milksheikh; I need to start paying Penny fifty grand a month, or I'll have the rest of the house taken off me; I need to start repairing the hole I've made in my own finances; and you need to do the same for your business overdraft. So wrong Birdie, the job on Bugbear is more important than ever. Any source of cash anywhere is as important as it's ever been right now.'

'Yeah, if you put it like that, I see what you... how are we going to raise a bet though?'

'Let's just get over the line on this first and see what we've got when that's done.'

Slightly chastised, Birkett went back to his books, then said, 'Don't forget, we've got that good thing, Pogle, running in a few days, we'll raise a bit on the back of that, you know, little fish, build it up.'

Freddie continued with his work, nodding to acknowledge Birkett's point.

'You don't fancy keeping a little bit back and going all in on Pogle do you?' asked Birkett.

Freddie stopped again. 'No,' he said, borrowing from Felix's lexicon again, 'don't desire it all on day one. Show patience, do it right, and expect it all in the end.'

'Yeah, you're right,' said Birkett, 'stick to the plan.'

'Then,' said Freddie to himself, 'all I have to do is find another seven hundred grand to pay my clients and all is well with the world.'

'Well, if we get this deal done, you'll be able to do that borrow from the future thing to pay them off,' he said.

'Maybe,' he said, 'if it all happens fast enough, I still might get out of this scrape with the skin on my back.'

TWENTY-FOUR

Birkett came in from the morning session and found Freddie at the office computer again, just as he had when he came down at five o'clock that morning.

'Still nothing?' he asked.

Freddie shook his head. 'Apart from this,' he said, reaching for his phone to show him a message from David. 'Tara should know about payment. I am out of loop now. You should call her perhaps?'

'That's what we got for our fifteen percent is it?' asked Birkett.

'Precisely.' The word brought Robert to mind, and it made him laugh.

'What is it?' asked Birkett.

'Nothing. I'm going to give Robert a call to see if there's any movement down there.'

There wasn't. And he could be sure of that he said because he'd been sitting at the kitchen table watching them doing all the jobs he should have been doing; and he'd done the same yesterday, and the same the day before. Air Hostess and her foal were still on the farm he told him.

'I'm sorry,' said Freddie, 'that's got to be really tough for you both.'

'Both?' said Robert. 'Both? There's only one of me now Freddie. Jules couldn't take it any longer. She's gone to her sister's in the west country... looking for work' he tagged on at the end.

'Oh Robert...' Freddie started, but Robert's sobs interrupted him.

'I've lost her, Freddie,' he said. He cried freely for a moment, until Freddie sensed him consciously pull himself together. 'And I'm going to have to go and find myself a job now too, I suppose.' Freddie looked up at Birkett and shook his head to indicate that it wasn't a happy phone call, and Birkett made a beckoning gesture in return. 'Come and stay with us, Robert,' he told him, 'be with friends. There's plenty to do here.'

Growing in frustration, Freddie next dialled David. 'You have to put your people in the picture and get them to do their duty,' he said.

'Look, I'm going through disciplinary,' David replied, 'shortly I won't have a job here. It won't work if I support your claim it will point to collusion.'

'Claim? Freddie shouted. 'It was a claim two weeks ago, David,' he said, 'it's a *right* now.'

'I'll send you some phone numbers, but don't be despondent, stick at it. It's how people like Tara work – they try to frighten you off. Don't make it easy for her by backing off.'

'Thanks,' said Freddie, and hung up. But as he did, the feeling that he was beginning to know too well came over him again, that he had given a large proportion of his remaining fortune to a very plausible man with absolutely no guarantees.

Birkett gave him a consoling grip of the shoulder as he passed behind him on the way to his afternoon nap. 'Don't be on it when I come back down,' he said.

Freddie went back to the screen began scouring the internet and social media for references to Tara Fitzsimmons, in the hope that it would give some clue to her whereabouts and contact details.

'At least Edward Hamilton, if that's who he is, had a LinkedIn and an Instagram account,' he thought, then suddenly experienced a shooting pain of panic as he contemplated the thought of Spencer and Hamilton working in tandem together. *No, impossible,* he thought.

He counselled himself to be patient while he waited for David's Anglo-French numbers to be messaged through and tried to use the time to drill down methodically into Tara's life.

An hour passed and he had learned nothing. Worse perhaps, there had been no message from David. He consoled himself with another call to Robert, just in case a horse box had departed with Air Hostess on board. Obviously, it hadn't. He called David again and he did not pick up.

He went back to tracking down Tara. And every ten minutes or so, each time he broke new ground, he would get up from his chair, circle the dining table, rehearsing the conversation he was about to have. Then believing himself to be calm and in control of his emotions made another abortive call to someone else in her empire.

Eventually, he took himself out to walk round the empty yard, trying not to disturb the sleeping horses, saying a quiet 'hello' to the odd one still looking out over their stable door. An hour passed and he returned to the house to make a lunch of cup-a-soup and toast, and to do something else to distract him from the constant round of disappointment.

He took his phone away from Birkett's desk, and called Felix's hospital. That call was no less disappointing, but it served to put his anxieties in perspective. Felix's body had not shown the hoped-for reduction in toxicity, and for the first time, they began to talk about long term damage to his body.

He put down his phone, and made himself inhale to a count of eight, and exhale to a count of five for the next fifteen minutes. 'I'm doing this for both of us son,' he said to Felix through their secure communication channel, 'but you've got to keep up your side of the bargain.'

There was still no message from David, and so he went back to his searches again, this time finding a number for Tara's bloodstock manager. He called him, but he seemed to resent the direct phone call as much as Tara would herself. He listened to Freddie's spiel then laughed and said, 'Tara's not selling any horses out of France,' before hanging up.

'There's nothing for it, Felix,' he said, and picked up the phone once more, to cash his last option.

Ced agreed to do his best for Freddie this one last time – but only because they weren't officially at the deadline date for subscriptions yet. But, he added, Freddie 'Had now entered the territory where he officially owed him a favour.'

About an hour or so later, still in the office, still without a message from David, and absent from evening stables, he received a text which had been forwarded on from Conrad. It gave Tara's *temp* number and said that he thought that her art adviser was still over. As soon as he received it, Freddie called the number, which wasn't answered. He ran out to the yard and got in his car.

Birkett called out after him, 'Ferdy! What's the matter son? You're making me scared.'

- 173 -

Freddie replied through the open window of his car as he left the yard, 'She's not responding, I'm going to face her down now.'

'Keep me posted,' he shouted to the back of the car as it sped out of the yard.

Freddie tried the number continually as he drove, but Tara didn't pick up, until eventually, as he gambled on left and southwards as he arrived at the M25, he heard her voice.

'You're persistent, whoever you are,' she said.

He sensed the disappointment in her voice as she heard his, and when he told her that he was within half an hour of central London, she said, 'Come to the project again. But you'd better hurry, we've dinner booked in an hour.' She didn't need to add, 'and I'm not waiting.'

About forty-five minutes later, he parked outside the same run-down building in which he'd met her the first time and was a sure as he could be that he hadn't been followed.

'She's on the roof,' said her security man, letting him in, indicating the stairs again.

He climbed the six sets of concrete stairs and emerged onto the flat roof off a short ladder from the top floor. The wind held the small door shut as he tried to push it open, and he felt like he'd forced it too firmly as he appeared, crawling, undignified, into the meeting he'd imposed on Tara.

She stood, hands on hips, waiting for him to appear, at first determined to enjoy his discomfort, which slowly turned to annoyance as he came to stand facing her.

'Why didn't you just phone?' she asked.

'Because you can get away with it on the phone. And you don't pick up.'

'Oh, he's come to look me in the eyes.'

'I'm here because there is not a single person in your organisation who will cooperate with me, and Anglo-French are so frightened of upsetting you, they're the same.'

'Must get some more helpers. Very interesting, thank you. You must send me an invoice for that advice Frederick,' she said. 'You're not an expert in art too, are you?'

Freddie resignedly shook his head.

'No, don't be like that. You're a clever bloke. I'd like a fresh opinion. You never know, it might make me like you.'

'Games,' he thought. He and Felix had seen them all. Usually, when they began trying to humiliate you, you knew you had them rattled.

'Do you know how difficult it is to acquire green art?' She asked him. 'Did he know of a work named Ice Watch?

Freddie stared at her, mute.

'Basically, the artist left thirty blocks of glacial ice to melt in public locations in London. Now it's art, and it's green, and it's making a point. It ticks all the boxes, but how do you own that?'

'Buy lots of it?' Freddie suggested.

She wasn't sure how to take the remark. 'In my game,' she said, then corrected it to, 'in our game… go back ten years, I'd say that about fifty percent of the self-appointed shrewdies had very clever things to say about bio-medics, or graphene, something like that. You know as well as me that if you'd bought every up and coming one of those stocks, you'd have gone bust in about five years. Calling the wave is all very well. But picking winners is something very different, isn't it?'

'What I meant,' said Freddie, 'is that you should bully some poor sod with no money into selling you his best assets for nothing, and if you buy enough of them, one of them will turn a profit to justify the whole thing.'

'Oh, like Robert you mean?'

'Robert, struggling artists. What do I care – if the greedy part of the market is pursuing the green part, we're all fucked.'

She stifled a laugh. 'Here's the thing: you thought you were stealing her off Robert. Don't deny it – I know how these things work. Unfortunately for you, you've been found out before you closed the deal, now you're going to have to give a bit of value back before she's yours. And that's to me. She's mine right now – not the bank's, not Robert's, mine. The price at which you stole her from Robert is no longer relevant.'

'No, that's not what I'm here for. I want to have my contract honoured. For goodness' sake Tara, you got Robert's stud for nothing, isn't that good enough for you?'

If you want the mare badly enough, you'd give me four hundred.'

Freddie laughed. 'Four hundred? You wouldn't have given much more for his whole stud.'

'No,' she said, 'I probably didn't. But it's how hedge funds work, I thought you knew that?'

'Tara,' he said, 'we've proved she's ours. You can't argue with it.'

She took a moment to reply, taking a little walk around the rooftop. 'OK, let's talk this through – to assert your rights you're going to have to sue me, and if you do, I'm going to join the bank in the action. Now ask yourself, how long is that going to take? And how much is it going to cost you – even if you win?'

Impotent with fury, Freddie took a break from the conversation next, going to the far rail, where he looked down at the ebbing Thames.

'Don't think about throwing me over – someone's always watching, and it'll take you ages to get her out of probate.' She walked towards him, 'Why not spare yourself the trouble and just give me that money now?'

She turned back to the door, so that he had to shout into her wake to keep her attention: 'You wouldn't have a case.'

'Oh, I think I would,' she said. 'I have bought an asset which has been overvalued by at least the price you agreed with Robert. An open market valuation might reveal that to be higher still, say I was to put her in the mare's sale in December.'

'She's not yours to do that with,' said Freddie.

'Listen, Frederick. Right now, she is. And she's not going anywhere 'til someone – you, the bank, Robert – makes me an acceptable offer for her.'

'Are you really saying that we have to pay you another one-forty?' he asked.

And Tara replied, 'I'm saying, make me an offer.'

It was all he was getting. It was an outrageous suggestion, but somehow it meant that the deal was in some way open. That was a form of progress he decided, so he banked the words and called the meeting over.

He re-ran the conversation all the way home, constantly berating himself for not having taken it in a better direction, to have extracted more certainty from her. What he would do to have Felix travelling back with him. He'd do that amused staccato laugh thing that he did, and tell him that they were never going to get anything different whatever tack they'd taken. He'd say that had Freddie come up with a different negotiation, so would she. They'd have ended up the same place. Felix always cut through the bullshit. He'd say, low ball her, leave it on the table, and be a constant pain in the arse, 'til she's had enough of you. Freddie laughed to himself. *If only I could be a bit more like that*, he thought.

TWENTY-FIVE

Freddie had begged off riding duties again, telling Birkett that as soon as it was office hours, he was going to go to the top at Anglo-French to demand delivery of the mare. His phone pinged at about seven thirty, and he grabbed it impatiently. But it wasn't from David, just another text from Penny which he left unread. Half an hour later it went again, this time from an unidentified number. He looked at that first, and read a message which said, 'Action not words.' Penny's read, 'See letter, can you please arrange to pay on or before the twenty-fourth.' Essentially the identical message, like a boxer's perfectly timed one-two combination. The meeting with Tara had been a low point from where he could not sink any further. Until receiving those reminders. He and Felix used to roll their eyes and laugh at their colleagues at the bank when they used phrases like, 'He's painted himself into the corner.' But now, suddenly, it had a resonance.

Birkett walked through the office in search of a cup of tea, making one for Freddie, then dropped a small pile of post onto the table as he delivered the mug.

'Thought they looked formal,' he said.

'Oh yeah,' said Freddie, 'I'm expecting a *Bank Error in my Favour* payment.'

Birkett looked at him oddly.

'Unless I'm very much mistaken, there should be a cheque for two hundred pounds in here.'

His expression changed to concern.

Freddie opened the letter, and saw that it was from Penny's solicitors, confirming the arrangement to start paying her fifty-k a month until the *clean-break* settlement had been achieved, and requesting the first payment on the twenty-fourth of June. He opened the next. It was brief, but it was from unknown solicitors to Tara requiring her to deliver up the horses that had been sold under contract before her purchase of Haras La Valleé Rose. It had been sent in his name, but without his authority. He threw it down on the table. 'For Christ's sake.' He shouted.

'Freddie, calm down, lad,' said Birkett, walking towards him, 'what is it?'

'Read that,' said Freddie, pointing to the letter.

Birkett shrugged when he'd read it. 'So what?' He didn't really understand the way lawyers spoke to each other. 'Everything he said was right, wasn't it? She needed someone like that to get after her, it was good, wasn't it?'

'Don't you see?' said Freddie. 'It's exactly what she wants us to do. I told you that last night. She wants us to take her to court. It'll cost more money than we've got, and she can afford to wait.'

'Who sent it, then?' He asked.

'Spencer,' Freddie replied, 'it's got an acknowledgement slip attached.'

'What? You think David's playing us?' he asked.

'That is something that sounds increasingly likely,' he replied.

Birkett had been shocked by the sight of the pale and haunted figure he'd seen as he came into the office. 'Why don't you get on the lorry and go with Pogo down to Newbury? You could do with a change of scene,' he said.

Freddie believed he had better things to do on the end of a phone, here at home, but Birkett would hear nothing of it.

'Go on, get out, we're going to have a winner. You won't make messages come any faster by sitting here waiting for them. He's six to four in the papers and they don't know what we know. Have as much on as we can afford. And enjoy yourself son. It'll be good to welcome a winner in. Go on. The lorry's ready. Go and get on it. Don't chuck anyone off – they can still get their extras, just go with them, and enjoy the day out.'

Freddie's face broke out into a smile for the first time in, how long? A week? 'Thank you, Birdie. You're a wise man – you know that don't you?'

'Get going now before I confiscate your phone too,' he said.

Freddie climbed into the cab of the lorry to make a line of three on the single bench seat of the horse box. Liam, head lad, driving, representing the trainer, Victor, to lead up the horse, him, the outsider of three.

Victor belonged on Liam and Davey's side of the power-play in the yard. Ostensibly a tramp, he was unkempt, always sort of half-shaved, and he wore the same pair of sweatpants with a hole in the backside to work every day. But Freddie had noticed a quiet intelligence about the *Shop Steward,* as he privately referred to him.

'Lads,' said Freddie as he settled in. Silence came the reply. His presence meant that the division of duties was no longer clear, that tips were no longer guaranteed to be given, or end up in the right hands if they were; that the overtime and per diems weren't as cut and dried as they'd been five minutes earlier.

He still hadn't phoned Anglo-French and it was difficult to set off leaving that undone, but otherwise he'd done as much as he could, so he switched off his phone and, propping his head against the passenger window, went into a deep sleep.

He woke as they pulled into the racecourse car park, and as soon as the horse was taken off the box, Freddie left the others alone to do their stuff without exchanging a single word.

He walked straight through the course up the grandstand steps and into the *owners and trainers,* looking to find a quiet space of his own in which to refuel and to continue chasing down the transaction. It was too early for a hot lunch, so he picked up a plate of salad, and went on his own to the farthest corner of the room.

Someone shuffled between the tables at the other end of the room and something about the way they looked over told him that they'd recognised him. He looked up, scared for a moment, until sensing that they were somehow familiar. They each consented to a small movement of their head to acknowledge the other.

He turned his attention back to lunch and thought to himself, 'Was that Warren, Conrad's partner?' He'd only met him once; he couldn't be sure. It hadn't been a warm greeting. But that would make sense, neither had his.

He finished lunch and set off back to the horse box deciding instead to make his calls and hide out there. Then, halfway across the flat tarmac in front of the stands he stopped. It was Warren. Did that mean that Tara might be here too? How would that be if she was here? How would they pick up the talk with others around?

He considered turning back to ask the question, then decided that his time would be better spent on the phone tracking down Anglo-French and getting the confirmation that the funds had arrived. David had still not messaged or called, and Freddie had all but given up on him as any use to them. As he turned back towards the car park, something caught his eye again – this time over to the right, in the direction of the paddock. It was Liam and he was talking with a small well-dressed, middle-aged, man who he thought he recognised too. Was it the man who had been at her side at Royal Ascot? Her racing manager, was it? They were talking together in the space between the stand and the paddock, and it was an animated discussion. Not arguing exactly, but there was an air of antagonism as each of them responded to the other. Then the man's phone rang; he answered it, and as he talked, Conrad and Warren came out of the restaurant and headed towards them. He hung up as they came close to shake their hands. The four of them continued the conversation that had been started by Liam and the racing manager, the man occasionally pointing towards Liam, as if he was making a point. Perhaps it was an argument. Perhaps he should intervene? If it had been anyone other than Liam, he might have considered doing that.

As the conversation broke up, he followed Conrad and Warren from a distance as they made their way up to a bar at the top of the grandstand, where they sat together alone and nursed a drink. Every now and then one of them would talk to someone on the phone, or check their phone for messages, but Tara never showed. Before long, he'd have to leave to be present as Pogle was brought to the paddock. He wasn't crucial to the work, but he'd be the one called to explain the problem if anything went wrong, being the senior representative. And should anything go wrong, it was a certainty that Liam would nominate him as the man in charge. And something was up.

He positioned himself so that he would spot the horse as it arrived, whilst trying to keep an eye on Warren and Conrad in their bar. He tried to look inconspicuous, entirely conscious of the fact that if anyone happened to be watching him, he looked the exact opposite. Who knew, someone could be watching him. As the thought crossed his mind, he shuffled closer to the protection of a bookies' pitch. Then, as time ticked on, he slipped further and further away from his line of sight on the bar, until, as race time drew closer, he finally left his post to go to the paddock.

Suddenly he recalled that this was one of their opportunities to add a little money to their survival fund. He checked the market on his phone and his heart sank to see that it was trading at five to four now, and that there wasn't much left at that price. He had a thousand on at the market price and kept the same amount back for later. If it went to evens then so be it, but he'd give it a chance to drift, as last-minute gambles on other horses took hold – it was a field of debutants and someone would like their horse – they'd convince themselves that perhaps none of the others were any good, or that their horse would be the only one fit enough to canter over the line. Pogle would never go odds on in a race like this, not on his racecourse debut from a yard like theirs.

As the parade ring filled with the rest of the field, he became more confident about Pogle's chance; he looked head and shoulders a better horse than the rest. Liam had been briefly by his side, but as the jockeys arrived, he left, saying, 'I'll let you play trainers and leg him up,' and went to talk with another jockey who Freddie took to be an old friend.

Freddie talked briefly with his own jockey about nothing very much, having confirmed that Birkett had relayed instructions to him by phone earlier.

'He's good, isn't he?' the young jockey asked, and Freddie nodded to say that he was.

Conrad and Warren entered the parade ring just then, as the last horse was leaving, and only Warren came over to say hello properly. He asked about Pogle's chances, and Freddie replied that he was by no means the good thing that the market indicated. Liam followed Victor out of the paddock onto the course and stayed there with him so that they'd be in the right place to collect him as he came back after the race.

Freddie checked his phone again and saw that Pogle had drifted out to seven to four, and he smiled as he put on the last of their stake, saying to himself that he wasn't such a bad judge after all. He made a quick mental calculation as to where a winning bet would put their survival fund, then closed his phone to look up at the big screen.

There was nothing unusual about the race. They went a nice even gallop, and for a race of debutants no horse bolted off in front, no horse dropped out an exaggerated last, they all just went steadily within themselves. There were eight runners and there'd be no excuses. They maintained the steady gallop for the first two furlongs of the straight and if he had a moment's concern it was that Pogle would get stuck behind horses on the fence as their race ended, but that was over-thinking it – when the race developed properly the gaps would come. This was a race with horses of all abilities, some of them just wouldn't be able to keep it up, and he'd be left with one, maybe two horses to aim at when it all got serious. The pace picked up a notch, and their young jockey perhaps sensing that the rail wasn't the place to be, edged him out slightly. As he did, the big screen showed Pogle cantering over the rest of them, seeming to take one stride for their two, until it became a question of not if, but how far. Then, instead of sitting on the tail of the horse in front and waiting, so well was he going that the jockey pulled his horse out wide and set off for home. He must have gone about fifty yards or so before he stopped. Not stopped dead, but stopped in a racing sense, stopped racing. His jockey tried to roust him as the field, and the race, went by, but it was too late. He laboured on to finish a very ordinary looking fifth of eight.

It wasn't possible. Since he'd been gelded, he was about the best two-year-old in the yard at the moment. He was far better than that. He was far better than every other horse in the race. But there was the evidence, fifth. All bets down.

He watched the replay over again as they re-ran it, trying to detect that moment that it all went wrong. He wasn't lame. He could see him walking back into the paddock with Victor and Liam and he was as sound as a pound, blowing a bit but not particularly so. He walked over towards them, so that he could catch the jockey before he disappeared but as he picked up his stride, he felt a tap on his shoulder. It was Conrad, who handed him his phone.

'Tara would like to speak to you,' he said.

He put the phone to his ear and heard Tara's voice: 'Is that a present to make up for the nasty letter from your lawyers?' she asked.

'What?'

'Didn't Conrad tell you? We took two hundred and fifty out of the market off that ungenuine horse of yours.' He looked at Conrad as he digested her words and saw a broad grin returned to him.

'Are you telling me, you…? You'd better not be saying that, Tara. Do you really think you can afford any more trouble?'

She laughed. 'I'm not saying anything, apart from thanks. I really feel that you're trying to make a big effort to pay me for my horses – but we can't do it this way. It'll have to be something more formal than this. I'll take this today as a gesture of goodwill to say that negotiations have reopened.'

He'd arrived at the pre-parade where they were unsaddling Pogle, Conrad still following behind, with his arm outstretched for the return of his phone.

Freddie ended the call then threw the phone as far as he could, over and beyond the saddling boxes.

'That's a five hundred quid, top-spec, phone,' said Conrad.

'And you are a five-star, top-spec, cunt,' said Freddie in return. They swapped hard, cold stares but nothing came of it. Conrad towered over his smaller adversary, but he wasn't a fighter. Freddie prayed for him to take the first swing.

Without speaking to Liam or Victor, he took the young jockey by the silks at his neck and walked with him back to the weighing room and, not loosening his grip, requested the clerk of scales for an audience with the stewards.

The clerk made a long slow sigh, then raised his eyebrows, as if to say, *if you insist*. He called the secretary to the stewards to make the appointment, then his own, to escort the two of them to their audience. They went by lift to the third floor then followed the secretary along a sterile corridor. It could have been a cheap hotel, a hospital perhaps, then he tapped lightly on a door, and hearing no response pushed at it gently and ushered them into an ante room to the stewards' quarters. It was wood panelled, and you could see that the actual stewards' room beyond it was decorated in the same way. Freddie laughed to himself; it was incongruous within the modern building like the dining room at Robert's house. The thought brought him round a little. He took his seat next to his accused, who maintained his stony-faced silence, and Freddie began to wonder whether he'd be able to communicate his sense of injustice to the stewards in the same way that it had struck him. He suddenly became conscious of a decreased heart rate, and only then recognised the anxiety he'd brought with him to the meeting. The door opened, and they were summoned inside.

He made his report to the stewards saying that the jockey rode against instructions to get the horse beaten on the orders of Tara Fitzsimmons, who had just won a quarter of a million pounds by laying it.

It was a serious allegation, he was warned, and did he want to reflect for a moment before making it formally. Freddie said that he didn't. Nevertheless, they gave him a moment, and interviewed the jockey while they did. His evidence was that the horse stopped when it hit daylight, and that he hadn't expected it. He said that he'd been asked to keep the horse covered up until late in the race but that he hadn't been specifically told not to put it out into the clear on its own. And the horse was going so well he said, compared with all the others, he thought he had them beat and was just planning to ride him out hands and heels to the line, when suddenly he stopped. It made him look foolish he admitted, but he didn't know that the horse would behave like that. He'd just been talking to the trainer's head lad, who was here, and who had confirmed that the horse could do that.

'He's the one who trains it, he told me.'

'Was he with you in the paddock?' he was asked, and he said, 'No, it was this gentleman.'

All eyes turned to Freddie.

'Mr Coward gave the instructions by telephone sir,' said Freddie, and the jockey confirmed that this was so.

'Had he said anything about this characteristic of his horse?'

'No sir, he didn't really, specific like. But they had him gelded early 'cos he was quirky, they said.'

The spokesman turned to Freddie again and said I think we'll take some evidence from your head lad. Could I suggest that you take a walk round the grandstand while we do?'

Back at the horse box, as they loaded Pogle for the long journey home, Liam was eager to show that he'd found the whole thing hilarious, then, true to form, that he was also very angry indeed. Throwing him under the bus with the stewards was about as disloyal behaviour as he'd ever come across.

Freddie didn't respond and watched in silence as Liam and Victor loaded the horse. The central partition was swung into place and secured, by Victor, who left by the ramp, then turned to push it back up and secure it as the side of the horse box. That done, Liam jumped into the small door between the horses' stalls and the wall of the front cabin to store the travelling kit and put up a hay net.

As soon as he did, Freddie locked him into the space, so that he'd travel home alone with just the horse for company. Without consulting Victor, he jumped into the driver's seat, and set off.

A day which had begun as badly as it possibly could, took an unexpected turn downwards early in the morning, had somehow managed to confound all possible predictions and finish in a yet worse place still.

He had not a morsel of energy or desire to continue to chase down their money. And his phone only rang a couple of times. When it did, he ordered Victor to answer it and put it on loudspeaker. He made no apologies and gave no thanks to Victor as the calls ended. Neither was from David Spencer nor any of his colleagues at Anglo-French, just Birkett and Robert, and he told each of them that he would prefer to talk to them face to face when they next met rather than in front of people that could not be trusted. If that turned out to be a harsh judgment on Victor, so be it. It wasn't a bad message for him to take back to the yard.

Birkett was there to meet the horse box as they pulled into the yard, and as Freddie descended from it, he held his hands aloft as if to surrender, guilty, to the justified onslaught that was coming his way. Victor busied himself with disembarking the horse, Liam was not referred to, and until the small side door in the horse box was opened, remained unseen.

'I'm sorry Birdie, I've dropped a bollock. What do you know?'

Before he answered the direct question, Birkett said, 'Yeah but you didn't tell them that the fucking horse would stop if he hit clean air, did you?'

'You'll want to talk to him about this,' said Freddie, and opened the side door to reveal Liam filthy and angry. It made Birkett smile for a second, but he said nothing. Liam seemed too determined to jump out on to Freddie to settle their differences, but Birkett put his hand on his shoulder from behind, saying, 'Don't you fucking dare. Be at my office in the morning to explain yourself, and it better be good.'

'Come into the house,' he said to Freddie, 'and tell me everything there.'

It had all been talked over many times when Robert landed in the yard, and so a version of the story was told again for his benefit.

His news brought little extra joy. He confirmed that Jules was settled with her sister in the West Country. A tear formed in his eye as he said the words, which was ignored by Birkett and Freddie, until he added, 'I can't stand staying there on my own, in the old place, looking out on all of them, all my little babbies.'

He dried his eyes, then said, 'How about I ride a few lots for you while I'm here? Get my eye back in – I might have to go looking for a job myself now.'

Birkett stretched out his arm to take Robert by the shoulders and said, 'I can't afford to pay you much Robert, but yes you can. To me you'd be more useful keeping an eye on that mare back at your stud, but I'd be the same myself, I'd want away. You're staying here with us, for as long as you need.'

As Birkett led him away to the back of the house to take him to his quarters for the night, he looked back towards Freddie. They both thought the same thing at the same time, 'Is it time to tell him?' No words were exchanged, not even a shake of the head, but they both knew that the answer was no. Not so much because it was a gratuitous act of generosity that wasn't needed, but more out of the sense that they were less sure than ever that they had anything to offer. They needed to lick their own wounds first, and over the next few days they'd do that. Robert, and all the rest of it would follow on naturally as soon as that was settled.

TWENTY-SIX

Liam's version of events was that he had been specific about Pogle's quirks with the young jockey and that it was obvious that he had shared this information with the gamblers for whom he worked; when Freddie saw him talking to them, they were pumping him for information, which he was resisting. Short of any corroboration for either story, Birkett felt he had no choice but to accept his explanation, but he resisted Liam's pleas to have Freddie disciplined. 'Just do yourself a favour and stay away from trouble like this from now on,' he said, and pointed to the office door.

'But he's got what he wanted,' Birkett confided to Freddie. Freddie looked puzzled. *How so?*

'You,' said Birkett, looking at his computer screen to read an email, 'for your, er what is it? That's it, intemperate actions, the stewards have decided that you do not represent the stable at the races for two calendar months.'

Freddie looked shocked.

'You've been *warned-off* lad, welcome to the club,' said Birkett, neither judging nor reprimanding.

Freddie struggled to discern whether Birkett was angered by the news, so settled for, 'I'm sorry Birdie,' to which Birkett did not reply.

Their attention turned to Robert, whose first job was to get them to the top in Anglo-French, and have their transaction confirmed. 'I'm sorry,' he said, 'I should have done this while I was still over there, but my head was spinning, and I couldn't think straight. The news that the payment had been registered, brought a collective calm on the office that had been missing for several days.

He also confirmed the news that David Spencer was no longer an employee of the bank, and that was why they decided, that he hadn't been responding.

'He'll be in touch when he's got himself a new phone,' said Birkett. But Freddie knew already that his social media footprint was lighter still than that of Edward Hamilton – besides his passport shot and a short bio on the bank's *Our Team* page, he'd found nothing else which would help track the man down.

'I'm not sure about that bugger,' said Robert, 'I've always thought that he'd just go to the highest bidder. I think he's probably done what he's going to do for you.'

'He might think he has,' said Freddie, 'but I want more than that from him for my fifteen percent. Give me Alan's number, I'm going to find out where he is.'

Alan picked up but that was where the good news ended. He had no news of David Spencer, didn't know he'd left the bank, and as for the supplementary, no, he also had no news about Edward Hamilton. He wouldn't, would he? Hamilton had disappeared owing him 'a not insignificant amount of money either.'

'He's just odd, isn't he?' said Freddie as he finished the call.

'He's quite a plausible salesman, you know,' said Robert.

Freddie shook his head, 'it's like he's reading a script, not talking,' he said.

They put Alan, David, and Edward behind them for a moment and continued to chat. It would be their first real conversation together. Neither man trusted Alan, David, or Tara, but Robert skewed more towards a visceral hatred of Alan, who he saw as the architect of his demise, Freddie – Tara; their separation from their wives was not quite the same matter, but the fact was they'd both been left by women they adored, and if either of them could turn back the clock and put one thing right, they'd choose that above all the others.

'I know the point that it all started to go wrong,' said Robert, 'the very point.' He laughed to himself, as if he was hearing the story for the first time.

'We had this colt. Alan had got hold of his mare, with the colt still inside her. Anyway, it turned into one of those *unlucky Alan Halliday* stories – you know, the pedigree, which was already quite good, got a tremendous boost after he got hold of her. So, we pull the colt out, and he's an absolute beauty – I mean a real beauty – everyone agreed. But for one fault – he had this hole, the size of a ten pence piece in his off-fore hoof. Now, how can that ever be my fault? He was just born that way – I couldn't do anything about it could I?'

Freddie shrugged and gave him a sympathetic shake of the head.

'Without that fault he was a million-dollar horse, with it, peanuts, we sold him for virtually nothing in the end. But from that moment, something went wrong. It was only recently, but the trust, it just ran out, like sand from an egg timer. Couldn't do a thing right for him from then on.'

'Did he keep the mare?' Freddie asked.

'What Spearmint? Yeah, she was the one of the first to go.'

'Spearmint?' asked Freddie. Robert nodded. 'That's funny,' he said.

'Why?' asked Robert.

'Because I bought the colt.'

Robert slapped the table. 'No!' he said.

'Nobody told me about the hole though.'

Robert sighed. 'Those things are easy to disguise with a bit of filler, I suppose,' he said, 'especially when you're buying them through an agent and don't have a close look at the horse yourself.' What was he going to do, Robert wanted to know? Ring him back? Was he saying that he thought Alan was behind it?

Freddie told him it was unlikely. Alan had just told him that Gordon and Edward had run off owing him a small sum. 'Hamilton just bought them cheap where he could and hiked the price to me,' he said. It disappointed Robert slightly because he thought that Alan might have a new enemy for a moment.

'You didn't see him, did you, down on the farm?'

'Who?' asked Robert.

'Edward Hamilton.'

'No,' said Robert, 'Alan often brought people down with him but no one I remember with that name – though he walked freely about the place, and sometimes I didn't know he was there until I stumbled on him – he liked people to think that it was his place too, and I kept away if he didn't introduce me.'

Robert enjoyed the novelty of racing routine again; it was the first time he'd experienced anything like it for many years. Financially he was destitute, but unlike Birkett and Freddie he seemed to be able to enjoy the moment a little better. He had no mortgage, no bank loans, no feed merchants' invoices. His wife was making her own money, and he was making his. No rent, hardly any shopping, just a car to run and a life to live. He wasn't happy, but he was tolerably satisfied with his lot.

The work of the yard now turned towards to the Newmarket July Festival – the Newmarket version of Royal Ascot. They'd have a few runners. Not Milksheikh, who'd recommenced road work with Birkett, and very occasionally, once he'd seen him ride, Robert. Slipshod would miss Newmarket to go for the Group I Sussex Stakes two weeks after the July Meeting, at Glorious Goodwood, in the expectation that the French horse wouldn't travel over. Pogle would be given another chance at Newmarket with a proper jockey.

Despite the best efforts of everyone to make it happen, Tara had still failed to deliver the mare. Their policy had altered now into asserting their rights by avoiding a court case and to wait until they had amassed some more money before they stepped up the pressure on her and the bank, as long as the mare was delivered before Milksheikh next ran, and that was still a little way off yet.

But amassing money felt a very long way off to Freddie. Another deadline had been missed with his wife; a sort of implied deadline had been missed with his former clients – though they had not bombarded him with angry messages as Penny had, but he recognised that he had now reached the phase of his strategy that was entirely based on homelessness. He wasn't present in his official residence, and he didn't officially live with Birkett. That way, he could still assert that he hadn't been formally served with proceedings, and with a little luck, avoid being recognised at all. His resistance amounted to no more than to remain anonymous for as long as he could hold out. He had as long as that lasted to wrestle himself out of his predicament.

On the Saturday lunchtime, just as morning stables finished, Birkett, Freddie, and Robert were taking a cup of tea on the terrace outside Birkett's office. Robert was trying for the third or fourth time that week to persuade Birkett to let him organise a car park picnic for all of Birkett's owners at the July Festival. He described lavish lunches set out on long trestles, and the impact it would have on his long suffering, neglected owners. As much as anything, it would have given him the chance to build a bridge with Jules, getting her up to help him pull it all together. It was her speciality he told them. They were always doing it for their clients in France. They loved it apparently, especially the English ones.

'Hey, that's what we'll do,' he said, 'we'll have runners in France, and take them over and do it there. Everywhere's nicer than here. They'll be bowled over. Honestly Birkett, they will, it's how you get loyal…'

Birkett's phone rang. As he answered he looked up alarmed at the two men. 'Yes,' he said, 'Yes. I understand. No, no, no, no. Oh we can, can we. I'm not sure.' He was silent for a while, then he said, 'OK, if it'll get us the mare, I'll have a think about it. Thanks Tara.' Freddie's eyes almost popped out of his head. 'Birdie?'

'We've had an offer.'

'Go on.'

'Not like you're thinking,' he said.

'What? She didn't talk about sending us the horses?'

'She didn't son. In her words, she's proposing a deal to put the negotiation back on track.'

Robert and Freddie edged their chairs up closer to Birkett's end of the table. They looked at him, unspeaking.

'There's a mile handicap at Newmarket next week. It's like their version of the Hunt Cup. I don't know what it's called anymore – some sponsor or other. You know it?'

Both men nodded.

'Entries close in about half an hour. She's got a horse in it they think'll win.'

They shrugged as if to say, *interesting, but what's that got to do with us?*

'She wants me to put Slipshod in the race.'

'What? That's mad,' said Freddie. Something made him turn and look to see if Liam had overheard.

'I know son, but he'll be clear top rated which means her horse will get in around about bottom weight. She said it's not a big horse, and that's the only thing they're worried about, that it won't carry weight.' Both Freddie and Robert looked slightly underwhelmed by the news.

'It's not all one-way traffic,' he added, 'as she said herself, we'll be able to have a bet. But she did give us a bit of a stern warning: we're to wait until half an hour before the race, or else she'll consider it a rejection of her olive branch.'

'That's her idea of an offer, is it?' said Robert.

They each sat in silence for a moment, trying to fathom the offer. Could it even be called an offer?

Birkett broke the silence. 'I'm going to do it,' he said.

'Birdie, you can't. You're going to ruin the horse for Goodwood. Not to mention our plans for Milksheikh and him. We can't,' said Freddie.

'It's our only chance to get those horses without a hassle. And we need a bet. It'll help us raise the funds we need to do it.'

They fell into a silent contemplation for a moment, each wondering what it was they'd really been offered, and what they might reasonably insist upon as payment if they complied.

Freddie voiced this concern, saying, 'If we're not precise about Tara's obligation, this deal amounts to no more than a charitable gesture on our part.' He implored Birkett to text her back with terms. Birkett seemed reluctant, as if he had picked up a tone in their conversation that the others had not grasped.

'What do I get out of all this?' said Robert suddenly, 'a free bet on Tara's horse? They were my horses you know. I've lost the lot, and my compensation is a bet, once everyone else has picked over the prices. That's just great that is.'

'We need that stake for Bugbear don't forget,' Birkett said to Freddie, ignoring Robert's outburst.

'Bugbear? What's this?' asked Robert.

Birkett shushed him and beckoned him to come into the house.

'Let's have a glass of whiskey,' he said. Then, as they went towards the house, he put his arm around Robert and said, 'I think you should have a proper job here, there's plenty you can turn your hand to yet.' And he shouted back To Freddie, 'I'll let you tell Liam. Say it's for Tara – he likes her better than us.'

Freddie immediately set off on a tour of the yard. He knew that it was unlikely that he'd find Liam still there, but he wanted to stew on the offer for a moment. Birkett had handled it poorly. He should have extracted more from her. That was why she rang him, he supposed, that he wouldn't be ready for her as Freddie now was. He didn't know exactly what she'd said to him, and it would be difficult to make him re-hash the conversation. It would sound judgmental, and now, more than ever, he needed a good loyal team around him.

His phone rang. It was from the hospital. If he was to visit Felix, now would be a good time, they said. He declined their offer, he had to. Hiding here, beneath the radar was the single option available to him. He put the phone back in his pocket and went to find Milksheikh in his box. He put his arms around him and told him the whole story, then broke down. He stayed with the horse, sitting in the corner of his box, until evening stables began, and he could hear people returning to work again.

TWENTY-SEVEN

The Newmarket July Course is pretty and quaint in comparison to its contemporary counterpart on the other side of the gallops. Still hanging on to its original Victorian stands, it is of a different scale to the commercial enterprise that is its sister course.

Freddie ambled from the security of Robert's hastily arranged owner's picnic on the grass parking area under the trees next to the thatch-roofed entrance. A short walk in a large crowd.

Only open in summer it was the first time this season he'd visited the place, making it the first time, in, say, twenty odd years since he'd last been here. Yet it looked just as he remembered it, the shady copse of the pre-parade, the old-fashioned plates showing runners and riders, marquees everywhere, it brought back so many jolting memories of his riding days, just before the world turned digital.

The largesse shown by Tara Fitzsimmons in sharing a winner with Birkett was not quite as generous as it had first appeared. She had three horses in the race and offered no further clues as to which was the one. When they'd declared, Birkett's people were expecting the four original entries to be reduced to one. They weren't, and there was no phone call.

Liam had done no more than work to rule since he'd heard the news of Slipshod's running in the race. He hadn't yet thought of anything nasty enough to do to take his revenge, though he reserved his greatest anger for the owners, whose idea it had been apparently. They had been easily persuaded, Birkett telling them that the horse was too fresh and needed a run to put him right for Goodwood. Freddie had simply upped their contribution to the idea when he broke the news to Liam via Davey. Liam saddled the horse and made his way into the paddock, determined not to stand as part of the group with Birkett, the owners, Freddie, and Robert, and stayed instead with the lad who'd brought one of Tara's other horses, until Birkett called him over to join them.

Robert was just setting off on his own recce as Liam arrived, having agreed to search out David Spencer who had been spotted earlier with Alan Halliday.

Tara stood in a group away from all her trainers, with Conrad and Warren, who between them gave off an unmistakable vibe of 'Do not approach.' Two close protection guards stood at a discreet distance to reinforce the message.

Liam joined the group and Birkett immediately asked the usual, 'What do you know?'

'Ah so I'm in the know now, am I?'

'I don't know, are you?' asked Birkett.

Liam stood in dumb insolence.

'Which one of Tara's horses is off?' asked Birkett. 'It's supposed to be the small one down the bottom of the weights, but all three look like that.'

Liam merely smiled.

'She's winning with one of them, which is it?'

Yet still nothing came from Liam. Birkett checked that the owners weren't listening, and turning his back to them, he said, 'That's what this is about. It's not my decision. Slipshod's in to help Tara's horse win. We're trying to find out which one it is. Do you know?'

'Well, it's nice to know you're consulting me,' he said. 'There was me, thinking that you didn't care.'

'For fuck's sake man,' Birkett hissed at him. 'We're all having our dicks pulled, go and ask your mate, and come back here before the race so that we can get on.'

Robert, finding Alan and David together, invited David to join them, which he did; Alan wasn't included but followed anyway. He deposited them with Birkett and Freddie, and said, 'Right I'm going to tackle that lot now,' and made a beeline for Tara.

Freddie confided to Birkett, 'You've got Robert working like a good 'un for you, what's your secret? Whiskey or ginger snaps?'

He did it as much as to be rude in front of Alan and David, but Birkett's reply took him by surprise.

'I've put him on points.' He spoke behind his hand.

Freddie looked surprised.

'It was your idea, wasn't it?' said Birkett. It was, it was just the timing surprised him.

'He'll be useful enough in his place. They used to be his horses you know, the poor bugger.'

Freddie acknowledged the point without speaking, then turned to look at David, edging closer to him. 'I've been trying to track you down for ages, where've you been?' he asked *sotto voce*.

'I've got to work you know, gun for hire,' David replied.

'I've been looking for a gun, to point at Tara,' he said, 'She's been a nightm…'

David's eyes told Freddie to stop talking. He looked up and saw that Alan had engaged Birkett's owners in a conversation. Nothing had been noticed.

'Just give us your new number then – you could have called us,' he said. 'How long are you here?'

David gestured three with his fingers of his other hand as he discretely passed Freddie a card with the other.

'I'll ring you tomorrow,' he said. 'Pick up.' Then he added, spitting it out in a harsh whisper, 'Lawyer's letters David? What the fuck?'

David replied as if he were answering a different question, in case Alan overheard it. 'A favour from a mate,' he said, 'you're welcome.'

Robert returned, and checking first that Alan was out of earshot, said, 'Nothing doing. I couldn't get close to her, but the boys said she thinks she's given us the crown jewels already.'

Birkett left to leg up his jockey and came back shortly afterwards with Liam at his side. 'Have you found out Liam?' asked Robert, but Liam simply smiled and said, 'I haven't heard a dickie bird.'

'What's going on?' asked David, and the three men shared a glance then took a pace aside to make a huddle with him. It was all news to him too – it was the most concrete proof yet that he wasn't in league with Tara. And so, they decided to pool their meagre funds and to split the stake evenly between Tara's three horses. They watched Liam disappear into the distance with his friend, the lad from one of Tara's stables, and David said, 'But he knows, doesn't he?'

Birkett said, 'Don't worry about him. One side of his brain has fallen out with the other.'

As the horses cantered to post, the group of them decided to stay put in the paddock and watch the race on the large screen next to the old-fashioned runners' board on the back wall of the head on stand.

They moved closer to it as the horses were loaded and as they did, found themselves close to Tara's group. Conrad circled behind Tara to put bodies between him and Freddie, which left Tara the closest to him.

She turned to Freddie and said, 'Anyone would think that you were stalking me. I thought you'd been warned-off?'

'I'm not representing the yard – merely spectating. And you know me,' he said, 'I'm always searching for a bit of craic.'
She looked at him expecting a suppressed a smile but saw only a dead expression as he returned her stare.

'And you're avoiding me,' he added.

'The classic response of the stalker. Or is it racing tips you're after?'

'Why don't you just own up to your responsibilities instead? If you don't want your intermediaries to see you climb down, just give me your number and we'll keep it between us two.'

'Now you're starting to sound dangerous,' she said and made a theatrical glance towards her security men. She sighed and turned to face the screen.

Birkett joined them. 'You didn't ask about riding plans,' he said to Tara.

Looking ahead at the screen, she replied, 'It doesn't matter,' then walked away to watch the race with her advisors, to make them two separate groups again.

And she was right. One of her horses made all, and just as he hit the rising ground for the final furlong and a half, and you thought that he'd capitulate, and the horse for whom he'd set up the race would come through and take it up, he went away again to win by a couple of lengths. Slipshod ran well, being held up as was customary, finished like a train, and at one point looked like he'd overhaul Tara's horse, until the weight told, and his run petered out halfway up the hill. He was clear third, a gargantuan effort under the welter weight he carried, and Birkett and his owners were as happy as they might be in the circumstances.

'Jesus, he was a good thing off that weight,' Tara said to Birkett as she set off for the winners' enclosure.

Birkett, Freddie, and Robert waited where they were to walk in with their gallant horse, but the smiling Liam appeared from nowhere to take the rein before they could get close.

'He's too good for you lot to ruin,' he said out of the side of his mouth to his boss, then strutted on ahead to take his place alongside the winner.

The prizes were doled out, the 'horses away' instruction given, and the winners' enclosure slowly emptied. As it did, Birkett, lagging behind his group in his slow bow-legged amble, felt a tap on the shoulder and turned round to see Tara again.

'Well done,' he said, 'you played it well.'

'Ah, it's easy this game,' she replied.

'So, we've got a deal?' tried Birkett.

She stopped walking. 'Yeah, a deal's a deal.'

'We can have the mare?'

'Yeah, she's yours. As I keep telling Frederick, all you've got to do is pay me what you paid Robert for her, then you can pick her up. Provided you train three of mine free for a year.'

Birkett blanched at the proposition, trying to compute all the figures in one go, he looked around desperately for Freddie to help him out before replying. He'd hardly begun to conjure with the consequences of agreeing to pay another hundred and forty thousand pounds, let alone the free training – *was he to calculate the cost to him, or the price he would charge?* when she said, 'Well? Agreed?'

He gave it no more thought, held out his hand, and said, 'Yes Tara, agreed.'

'Good,' she said, 'that's done.'

At a distance Freddie looked on. Not at the potentially life changing transaction that had just taken place, but at the entourage that had waited in the parade ring, and now lagged behind as Tara moved on elsewhere. Conrad and Warren headed that party, Alan and David meandered slowly in the same direction, heads close together, and two close protection guards, one of whom Freddie had convinced himself he recognised from Saint Cloud, coordinated their work like two sheep dogs in tandem.

What did this mean? A shiver went down his spine as he contemplated the presence of his ex-clients, and worse, that they were somehow in cahoots with Tara, and so always knew where he'd be.

He followed them to the rear of the first and largest of the Victorian grandstands and watched them disappear into a guarded opening which took them into a concrete stairwell. He couldn't quite get close enough to see accurately, but the body language of the guard suggested that they then went up a flight of stairs. Other people went through the same doorway too, but he didn't want to risk being refused entry, and so using his local knowledge, he took himself to the front of the stands and made his way to the top of the old-fashioned terracing. Once there, he located a doorway which he knew to be at the top of the stairwell into which he'd watched the group disappear below. The stairs were divided into sets of about ten or so wide concrete steps which kept switching back on themselves at the large half-landings; and on each of those landings there was a door at either end with the name of the host of the party pinned to it. He checked each name en-passant as he skipped from one landing to the next, until, on the third landing down, the door to the left had a notice which read, *Marlborough Thoroughbreds* – the name of Ced and Conrad's scheme wasn't it? That would explain the eclectic mix of people here today all heading in the same direction. He hadn't heard from Ced, but that channel had been taken off air recently.

As he arrived on the landing, the door was being held open for a couple to leave by a guard, and he quickly jumped back to the set of stairs behind him, out of sight, listening for any voices he might recognise; ready to move if anyone else came by; ready to follow, if they sounded interesting. He wasn't sure exactly what he was going to prove by being here, but it felt that this was the closest he'd been for a long time to understanding something about the events in which he was embroiled and the people who had an influence upon them, particularly David – he might find out something crucial about David today. Perhaps he should just enter the party? He probably knew a good proportion of the people in there, but that five percent chance of being refused entry held him back – here he is again Freddie Lyons, the troublemaker, the man who welches on his debts, the soon to be bankrupt, the man who drove his wife away. God, Penny might be there. Imagine that showdown. No, he'd stick with the spying for now.

Another couple left the box. He listened, then gave them up, but just as he went back to his station, the door swung back again.

This time the leaver came towards him. He quickly mounted the steps to the next flight, then stopped halfway up to turn back, as if he was descending. At the landing, as he turned to face the flight below, a man, head down, was walking towards him, gripping the handrail to keep to the inner. He sensed Freddie's presence and looked up. It was Edward Hamilton.

For how long did they lock eyes? It felt like seconds, yet it must have been fractions. Hamilton spun a hundred and eighty degrees and made to get away; instinctively Freddie grabbed for him but clutched only at fresh air. Hamilton went careering down the stairs as fast as he could, not quite in control of his balance. The adrenalin surged in Freddie, he quickly looked about him and seeing nobody, went after him. The *Marlborough Thoroughbreds* door just closed as he arrived outside – had he dodged into that? Surely he didn't have the time to do that? If he had, what did it mean? All these random, scary thoughts raced through his mind at once. He darted quickly to the ground floor and looked out past the security guard to see if there was any sign of Hamilton out in the crowd. It was busy and he couldn't say for sure, but he felt increasingly sure that he hadn't escaped that way. He returned to the first floor, and stood outside the Marlborough Thoroughbred's door for a moment longer. *What was stopping him?* God, the man had taken him for millions. Of course, he was going in. He took a deep breath and paused for a moment longer to consider everyone he might meet on the other side of the door and how he might respond to each of them. The door opened. The man on the door, letting no-one out and no-one in, looked at Freddie and grinned. Did he know him from somewhere? Freddie felt a tap on his shoulder. He turned to see two men in lounge suits standing to either side of him. They were wearing the ear pieces that gave them away as *security*.

'Mr Frederick Lyons?' asked one of them.

Freddie nodded.

'I represent the B.H.A., I am sorry sir, but I have to inform you that you have been served with a warning-off notice which is still current, and I must ask you to leave now.'

'But, I'm not…' he began, then gave up his case.

The two men escorted him down the stairs, out of the building and to the nearest entrance. They took him outside the course and watched as he walked away, making sure that he wasn't minded to hang around, or try his luck at another entry point.

Freddie occasionally turned to watch them as they did this, and so, eventually, reconciling himself to the position he was in, kept walking. Forty-five minutes later he was back at the yard.

TWENTY-EIGHT

The three comrades, all shareholders in the same scheme, sat down for what Robert would have a *celebration dinner*. His original suggestion to treat themselves to a meal out having been refused by Freddie, had seen him nip over out to Waitrose at the last moment to rustle something up, 'A la Francaise,' as he put it. He'd made it, so it was his right to give it a name.

Freddie felt that an explanation was required for his anti-social behaviour, and so, as they ate, he filled in Robert about all the things that were making him that way. It served to bring Birkett up to date too, if not remind him about the additional strain under which he lived. When he came to the final revelation about Edward Hamilton, the pair of them stopped eating and turned to look open mouthed at Freddie. Then silence.

'You know,' he said, 'how these projects in which we find ourselves define our lives? Well, in mine, the best possible opportunity to recoup my lost fortune has maybe just disappeared forever.'

Another silence, then Birkett raised his glass and said, 'Second best chance.' Robert laughed and clinked Birkett's glass, and they left them there, together in the air, until eventually Freddie consented to do the same.

'You know what Felix always said about times like this?' He said, '...that if we all sat round a table and laid our troubles before us, we'd each sooner pick up our own again than go home with anyone else's.'

Birkett and Robert both nodded as if to say, *that was true enough*.

'Well,' he continued, 'I'd swap both of yours put together than have my own.'

It was a brave call in the company of a bankrupt and racehorse trainer, who had said of his own predicament, that he was a funeral away from ruin himself.

'Oh, for God's sake,' said Robert, 'you're starting to sound as bad as me. We've had a winner, and we're getting our horses back.' And he raised his glass again.

'Well said, lad,' said Birkett.

Freddie smiled to himself. 'One more such victory like that and we will be done for.' The other two didn't pick up on the reference, so he added, 'We've been rinsed boys. Tara has taken two hundred and fifty grand off us laying Pogle, she's used us today to land another monster bet, she's sold us an unproven mare and foal for twice as much as they're currently worth and add to that we've to train three of her horses free for a year.'

'Well, when you put it like that,' said Robert, trying to draw a laugh. But Freddie wanted to make his point.

'I do Robert – and don't forget we've hardly got a penny between us to pay her so it probably won't happen anyway. I suspect that she was advised that she didn't have a leg to stand on, and so decided to extract every last penny of value out of us before finally conceding the case. And she's done it all without the expense of going to court.'

He'd brought the mood down enough, but Birkett didn't want to jump on him. He was having it tough poor lad. He made a 'settle down' gesture with his hand in Freddie's direction, and when he was sure that he'd stopped talking, he said, 'Hey! Listen to me. Is this how we're going to live our lives boys? This is still the greatest opportunity we'll ever have. We'll get over our little problems, not because we know how to yet, but because we'll look after each other until we find a way.'

It didn't really convince Freddie, but he knew that Birkett was right in one sense – he wasn't going to get out of this all on his own.

Robert simply looked at Birkett in awestruck admiration. He managed to cough out, 'Hear, hear,' then raised his glass one more time. And he did it solemnly, as if to say, 'This time, I really mean it.'

Freddie was in the kitchen scouring the internet for news when Birkett came down the next morning.

'I thought that was you, what are you on with?' he asked.

'Seeing if there's any news on Edward Hamilton,' he said.

'Hey!' said Birkett, turning on him, pointing, 'What did you promise us – and yourself by the way – last night? We've got a job to do, and you're to stay out of trouble.'

He looked at him until he closed the lid of the laptop.

'If he's as bad as you say he is, there'll be others after him too, some of them at that party, and they've all got plenty of money. If he's still breathing, one of them will have him tucked away at home before you ever get to him.'

'It's just so hard, Birkett. If I lose Hamilton, I've lost the only link to my money.'

'I know it's hard son. But do like your buddy says, try looking forward.'

Freddie sighed. 'I'm doing it for him, Birdie, I've promised him. That's my side of the bargain.'

Birkett's face brightened. 'Has he started improving?'

'No,' said Freddie, 'I mean I promised him in my prayers.'

Birkett was at a loss for a response. He made do with putting a consoling hand on Freddie's shoulder.

'No breakfast?' he tried.

'No, I'm nearly back to my old fighting weight and I want to keep going,' said Freddie, 'you're a hard taskmaster, I'd forgotten.'

'As long as it's not for fighting.'

'It's for Felix,' Freddie replied.

Birkett nodded, 'Have you done the first lot list yet?'

He shook his head.

'Come on Ferdy, we're here to work lad.'

David Spencer arrived at second lot break. He could have been welcomed as pariah or prodigal, but he didn't wait to find out, he simply assumed to act as advisor and confidante as if his role in their scheme had never been in issue. And as the morning drew to a close, and all went quiet, the horses fed, and the staff left for home, he sat down with Birkett, Freddie, and Robert to discuss their situation properly.

Freddie explained the case. He tried to put the unexpected demand for an additional hundred and forty thousand pounds in a way that sounded like a complaint against David's original negotiation to secure the horses for them. But it didn't register with David that way.

Turning to Birkett he said, 'You agreed to pay her the one forty before picking up the horses I guess?'

'We, er, I did,' said Birkett.

Robert started to talk about how unconscionable it was that Tara just arbitrarily doubled the price, and a digression began about that and other injustices, which Freddie brought to an end by saying blankly to David, 'How do we know that we can we trust you?'

'Hold on,' said David, 'I'm sensing a little hostility here.'

'Well, you did go missing before the deal was done,' said Freddie.

'Look,' he said, 'I got that deal through for you whilst I was acting as if I worked for the bank. I handled it professionally, and discreetly. No one batted an eye, did they? – well, did they?'

They chorused their agreement.

'And I kept up the pretence – how would it have been if I'd been seen as the advocate for your deal, then as soon as I'd left, I teamed up with you?' He paused, but before anyone could answer, went on, 'And when I got sacked, I received thirty seconds' notice. My phone was taken, I had no contacts, nothing. I walked out in the clothes I was wearing. And all of that was for your deal that never was.' He gave them all a long hard stare.

'What brings you here now then?' asked Birkett.

'I see opportunity,' said David, 'I met Freddie in France, and I know you'll achieve more with my help.'

'It's just that you seem...'

'Conflicted?' said David.

'Yes,' said Freddie.

'Here's how it is,' said David, 'when you're as crooked as me, you've got to play straight.'

It brought a smile to Freddie's face, and the others decided to let the line of questioning drop too. A line had been drawn, and everything that happened next would fall after that defining moment.

'So, when do you next expect to be in funds?' he asked.

'After the middle of August,' Birkett somewhat sheepishly replied.

'That's a bit off,' said David.

He thought to himself for a moment, smiling quietly, while they waited for him to speak again.

'Tell me how you're going to do it,' he said, and Birkett took up the story of Bugbear, and the worst race of the year at Sedgefield in August.

'Not Milksheikh then? That was the other job, wasn't it?'

'Milksheikh is next running in a Group III in France,' said Birkett. 'We think he'll be hard to beat, but the rest of the world are waiting for him too. Besides it's France, it might only draw a few runners.'

'OK,' said David, drumming his fingers on the table as he thought. 'How certain are you?'

'About the horse and the race, very,' said Birkett. 'About the stake not certain at all.'

'What are you planning to do? Win the money, take a suitcase to… er, your old stud Robert, and drive back with the horses?'

'Basically, yes,' said Freddie.

'You haven't tried asking her to send them and you pay later?'

Freddie laughed. 'We don't want to show her any weaknesses or any reason to back out of the deal,' he said.

'They really mean a lot to you, don't they?' said David, 'I know you've told me before Freddie, but Birkett, will you take me through the story from your end? I'm sorry, this may be painful to hear Robert.'

Robert waived away his concerns.

So Birkett told David the story from the beginning, and as he finished, Freddie said, 'You tell Alan Halliday that, and I will personally throw you both in the Channel.'

'Alan might help,' he said.

A quick glance around the table told him that the idea had not gone down well.

'I was thinking about this,' said David, 'I'm running the finances for Conrad, Cedric, and Alan on their new bloodstock scheme, *Marlborough Thoroughbreds* – you're participating aren't you, Freddie?'

'Was,' said Freddie.

'Oh yeah, you've fallen out, haven't you? Well, all the money's in, just about. How about if they lent you the one forty for a while? Most of the raise is to be spent on training the horses, so they won't need it for a long time. In fact, if their horses win any prize money – which they will, they won't need it at all, and it'll just sit there as an unused cash balance.'

A collective gulp went round the table. 'Would they need to know?' they all wanted to know.

'They should – and if they did, they'd be asking for points – especially if they knew it was for your benefit Robert – and if they knew it was for your benefit, Freddie, they'd refuse – but I think I could get round that.'

Slowly, a smile went round the table.

'How would it work?' asked Freddie.

'Well, I'd organise it,' said David. 'You'd get your money and acquire your horses. Then when you're next in funds, hopefully when you've landed your gamble, the money is paid back, and no one would know.'

He looked at their faces. What, that simple? They wanted to object but couldn't find a reason.

'And – I can see you're all dying to ask – if the gamble isn't landed, well by then you'll own the horses, so you can either sell them, or take a loan against their future earnings to pay off the loan to Ced. If not that, you salvage what you can out of the equity in your respective properties to pay it off.'

It seemed so simple, and there was an element of justice in it which appealed, but imagine if it got out? Imagine, thought Freddie, the leverage that David would have over them once they were compromised? Besides, it was plain illegal what he was proposing, and he was in enough trouble as it was.

'I'm not sure,' said Freddie. 'It feels like a step too far.'

'It's only what banks do,' said Birkett. 'It's just that we're in the bank of David with two clients. That's all.'

'You just have to ask yourself whether you can afford not to do it now,' David suggested.

Birkett agreed. 'We can't afford to delay,' he said, 'we'll be running Milksheikh by early September, and she'll see for herself what it's all about.'

'That's right,' said David. 'It's up to you, I'm here to help – whatever you do,' he added.

Birkett cocked his jaw as if to ask, '*Whatever?* – what do you mean by that?' and David answered: 'I've told you what I can do, if you want to get the cash now to close the deal – fine, we can do that – park that for now. But whichever way you go right now, you're planning on paying back the loan, or perhaps even financing the deal yourselves, by landing a gamble. For that, you'll need someone who knows how to get a lot of money on in a short space of time at a country backwater like Sedgefield – which you'll find is not the same proposition as trying to win two million quid at Royal Ascot.'

Robert said, 'You what?' and laughed. He hadn't yet appreciated that he was in this sort of company.

'And...' continued David, 'I get the impression that you might need a bit of help in raising a stake for that too. I can help with both.'

'What do you cost?' asked Robert. It wasn't his question to ask, but he wanted him to know that until he proved otherwise, Robert was a long way from being prepared to accept that David was on his side.

'OK, so if I help you organise the gamble, I'm in it for my share of the bet. And if we go that route then my fee for doing it will be that you've got to give me a fair price to buy into your bloodstock deal afterwards.'

He looked round the table and the three of them gave a vaguely positive nod of the head.

'If I organise it the other way by providing the finance, I want points in the deal from the outset, but I'll need more that way. I know it's your gig,' he said, 'and I won't be greedy. I just want a fair shake.'

'It all sounds right,' said Freddie speaking for all of them. 'We'll have to have a little chat between us to decide how we want to do it, but we'll use you, whichever way we go.'

Robert and Birkett turned to look at Freddie, as if he'd been hasty, then he added, 'What I have in mind, will need four of us. It's a good job you turned up.'

A horse box drew into the yard carrying Tara's colours. It contained three horses and a young jockey.

'Here we are,' said the jockey as they went to meet him.

'We?' said Birkett. 'Who are you?'

'I'm Brodie Fitzpatrick,' he said. 'You get me too.'

'Well Brodie, get them off and put them in the paddock for now, I'll show you where they're going to go when you've done that. We haven't got any boxes ready; we didn't expect you yet.'

On the way back to the house David took Birkett by the arm and asked, 'What are they?'

'They,' said Birkett, stopping to face him, 'are three of Tara's horses that I have offered to train for free for a year.'

'Text her to say that they've arrived, and when you do, confirm the terms of the deal she gave you yesterday. Add nothing and take nothing away but put it on the record. And do it now. If you haven't got her number send the same message to Brodie and tell him to send it on.'

Later that evening, when just the three of them sat together to share a glass of whiskey, Robert and Birkett agreed that had they behaved a little more like David, they'd have dealt with Tara better. Freddie disagreed. He knew her type from old, and neither he, nor David were built her way. She was one of those who would take every ounce of value out of a generous deal, then push for more. They were so hard to manage at the bank, people like her. You'd spoil good relationships with reliable people to push for the unreasonable change in terms for them, then the next morning, they'd be on the phone, complaining, asking for more.

They agreed that demanding the training three horses for free was just such an example.

'Perhaps,' said Freddie, 'but sending Brodie definitely is.'

Birkett refilled their glasses for a final round. His words didn't quite match his thoughts, but they went along the lines of: *if they were to obsess about getting even with Tara, they'd never win anything.* 'Our fight is to win our own game,' he said. They clinked their glasses, downed the whiskey in one gulp, and for the first time in a long time set off to bed full of resolve.

Only Freddie lingered. He didn't want to bring the mood down but he had to take a step out of the growing euphoria to spend a moment alone with Felix. Robert was a great person to have around the place but his endlessly positivity tended to block out the light.

He sat at Birkett's computer, turned it on, and imagining Felix imploring him to go back to basics, sketched out a SWAT analysis of their predicament. Slightly drunk and quickly despondent, he soon gave up. He closed his eyes and tried to take himself back to the little cubby-hole office they shared at the bank and brought all his resolve and concentration to visualise one of their conversations where they had to employ a great leap of imagination to solve an intractable problem.

But no inspiration came. He was tired and likely to be far drunker than he reckoned. 'OK, Felix,' he said finally, 'one last go for you,' and he simply wrote a long list of every possible scenario by which he might raise the funds to get himself out of trouble.

TWENTY-NINE

That first week following David's arrival brought its challenges for Freddie. For all his façade reflected confidence, behind it the uncertainty grew. Eventually they might hit their stride as a partnership, Freddie's CEO worrying everything right, to David's chairman, bringing opportunity and new ways of doing things. But until then, they looked like an oddly cast pair, David only recently the rogue, was becoming the one that the others started to look to for calm and comfort, while the same qualities seemed to leach away out of Freddie with each new day. He had lost weight but now he looked haunted rather than healthy.

Increasingly he kept his own hours too, and would be the first to bed, and first up each day, keeping to himself throughout the daylight hours, with only their recently instituted lunchtime meetings providing an anchor point for the day.

Agony was etched on his face when he eventually interrupted one of those early meetings to say, 'We're not going to borrow from Alan and Conrad's fund.' In the intervening period Birkett and Robert had come round to the idea and he saw their disappointment with his decision. 'If it all goes wrong, it still remains a last option for us. But we'll look at it with different eyes then. I'm just saying no for now. I want to get it off the table.'

The truth was he'd spent the previous nights going through every possible future scenario, from every possible angle. He'd decided that if the gamble failed, he would then ask David to loan them the money, and once that was done, he'd ask him to make another financial arrangement for him alone, whereby he drew a line of credit from the projected future earnings of the family, to pay off his creditors. If the gamble succeeded, he would ask David to top up the shortfall from his winnings by dipping into the fund for the same purposes.

Once that matter was off the table, over the following days, the four of them, five if you counted Brodie, and six if you included his new best friend Liam, started to fall into something of a routine.

Robert was immersed in his new job, seeming only to be able to look forward. As soon as Freddie stopped going to the races, Robert stepped in. Certain owners loved him, and he loved looking after the horses and taking them to and fro. Birkett never doubted for a moment that he could be trusted. The odd member of staff was put out by not getting the away days that supplemented their wages, but Robert had a winning way with them too, and grudges were never held for long.

Of all of them, Liam should have felt most aggrieved because he did most of the box driving until Freddie and Robert turned up, and he no longer had the pick of where he went. When Davey dared to bring up the subject, he chose to describe it as a welcome reprieve for all the months and years he had been put upon and exploited. He had still not properly avenged their decision to exploit Slipshod at Newmarket, which was made worse by his finishing only third at Goodwood in a race where the good French horse did not turn up, but he was happy that he would run next in a Group III in France, in the same race as Milksheikh, and there, they'd find out which one of them meant most to the stable. That was one of the recurring themes of his many conversations with Brodie, with whom he sensed a kindred spirit.

David Spencer came to the yard infrequently to begin with, but as D-Day for Bugbear loomed, and the day on which Milksheikh's half-brother would pass through the ring came closer, he was present three or four days out of six. When he was there, he used Birkett's office as his own, but always brought with him his own much more powerful armoury of computers and equipment.

The logistics of organising the purchase of the half-brother were only complicated to a point. His view, which won out, was to have a local agent do the bidding. Their presence would indicate more strongly than was prudent their interest in the horse; particularly to Tara, who could buy the horse just to give herself a stake in their project.

Once purchased, the horse would be signed for by the agent, and then, in about three weeks or so, before paying, he'd sign it over to them. It would help keep it anonymous, and it would give them that little bit more time to pay, if they needed it by then. Their last resort would be to sell the horse to a syndicate of existing owners.

As to the gamble on Bugbear, there were two options. The first was that Birkett, Freddie, and Robert, starting with a small heap of winnings from Tara's horse at Newmarket together with a few winners and some placed horses of their own, to which they'd add every penny they could scrape together by avoiding paying any bills, would grow it organically into something that resembled a stake.

Throughout this planning and scheming, David constantly reminded them that they would not be getting thirty-threes or forties for Bugbear at Sedgefield, as they had at Royal Ascot, but they continued to live in hope. And something about the way they approached the bet told David that they were naïve beyond comprehension, or that there was something about it that they had kept from him. Either way, he worried for them.

'As a flat trainer of a certain note,' he said to Birkett in one of their meetings, 'it'll catch the eye of most people that you even have a runner in a race like that. That it's a seller will make it stand out a mile. You'll be lucky to see ten to one offered for openers, and that will disappear quickly if any of this bet gets out.'

'You don't believe in this bet, do you?' Freddie asked, and David replied that he had great faith in their collective ability, but he didn't believe that they would have anywhere near sufficient stake to be able to realise the sum required to pay Tara. And so, the second option came into view.

'Perhaps I'm being naïve,' said David, 'but hear me out – I can help here. I've been here before.'

He explained an alternative strategy for the gamble, which was that *his investors* as he called them, would lodge funds with him. And their terms were simple: they got half of the bounty if their funds were used. A horse backed at ten to one, would yield five to one to Birkett, Freddie, and Robert, and the same price to the investor.

He did not promise his clients that their funds would be used, but they would find out where, and by how much they were invested, by a simple text message as soon as 'They're off!' was sounded in the race in question, so that they could not spoil the price or influence the outcome. He'd prepare a text to send to all of them, which would read something like: '75% invested @ 8.2, Bugbear, 2.50 Sedgefield.' In that way, they were informed before the outcome was known in a way that could be audited, and neither side could cheat the transaction.

It was a good system and it had worked well previously, though it had not been frequently used. And it meant that the funds were there depending on how much it was that the boys needed to make. 'Say you wanted to clear half a million,' he said. 'You will never achieve that in a month of Sundays with your own stake as it stands now.'

Freddie gave a cautious go ahead to it all. He was reluctant to share the spoils with anyone else, but he could see a means by which it could work.

'Let's get back to you on the detail there,' he said. And left it at that.

THIRTY

Birkett was up first on that morning. He went out onto the terrace as usual with his first lot list and from there, after taking in the air and casting his beady eye over each corner of the yard, to the main noticeboard, where he was stopped in his tracks by the full-beam glare of a 4x4 coming down the gravel drive towards him. He stood still in the drive, shielding his eyes from the light as the vehicle drew to a halt a couple of feet in front of him. A police officer came out from the passenger side and asked, 'Frederick Lyons?'

Birkett replied that he'd fetch him for them, pinned up the list and returned to the house. Freddie excused himself for a moment and took a couple of seconds to gather some personal effects from his bedroom: watch, phone, reading glasses. He put on a V-neck pullover and came down to meet the officers.

David hadn't yet arrived at the yard; the rest of the staff were straining to strike that balance between prurience and concern. The police officer, standing inside the office, informed Freddie that they needed to speak to him 'About certain matters,' and that it would be better, all things considered, if he'd be prepared to come with them now to the station. They'd have him back before midday.

Freddie consented. Birkett took down the lot-list to make a hasty revision or two, wished him well, and told him to ring him when it was all over for a lift back.

'No need sir, we'll have him back shortly,' replied the officer. He followed Freddie to the car, and offered him the back seat, then climbed in besides him. The car made a slow circle in the yard, then left.

He was placed in an interview room with a cup of tea and left to stew on his thoughts for quarter of an hour or so, until eventually, three men entered the room, one in uniform, two in casual clothes. One of them he recognised, Inspector Grandcollot from Deauville, the other introduced himself as Detective Inspector Rayner.

'Two of you?' asked Freddie, and Grandcollot replied that it needn't have been, had he not breached his promise not to leave the area.

'I'm sorry, I needed a job,' he mumbled.

But Grandcollot did not understand why he had not been able to come and see him to discuss that. Freddie refrained from answering.

Both men looked solemn, they drew back their chairs, and came to sit, facing Freddie.

'I have some serious news for you Mr Lyons,' said Grandcollot.

Freddie stared back blankly.

'It concerns your partner, Felix Diaz.'

They seemed to exchange a brief glance. 'I am sorry to have to tell you that he died during the night.'

Freddie put his left hand to his face, his elbow propped on the desk between them. He bit hard on his bottom lip to stem the flow of tears but could not stop his hand shaking as he moved it to cover his mouth. Grandcollot and Rayner gave him a few moments to digest the news.

'Mr Lyons,' said Grandcollot eventually, 'you will realise of course that this is now a murder enquiry.'

'Yes,' he said, of course it was a murder enquiry, before that it was a GBH enquiry, or attempted murder, whatever they called it. The same people did it. How did his death change anything?

'You were one of the last to see him alive,' said Rayner.

'Just a minute,' said Freddie, 'we've been through all this.'

'Yes, we have those records,' said Grandcollot, 'but our investigation develops. We know that he was injected with a lethal agent. We know the point of entry on his body. His death was most certainly deliberate.'

Freddie nodded, he'd always thought that was the case, then Rayner came back in: 'And we know that you argued with him a few minutes before he was attacked.'

'What? How would I know where to buy *Novichok*? We didn't argue, that's preposterous.'

Grandcollot said, 'With the right contacts it can be acquired.'

He had talked over Rayner, who was was saying, 'Well, a strongly worded disagreement, but still...'

'We did no such thing,' said Freddie, 'we never had a cross word. Ever. That's why we did what we did together. Who told you that?'

Grandcollot raised his hand. 'You had lost some money?'

'Sorry?'

'You'd lost a lot of money in the bloodstock markets. That was the day you realised your losses.'

'Yeah, we had.'

'Were you both due to meet your client, or just Felix?' Rayner put in.

'Just him.'

'Why?'

'Why? It's the way it fell. He'd called him. He'd been talking to him I suppose, held the relationship at the time. It could have been either of us. I'd been at the sales. Haven't I said all this before?'

'How did it go down?' asked Rayner, 'when you reported the loss?'

'It was… I don't know… it's just how it was. I didn't hear. I was waiting to hear. It seemed OK from what he told me of their phone call.'

'You know a man called Hamilton? Edward Hamilton,' asked Grandcollot.

'What? Yeah, of course.'

'Did you meet him?' asked Rayner

'No.'

The two detectives paused for a moment.

Grandcollot picked it up: 'Your client – the one that met Felix on the night he was attacked. Did you meet him last week? At Newmarket races?'

'No. He was my client, past tense.'

'You see, we can put you all at Newmarket at about the same time. You all know each other, but you say you didn't meet? Didn't bump into each other?'

Perhaps they had him on CCTV. 'Look, you'll have to explain what this is all about. How does it help you find Felix's killer?'

'Are you still in contact with your Russian clients?' asked Rayner.

'No. I mean, I haven't... I mean, I don't do that anymore.'

'We will need to look more closely at your records, your transactions with them. Will you be able to provide these for us?'

'They're in France. I er...'

'When are you next there?'

'Er, in two- or three-weeks' time. I er...'

'Good, I will arrange to meet you there,' said Grandcollot.

'He owed you money, Hamilton?' asked Rayner.

Freddie hung his head and groaned. 'Oh Jesus.'

'...or did you work with him?'

'What?'

Rayner shrugged.

'Of course I didn't work with him, who told you that?'

'So, he owes you then, how much?'

What was this? Was this what they called robust questioning, or was he really implicated? Was there a view of the facts, that could be reasonably construed to put him at the heart of some sort of conspiracy? Every instinct told him to take on the argument and explain why they were mistaken, but the desire to explain would only lead to an unprepared for discussion about his relationship with his clients. And that wasn't going to happen – it was bad enough to have to turn over records.

'Aren't you supposed to offer me the chance to see a solicitor?'

Grandcollot apologised. 'Sorry, it is my understanding of the regulations which is at fault. I wanted to bring you the news, and to tell you where we are with the enquiry. Of course you may go, but I must ask that you tell myself or Mr Rayner if you see Mr Hamilton or your Russian clients.'

Freddie nodded.

'...and a promise not to move from here without reporting to police at either end of his journey. Here is my number again.'

Freddie nodded again.

'En ce cas, I will see you in about two weeks' time, when you next return to France,' he said.

'Can I let you know in a couple of days? I don't know exactly myself yet,' he asked.

'I expect a call, otherwise, I will collect you again,' Grandcollot said, thrusting a business card into Freddie's hand.

Freddie stood up and shook hands with both men. 'Will you be putting a guard on the stables?' he asked, and when they both laughed, he decided to laugh too.

The police car couldn't make it all the way back down the drive, a small flat-back truck, with his car already winched onto it, blocked the way. Freddie got out of the car and left the policeman to back his way out of the situation best he could. As he approached the yard he was struck by the maelstrom of noise and voices and faces.

'Here he is,' he heard someone say, then a moment later a small bespectacled man appeared from the crowd and said, 'Frederick Lyons?'

Freddie replied, 'Yes,' and the small man handed him a bunch of documents.

'You are hereby served,' he said.

He looked down to the court bundle, shook his head and sighed.

'Get in here will you Freddie,' shouted Birkett, walking towards him, beckoning, 'tell this fucking idiot what's what will you?'

Two casually dressed men, the same size and scope as the close protection guards he'd met in St Cloud, were on their way out of Birkett's office. One of them was clutching an old-fashioned briefcase, and Freddie's heart skipped a beat as he saw it.

'That's mine, you cunt,' said Birkett, grabbing it off him as he passed him on the way to the house. The man resisted but Birkett won out. 'Show these fuckers what's yours and get them out of here,' he said.

The other man took a pace towards Freddie and showed him some documents. 'We're ordered to take back your possessions to the value of the amount in the document,' he said.

Freddie laughed, and said, 'Good luck with that.'

'I'd like you to identify which of these computers belongs to you,' he said. He gestured for them to go into the office.

'I can save you some time there,' said Freddie. 'I have the clothes that I'm wearing, and those hanging in my wardrobe. There are some items in the bathroom which are mine, but, and I make this plea to you as a fellow being – you are human aren't you? Please leave me a little after-shave.'

'This way please sir,' said the man.

Freddie stopped where he was standing and drew in his breath. David had appeared from the office, clutching his computer, Robert stopped what he was doing and turned to look at Freddie. Birkett moved to stand by his own computer.

'Just fuck off,' said Freddie.

David laughed and the man turned round menacingly.

Freddie's phone pinged and he immediately said, 'it's rented, you can't have it.'

David laughed again, and the man, unsure of himself for the first time that morning, took a moment to consider how best to assert his jurisdiction over the situation. He went back into the office to see which of the computers remained unclaimed. None were.

He came out onto the terrace again, seeming set on upgrading the negotiation with Freddie. As he did, he tripped, or somebody tripped him and he went careering forwards, trying but failing to regain his balance as he did, before landing chin first on the small brick wall which protruded into that end of the terrace.

His colleague reappeared with Freddie's travelling bag and he tried to push through the four of them, who had not moved to help his stricken mate, who was still struggling to shake off the impact of the blow, still on all fours, breathing deeply, trying to regain his equilibrium. He went to put the bag down, but David stepped into his path and said:

'Put that back inside first.'

The man smirked and locked eyes with David, but David took a step towards him, and as he did, the other three men went a pace closer too. He said, 'My partner...'

'The bag,' said David.

He turned and placed the bag inside the office.

'Back upstairs,' David told him.

Birkett, David, and Robert went back into the office to see that he'd done as he was told, and as they did, Freddie swiftly, unnoticed, swept his foot under the stricken man's arms and sent him chin first onto the hard surface.

His mate came back again and as he crouched to tend to him, Birkett shoved him gently in the back and said, 'Get that truck away first, we're running a business here.'

The man snarled, as if to say that he could pick off Birkett any time he chose. Then he noticed first David, then Freddie cock their fists, ready for the next stage if that was what it was going to be. He thought better of it and got up to gather his stuff and take it back to the lorry. Once done, he came back to his colleague but struggled to pick him up alone. He turned to ask for help, and the four of them, in a close semi-circle around the two men did not move, until eventually, Robert broke ranks to pick up a bucket and fill it from the fountain. He returned and threw it over the man on the ground.

'That's all the help you're getting,' he said.

'You've got five minutes,' Birkett added, 'otherwise he's going out of here on the end of tow rope.'

The four men then left them to it, went inside and locked the door behind them – a tiny moment of triumph in a tidal wave of woe.

'For fuck's sake, Freddie,' said Birkett, but Freddie's reaction told them that he could have done nothing about the events of that morning.

He took them through the police interview, then suddenly realised: 'The briefcase, with our cash. Something made me hide it in the kitchen before I went with the police this morning. Was that it – that you grabbed off him?'

'Yes. And that's the last upset 'til the horse runs,' said Birkett.

Freddie held up his hands, mea culpa. 'I'll keep them away,' he said. Though how he'd do that, he had no idea.

All he wanted to do was to wish away the next couple of weeks so that he might know his fate. With that certainty whatever it might be, he would face his pursuers. *Pursuers?* He swallowed. His ex-wife was wreaking enough damage all on her own; the police were more frightening still; but what was really terrifying was the silence that came from his ex-clients.

The next day was quiet, but for the small matter of Tara's people chasing up payment. In the new mood that had settled over the place, they got short shrift from Birkett, who shouted down the phone, 'I've told you already I'm coming to France to pick them up in about a week, with the money – have them ready or woe be-fucking-tide you.'

'We should have treated them like that from the off,' said Freddie.

'At least we are now,' said Birkett.

THIRTY-ONE

As much as Brodie became absorbed into the daily rhythm of the place, he also stood apart. He was alone, round the back with his three horses. He mucked them, groomed them, fed them, rugged them up and rode them. Birkett was not allowed to have anything to do with their training. Sometimes Brodie tacked on to the end of the string if he was giving a horse a routine piece of work, and sometimes he'd ask if Birkett had anything that could work with one of his horses when it was going to do some faster work. But when he did, he described it by age, ability, and trip, and never its name. Similarly, Birkett would piggyback his schooling sessions, and so when Brodie took one of his horses to the schooling hurdles, Birkett would arrange for another jump jockey to come and ride Bugbear, or one of the others that he'd decided to put over hurdles so that Bugbear didn't stand out so much when he made his debut.

Brodie would take his hay, straw, and feed from Birkett's barn, but never an invoice went out, and never a payment came in. When eventually they wanted to put one of their horses in a race, Brodie came to the office door in the morning on which the entries were due, and told Birkett what to do. Similarly, on declarations day, three days later, he'd come and tell him to declare or to scratch, and if they were declaring, who to put up as jockey, or that he'd be riding it himself. When the horses went to the races, Brodie would drive, and Birkett would lend him someone to lead up the horse.

But the place felt busy in a way that it hadn't for a long time, and everyone was lost to their jobs. It suited Freddie, in his desire to block out all the external troubles that pursued him and to disappear from view. He'd shared too much already but he kept to himself the stultifying dread of his clients which grew to haunt him day and night.

Milksheikh had been moved from his isolated box and put into the main yard, and as he did, Freddie moved into his old box and set up camp for himself. He surfaced from that hideaway for work, meetings, and very little else. He was a concern to his friends, but they all had their eyes on a bigger prize and understood his desire to melt safely into the background.

Their quest for winners made it his job to scour the programme book to look for opportunities. He'd stopped going to the races but having ridden many of the horses in their work made sure that Robert was thoroughly briefed before he set off with them.

In that purposeful routine, their confidence in their plans grew, but then, as Bugbear's race grew closer, two events conspired to throw their quiet industry and resolve off track. With a week to go to the race, they were giving Bugbear his final blow out. Liam led the gallop on a horse that had recently run in a hurdle race. It hadn't won, but it had kept on well to the end, and they knew that it stayed the two-miles trip well. It was to be a steady piece of work over ten furlongs or so, and Bugbear was to take it up and put daylight between himself and the other horse at the end of the gallop. After three furlongs, Liam pulled up his mount, saying later that he thought it had gone wrong, and so left Freddie on Bugbear to make the most of what was now a meaningless gallop. He considered pulling up too, so that they could organise it all again tomorrow with another horse and another jockey, but he didn't want to disappoint his mount who had committed to the work by the time that Liam went through with his stunt, and so he rode it out.

It was too close to him running to organise another gallop, so they were to go there now, not quite sure that they had him absolutely cherry ripe.

Not unrelated perhaps to that event, was the second, when Brodie knocked on Birkett's door the next morning and said, 'Will you put Submariner in the Monkey Puzzle Handicap at Sedgefield please?'

It was the first point on the agenda in what had become their daily debriefs. They took place at twelve-thirty after the staff had gone home, and as soon as Robert, their domestique, could rustle them up some sandwiches and drinks.

Birkett's initial view was that they could talk Tara out of declaring her horse, but nobody else agreed. They didn't know, but if this was a plan, nothing would dissuade her from carrying it out. If it wasn't, it'd muck up their own gamble if they were to alert her to it. No, they had to sit and wait and see which way she went. In the meantime, they had to get prepared.

'Firstly,' said David, 'you're going to have to look to Plan B to raise the one-forty to buy the horses.'

A collective groan went round the table.

'Say we don't,' he went on, 'say we wait until sometime after the race to turn any money we might have won into cash. Then we take it to France, and then we hand it over to Tara in return for her horses. This is Tara, the unconscionable cheat – that's what you call her isn't it, Freddie? – we rely on her to play fair, when we have just ruined a gamble for her? I say, we get them now, and make them ours.'

Each man looked at the other.

'And then, if the gamble goes wrong, and we have no money, you'll have to prove that Milksheikh is as good as you think he is, then sell him. And in pretty short order too.'

Reluctantly they each acknowledged that he was right. Milksheikh or the mare, what a terrible choice to have to make. And so, the meeting decided that David would produce one hundred and forty thousand pounds cash for them, and that Freddie and Birkett would travel to France in one of Birkett's boxes to pick up Air Hostess and her foal on the day before the race.

In many ways it suited Freddie, because it took him under the radar, far and away to the deep countryside of France. He'd leave the yard in the back of the horse box, and ring Grandcollot once he was on the ferry to arrange the meet he'd promised.

THIRTY-TWO

Freddie, as he always did, took the new problems of the day back to Milksheikh's box each night, to add to those he already knew. He would retire by eight-thirty most nights. Then for the next few hours, wearing a head torch so that he could use his laptop, he'd read and research for as long as he could keep awake before surrendering to sleep. This way, he reasoned, he'd deny the chance to his mind to churn over thoughts of Felix, Hamilton, Penny, and his clients. He seemed to go through them like a list, ticking them off before moving on to the next, on one pass hating them for their incursion into his life; the next time hating himself for the mistakes he'd made in dealing with them, constantly replaying the key moments in their relationship to see how he should have done better.

Penny! Why did she still loom so large in his thoughts? Because she persisted, that's why. Because he didn't know what new idiocy she'd perpetrate next on him. He'd wronged her, sure, but God, enforcing the judgments? She knew by now he had nothing, what on earth was the point of trying to take his last few pennies? What good was the house to her? She'd be as unable to sell as he had been. Oh no! She'd know about the mortgage now. He got up again paced the box for a while, then went back to reading again, trying to eradicate extraneous thoughts, and bring on fatigue.

Milksheikh's secret box was landlocked and the light he created could not travel from it, but soon he became aware that his headlight was not the only light in the yard. He turned it off, then his laptop and went back to sit on the edge of his camp bed. Five minutes later he noticed the swirling light of a torch again. None of the horses stirred, but he was sure he could hear the sound of grit under shoes, imagining the intruder to be biding his time, standing in the shadows, looking about him, careful not to walk more than he needed to.

No lights now, but the sound of a man, yes it was a man, you could somehow discern the gait, began to walk again. A far-off whinny told him that one of the horses had noticed something. A motion sensitive spotlight came on. There was someone there.

The footsteps weren't disguised now, and the intruder walked steadily and openly towards the corner of the yard in which he lived. He crept from his camp bed and checked that the bolts were drawn on the box, then crawled to the nearest corner, imagining it a blind spot from the stable door.

A whispered voice came towards him: 'Psst.'

It repeated. He didn't answer.

'Psst, Freddie. Sorry to wake you.'

'Who is it?' he asked.

'Me, you fool, Robert. Just doing the night patrol.'

Freddie breathed again. He suddenly became aware of his heart, beating thunderously in his chest as he exhaled and started to calm down. He almost berated Robert then stopped himself, realising that he'd probably been doing this every night since Freddie had been living this way.

'Thank you, Robert. All's fine, mate.'

'That's good,' he whispered, trying not to disturb the horses, 'night night.'

Freddie heard his footsteps walk away, then returned to his camp bed. He was awake now. 'Night night.' What a lovely, decent, gentle man. The thought struck him cold - I was once like that. Was raised to be like that; should still be like that. He laughed to himself then said under his voice, 'But Robert has not been tainted by ambition, as I have.'

Penny was right. He'd had no right to play this game. Even Jonny could run rings round him, let alone someone smart like Edward Hamilton. What had made him think that he could take on sophisticated, timed-served professionals like them? His most significant asset was the arrogance borne of privilege that told him that his was the earth and everything that's in it. What was he? What had he actually achieved? He was one of those people who had breezed through his early life and had spent the middle part of it telling himself how clever he was. He'd got his job in investment banking on the basis of an ability to do fast mental arithmetic. That was it. That, and looking and sounding right were the essential qualifications. Then he'd been trained to do something that thousands of other people could have done equally well. A few years into that career and he was competent at something that was considered extremely important. He mattered. He and his colleagues, and the people he spoke to at other banks really mattered – they were at the heart of the economy – the shrewd bit at its very core. They all eventually bought into the idea that what they did was essential and that they alone possessed the exceptional qualities to do it right. Sure, his analytical skills improved over the years but no more so than someone who built roads or worked in a laboratory got better at what they did. He came out of that career thinking that he could turn his hand to anything and make a success of it. The truth was you came out of jobs like that unfit for anything. Those banks boasted that they only employed people with razor sharp minds. They paid salaries that were unimaginable in almost any other line of business on the basis that they had cornered the market for talent. They alone had skimmed the cream off the top and the rest of the working population were the also-rans in life. Yet the people he'd worked with wouldn't even be able to fathom out Birkett let alone keep up with him; people like Ced and Edward Hamilton would humiliate them for their lack of nous. David would wipe the floor with them. Nevertheless his, Felix's, their colleague's, their terrible arrogance grew. It was perhaps because they'd never had to extend themselves to get their position in life; they were bright, they passed exams, got into good universities, possessed good social skills, and just stayed on the conveyor belt. Then in time they came to regard those commonplace skills as somehow exclusively belonging to them believing that everybody else was lacking by comparison – they weren't bright, quick witted, and smart like them. God, he and Felix laughed up their sleeves at their colleagues – that they weren't quite as smart as them; that they 'got it' faster than them. They were just one notch further along, that was all. And so, they valued this thing, this being bright, completely unaware of the fact that millions of other people were bright too – the thing that they thought marked them out as special. And all the time, the real world grew. Those ordinary plodders who weren't good enough to get into investment banks when they did, those people who didn't file through Oxford and Cambridge because they couldn't pass their exams with the insouciant élan of Freddie and his friends, they plodded on and learnt how to do real things. They applied their God given brightness and turned themselves into people with professional skills that they put to work in the real world. Freddie's lot popped out of their hermetically sealed fantasies, bloated with hubris, certain that they could turn their hand to anything because they held in spades the only skill worth possessing: self-confidence. 'You caught us up and passed us by,' he said to himself. 'Everybody else worked and made progress by merit, we were lauded just for being ourselves. We were rewarded for what we'd inherited and for our undertaking not to change.'

He talked out loud like this to himself like until he became sick of his own voice, then stopped pacing and went back to his bed again, hoping that sleep would come soon to release him from these thoughts. He lay back on the camp bed fully expecting them to continue to file through his mind for hours to come, but in just a few moments anxiety-induced fatigue overwhelmed his body, and another day ended.

On most days, from his new accommodation, Freddie was the first to arrive in the yard. He'd splash himself awake with the fresh water in the fountain, then go to the tack room where he'd hidden a washbag, to complete his ablutions. This morning he slept on, for once not disturbed by the horses as they roused, until just after six-thirty when a piercing scream woke him with a start. He quickly pulled on some clothes and rushed out into the yard in the direction of the cry. Outside what he believed to be an unoccupied box in the far corner of the main yard he saw one of the girls, another early starter. As he came closer, he could see that her sobbing had turned into a silent, fearful, trembling. She pointed towards the empty box, unable to look at it, it's door now open. Freddie's thoughts jumped immediately to the horses, thinking that a new arrival been put in there unknown to him and had got loose. He suddenly halted to look around the yard, and saw Birkett and Robert heading in their direction. The open door did not compute. He placed a consoling hand across the stable lass's shoulders as he went past her, knowing that Robert and Birkett were shortly behind him to comfort her properly, then went on towards the box.

There was no horse, but on the freshly laid straw waiting for its next new occupant lay the body of Edward Hamilton with a pitchfork, standing erect, planted in his neck. Freddie recoiled at the sight. He looked briefly round the empty box and seeing nothing else, left to apprehend the others as they rushed towards the crime scene.

As more people arrived for first lot they were drawn towards the incident but Birkett held them at bay, putting Liam in charge, telling him to ignore the lots he'd pinned up on the board and to set to work in the other yard, using his discretion about what horses to take out and in what order.

He asked Freddie whether he had anything to do with what had happened, and when Freddie shook his head to answer, he took out his phone and called the police. He invited Robert to look at the body with him from a distance, then he ordered Robert to take Freddie and the girl back to the office and to look after them there until the police arrived.

Robert and Freddie were taken to the police station to make their statements. Freddie to be interviewed by Detective Rayner, the same junior officer that took a statement from the stable lass in the office would deal with Robert. Robert had recognised the body described as Edward Hamilton as an occasional visitor to his farm. He had to call Jules to get his name, and she was the one who eventually came up with Teddy Hamble. 'He only said it,' he told the officer. 'Didn't write it down. Always after bargains, I think. Never bought buggar all off us though,' he said.

Rayner raised his eyebrows at Freddie as he arrived to interview him, *here we are again, eh?* It felt like a nod to the football referees' totting up system, where a series of not-quite fouls eventually bring the offender a yellow card. The detective took a statement from him about the events of the morning and his whereabouts in the twenty-fours prior, in cold sobriety, as if taking a slow-motion dictation. They shared an insincere smile as the statement was completed. Rayner put down his pen, then spun the document towards Freddie for him to read and sign. Still no words were exchanged. Freddie signed the document and spun it back. As he did, Rayner locked eyes with him.

'You saw him, didn't you?' he said.

'No, when?' asked Freddie.

'At Newmarket. We have him on CCTV. We know he was there. And we know that you were too because you were thrown out.'

Freddie said nothing but nodded to say that it was true.

'So that's a yes then? What did you speak about?'

Freddie stuck to the line that he hadn't seen him in person and that no words had been exchanged. Rayner simply shook his head, 'Why lie?' he said.

- 231 -

Freddie insisted that he wasn't lying and offered up a little prayer that there were no CCTV cameras on the stairwell to show how close they'd come.

'I'm putting it to you,' said Rayner, 'that you got wind that Hamilton was going to be at Newmarket races on that day and that you, knowing that you were still under a warning-off notice, went there under the radar to track him down.'

'I did no such thing,' said Freddie, 'I went to watch our horse, I thought that I could go to watch – just as long as I wasn't working.'

Rayner laughed, then went on, as if Freddie hadn't spoken, '...showing your motive, to be revenged against him.'

Freddie took a moment, 'Is it time for me to ask for a lawyer?' he asked.

'You're just assisting the police with their enquiries.'

'Am I going to be charged with anything?' he asked.

'No.' said Rayner.

'Arrested?'

Rayner shook his head.

Nothing was said for a moment, then Freddie said, 'So I'm free to go?'

'If you like,' said Rayner, eventually.

Freddie pushed back his chair and got up to leave. He almost held out his hand, then decided against it. For a moment he considered requesting that Rayner hold him in custody until he got to the bottom of it all. He knew it was an absurd thought but he had reached the stage where he no longer felt safe wherever he was, and for a moment, solitary confinement with the odd moment of forced civility with Rayner felt attractive.

As he reached the door of the interview room, Rayner called out after him:

'Don't leave the country or this area, unless specifically requested to do so by the police. Is that understood?'

Without turning to look at him Freddie replied, 'OK,' then left the room.

He found Robert waiting for him at the desk with the junior officer, who was to drive them home.

'Everything OK?' said Robert sotto voce when he was sure the policeman's attention was elsewhere.

'Yeah,' said Freddie, 'been a tough morning, hasn't it?'

Robert grabbed his hand tightly and walked with him like that until they arrived at the police car. He allowed Freddie into the car first, then got in alongside him, where he grasped his hand again. They didn't speak, but if there was a better person than Robert to look after a man so undermined in his confidence as he now was, Freddie didn't know who that was. He squeezed Robert's hand to let him know how he felt, not quite able to find the words to say it.

THIRTY-THREE

When the day to make the declarations arrived, Brodie appeared at the office door just before second lot and said, 'We're going to take a chance in that Sedgefield race with Submariner. It doesn't look that hot, unless yours is a dark one?' He laughed.

Birkett declared both horses and sat to think for a moment. He knew that by his not saying, that Brodie intended to ride the horse, that being the default, but nevertheless he went into the yard later to check with him. Just in case.

It was there that he found out that Submariner in the Monkey Puzzle was a *job* that had been set up for months, and that changing yards for the horses had always been part of the plan.

'Oh, there's no doubt he won't run,' said Brodie, 'he's a good thing, and it's a rank bad race – it'll get your relationship off on the right foot.' Then he laughed, as if things like this were part of the great fun of life. 'Don't go spoiling the price now – that wouldn't go down too well,' he added, as Birkett made his way back to the office.

He told the news first to David, who was sat as his desk. They were talking it over still as Robert, then Freddie came in to find out what he knew.

'He's running, and they think they're going to win,' he told them. 'What should we do?'

They talked for a long time, and finally decided, having looked at the public form of Tara's horse, that she had underestimated Bugbear. He was thirty, forty pounds better than anything he'd shown in public. He hadn't raced for over a year, but he'd been to the races often as company for other horses; they'd given him a racecourse gallop as part of his prep. Only the ruined piece of work was a negative, and he'd been in work for almost all the season, doing in his gallops with Slipshod and Milksheikh, something the opposition on Monday couldn't dream of doing. Plus, if Tara was backing her horse, they'd get a decent gallop in the race, and more importantly, a price. No, they were still going. It wasn't quite the penalty kick that they'd imagined it to be a month or so ago, but they only had one horse to beat. A horse that for all they could see was worse than theirs. At the expected prices, there may even be a little opportunity to steal some each-way money, suggested Robert.

Freddie picked up on Robert's words. He had a point; they were taking too much risk for too little reward, weren't they? He'd been hoping that they'd declare Submariner, he told them.

Robert, David, and Birkett, almost as one, dropped the point that they wanted to make, and turned to look at Freddie.

'You scare me sometimes,' said Robert.

Freddie noticed Birkett look over to Robert as if to say, *me too.*

Freddie smiled, extended the pause, then he began.

They heard him out in a solemn silence.

Robert responded first. Beaming, he said, 'Genius.'

David leaned back on his chair and clapped slowly and deliberately to acknowledge the same thing.

Birkett said nothing, he simply moved his head from side to side in pure admiration. Freddie's suggestion only amounted to a small tweak to the arrangements, but it made everything work better. Gave the plan clarity. He hadn't spent those long nights in Milksheikh's box fretting his life away, he'd been thinking, and plotting and planning. A broad grin broke out over his face. His mate was back.

All agreed, they set about to finalise the details. Birkett and Freddie would set off later in the afternoon with the money to pick up the horses from France using Birkett's main horse box. They'd see them next on Tuesday night. Freddie would leave the yard under a horse blanket in the back of the empty horse box. They would not push their luck any further by doing the same at customs. There, they'd play it straight. He'd only be out of the country for a day or so and neither Rayner nor Grandcollot would notice or care about that. Apart from the *scene-of-crime* forensics, they'd heard nothing from the police since the incident; nothing at all from the two detectives, and as each new day went by and the day of the race came closer, they each, slowly at first, switched their attention from one event to the other. Particularly so Freddie who came to assume that the police investigation had turned up the evidence that took their gaze from him to the real perpetrators. Those real perpetrators were the real reason he had decided to leave the yard under a horse blanket.

David was to go elsewhere to manage his side of the business, so that none of it was associated with Birkett's stable. Robert was to be travelling head lad, but they'd hire a horse transporter to take the two horses to the races. Brodie would go up in that with one other lass to lead up Submariner. Robert would lead up Bugbear. There'd only be room for three in the horse transporter, including the driver, so Robert would follow in his own car.

They talked for a little while longer as Birkett delivered his detailed stipulations as to how the horses and the race were to be organised. They seemed incongruous on his lips, these meticulous instructions, but this time he hammered home each and every detail for Robert's trip.

Forty-five minutes later Birkett said to Robert, 'You're in charge now. I know you will, but to the T, Robert.'

Robert nodded his acceptance, no words, he was a little choked. He merely patted Birkett on his back as he said his goodbyes, and they all wished each other good luck for what was to come.

'And absolutely no cash bets by anyone. Especially on course,' said Birkett, 'don't forget to remind Alison, Robert.' He fixed his comrades with a steely glare and left the office.

THIRTY-FOUR

Robert met the horse box as it arrived at the course. 'All OK, Ali?' he asked.

She told him that they'd both been, 'Good as gold.'

'Exact,' he said. 'Champion. Bobby Hamley,' he said, thrusting out his hand towards Brodie. 'I've seen you here and there, but we've never been introduced.'

They shook hands, and Robert said, 'OK you two get the horses settled in. I'll take the colours and declare them both if you like.'

Brodie said, 'No thanks Bobby. Tara prefers it if we do all of that stuff. No offence, just that she'd kill me if she found out.'

'No problem,' said Robert, 'I'll still do ours.' He went on his way, then ran back to catch them as they led the horses into the racecourse stables. 'Do us a favour and weigh out as soon as you can when the time comes. It's a nightmare doing two and I'm leading one up, so the earlier the better.'

'Sure thing Bob,' said Brodie, laughing at the fussy little red-faced man.

Birkett's empty horse box was ushered into the lane for vehicles carrying livestock as it disembarked the ferry at Caen, and they took their place in a long queue. After fifteen minutes or so, the passenger door was unexpectedly opened from the outside. Inspector Grandcollot greeted them.

'I was expecting a call,' he said.

Freddie replied, 'I was going to ring you as soon as we got through customs.'

'I am sure,' he said, 'please follow me. Your colleague can park when he gets to the front of the queue.'

As soon as the second race was run, Robert and Alison went to fetch the saddles from the weighing room. Both jockeys, Brodie now in the striking red and green silks of Tara Fitzsimmons, and

Gilbert Godly, nearly as old as Birkett by the look of him, in the far less conspicuous brown and yellow hoops of Birkett's so-called stud, were hanging on the rail, ready with their saddles.

'Thanks lads,' said Robert. Then as they went out onto the course again, Robert handed Bugbear's saddle to Alison. 'Keep them separate,' he said, 'you look after ours. I once got them mixed up years ago and I never want to do that again.'

They walked together back towards the racecourse stables, where Robert had earlier secured permission for them to saddle the horses, they being light a man. Halfway there he begged Alison to stop a moment. He leaned on the paddock rail blowing hard, unable to put together a complete sentence.

'Should I get help?' asked Alison, but he managed to raise his hand to tell her 'No, he'd be OK.'

He stood a moment longer, trying to regain his breath. Eventually, slowly, it became more regulated, and he could stand up straight again.

'It might all be getting a bit much for me,' he said, 'I've had trouble with the ticker before.' He blew hard again, the strain of saying the sentence seemed to take more out of him than he thought it would.

He took long deliberate breaths then said, 'Do me a favour Ali. Go back to the weighing room and get Brodie to help you tack them up. I'll be all right here for a moment, just run and get him.' He saw fear and panic reflected in her eyes, and suddenly became aware of how sudden, how dramatic that change had come over him. He counselled himself again that he should do nothing quickly, that he must concentrate on one thing: breathing. Deep slow breaths. That would be enough for now.

He pitied poor Alison. She was only a young girl and wasn't ready for stuff like this. He should have told Birkett to send someone more experienced, someone like Victor, who would panic less and step up more. She should have been back at the yard with the rest of them, enjoying Bugbear's big day that way. Not with him in the heat of it all, going through all this.

Alison's workmates were nearly all crammed into the small office. The bosses weren't here, and they too shared the anticipation of what would be a popular winner. Something about the horse, maybe his work with the two stable stars, marked it out to them as important somehow, that he, the horse that everyone loved, got his win, and started to have a career of his own. Well, all bar one of them thought this way. Even Davey had invested on behalf of his sisters. Liam was firmly in the other camp. Tara Fitzsimmons's was a pro-outfit. They knew how to line up horses for gambles, and they knew what it took to win a race like this. Though none of them were privy to the coup, most of those present had taken a small bet on Bugbear and just one of their number, had taken quite a hefty tilt at the ring on the back of Submariner.

Robert handed the saddle to Brodie, made his apologies, and went to find a lad to whom he could pay twenty quid to lead up Bugbear for him. Then he went to find a quiet place to watch the race, far away from the crowds, where he could take his time and breathe easy.

In an interview room at Ouistreham Port, Caen, Freddie was being grilled by Grandcollot. Birkett waited in the empty lobby, kicking his heels. His IT skills had improved under Freddie's tuition but he didn't know how to watch a race on his phone from France. They'd be off soon.

The door opened and Freddie appeared. 'I'm going to have to stay a little longer Birdie,' he said, 'he's going to run me back. You'd better get on and I'll catch you up. The horses can overnight at my place – but grab some bags of feed off them when you pick them up.'

'Is it not going well?' Birkett asked.

'Not yet,' said Freddie, offering him a weak smile.

Grandcollot appeared at the door and cleared his throat.

'Yes, sorry,' said Freddie, continuing on his way to the *gents*.

Birkett and Grandcollot exchanged smiles without speaking, and together they endured a prolonged silence until Freddie reappeared. He and Grandcollot set off in the direction of the interview room. As they did, Birkett made a noise which he turned into an 'Er...'.

The other two stopped and looked at him curiously.

'My phone. I don't know how to use it here; would you mind if Freddie showed me before I left?' he asked the detective.

Grandcollot gave a short jolt back with his head which communicated, 'Go on, be quick.'

'The race is off,' Birkett whispered from the side of his mouth. Freddie took the instruction and found the live race for him. He stayed to watch it himself for as long as he could, until finally Grandcollot's patience ran out and he insisted that Freddie re-join him.

Freddie left the race as they went down the back straight for the second time. It was at the point just before Brodie kicked his horse in the belly and went three or four lengths in front of the next horse, to go further ahead, defying any of them to try and bridge the gap. That second horse was Bugbear, and as everyone in the office said, he'd stay all day. He'd keep trying, and as long as his jockey kept asking for more, he'd keep giving, and never stop. At the top of the hill, the two horses had pulled clear, and it seemed inevitable now that Bugbear would start to wear down the long-time leader. As Submariner breasted the rise, his rider suddenly sat down into him and urged him up the last of the hill and round the bend. And as he did, there was a murmur in the stands, and a muted cheer in Birkett's office. Bugbear bounded over the crest of the rise and took the bend as if on wheels. He closed as the horses set off downhill, now with the winning post visible in the far distance. On he went, getting closer with every stride, and though Submariner went well, the momentum was with Bugbear.

Birkett could hardly bear to watch those closing moments alone. Freddie himself had been both petrified and fascinated, but as he left, all was well. Now it was the business end and Birkett had to endure it all on his own. Down they came to the last, the downhill section turning to uphill in a matter of strides. Submariner flew the final hurdle and Bugbear now only a half a length behind flicked the top of it. It didn't stop his momentum, but something about the jump galvanised Submariner, and off he went, suddenly a fresh horse again bounding on up run to the line. Bugbear was sent to the stands' rails, to give him something to run at but his stamina began to ebb, and the two horses, with the width of the track between them, who seemed for a fleeting instant to be almost level, were in fact anything but. Submariner was a good three or four lengths to the good and going away, and poor Bugbear, gallant and brave as he was, was no match for Tara's horse. That last two hundred yards seemed to last forever, as Bugbear, now going up and down on the spot, laboured

- 240 -

for an age to get up to the post. Submariner was pulling up as his opponent finally walked over the line, still miles in front of the third horse, but a mile behind the winner.

Some people in the office cried. Liam did not quite jump for joy, but for anyone who cared to look it was clear to see what the result had meant to him. He, after all, had supplied the crucial intelligence that to get Bugbear beaten you had to deny him the lead.

Birkett sighed and said out loud saying, 'I never want to go through anything like that in my life again.' He kept the pictures running as he went back to find his lorry, wondering whether he could somehow get the message through to Freddie, wherever he was.

By the time the winner and second had made their way into the winners' enclosure, Robert was already in his car. Feeling fine now, he could still have done without the drama of the last five minutes.

Birkett's phone immediately began to ping with messages of commiseration, mainly from his staff, unsure whether he'd managed to see the race.

Tara was in an auction room in London. She watched the race on her phone, smiled, then snapped it shut as soon as Submariner crossed the line. She began to receive messages of congratulations, so she pulled out the phone again and switched it off.

One of those was from Conrad, who had watched the race in a nearby bar with Warren. They shared a fist bump as Submariner powered up the hill, then Conrad exhaled in relief at a long-planned job finally being executed. Receiving no reply from Tara, he texted her racing manager to compare notes about the success.

Robert pulled into a lay-by a few hundred yards from the course and wound down his window. He could just make out the noise of the racecourse, and waited there for a few minutes, hoping, knowing somehow. Then he heard it: the warning alarm that indicates a Stewards' Enquiry. He only just strained to hear it and wasn't sure that he could follow it all from where he'd parked and so dialled a racing commentary service on his phone and held that to his left ear.

In France, Birkett heard the news of the enquiry, then turned off the Racing Channel on his phone. Then he opened up a Betting

Exchange app, where he saw one of the accounts David had set up for them with bets matched at a thousand to one on Bugbear. He logged out, then logged back into another and saw the same thing. Then he received a text from David to say *log out of all accounts.* He dared smile for a moment, then thought better of it.

The news came in on Robert's phone that there was an objection by the clerk of the scales to the winner, and shortly afterwards he caught another loudspeaker announcement from the course reminding punters to keep hold of all betting slips.

His roar of delight meant that he didn't quite get the next update on his phone but before long it was made certain by another announcement from the course:

'The winner has been disqualified for failing to draw the weight,' it said. 'The places are reversed, Bugbear is promoted to first place, Submariner is disqualified and placed last.' At the news of the disqualification Robert shouted his thanks to the heavens. Then he took out five individual lead tablets, each weighing one pound, from his pocket, and threw them into the undergrowth, before setting off on the road home.

Ten minutes later, Birkett logged back into the accounts and saw that the balances had been reduced to zero. He could think of nothing better to do than sound his horn, doing his best to make it sound like a victory salute, hoping that somewhere in the building next to him, Freddie would hear, and understand what had happened.

He could hear and for a moment wondered what the mad noise was all about. He never quite connected it with Birkett, even though he recognised it as a sort of victory salute, like when all the young people go out into the capital after their team's won the World Cup, leaning on their horns, making noise out of pure joy. Grandcollot's admonitory stare brought him back into the room and the interview.

'You see,' said Grandcollot, 'it's your style, the pitchfork, isn't it? Your go-to weapon.'

Freddie's patience was beginning to run out. He hadn't murdered Hamilton, much as he'd wanted to – he was happy for that to be known, he'd have liked nothing better than to push a pitchfork through Hamilton's neck. But he'd never had so much as a sliver of an opportunity to do so, and he knew that Grandcollot knew that too. Yet still the old man questioned him as if he was in the frame.

'What?' he said, witheringly.

'Gordon Melville, Liam Williamson, and now pauvre Edward Hamilton. All have found themselves at the end of a pitchfork held by you.'

'Hamilton hasn't,' said Freddie, then regretted jumping in so precipitously to confirm that the other two had.

Grandcollot allowed himself a little smile.

'We know that he defrauded you. That is public domain thanks to your wife's proceedings, we know that you are, shall we say, emotional with your partner in hospital. And we know that you are under terrible financial pressure. In such circumstances, mistakes are made. Revenge is sought. Recuperation looked for.'

Freddie shook his head, Grandcollot went on:

'Now, we see also that you alone perhaps cannot do this thing – you have had your difficulties, we know that. But someone may help you Monsieur Lyons. Someone who was interested to work alongside you to get your money back. Their money, perhaps. Or to invest in you for a share of your money?'

'What are you…' he started, but Grandcollot cut across him again:

'Someone who likes your methods. The accident with the pitchfork. The list is very short, there are your clients, there are your bloodstock contacts, there are very few others. Enlighten me.'

What is this? thought Freddie. *Is it an absurd joke?*

'I can't help you.' he said, it sounded more desperate than he would have liked. 'I have spent the last year running away and hiding from everyone you mention. I'm scared of them. I don't have the money they want from me. I've avoided them, not conspired with them.'

'Well, Monsieur Lyons,' said Grandcollot, 'we should take a little break, and perhaps I might suggest that you use this time to think very hard about who would want to make it look like you did this thing. And if you are to insist that you have nothing to do with this thing, then you must trust me. You must be open with me.'

Robert, whose share in the bet alone had made up for all that he'd lost through the bank to Tara, could hardly speak for crying.

'It's the best thing that has ever happened to me,' he said on the phone to Birkett, though his joy was tempered by his concern for Freddie. 'Oh no, actually…' then, 'Yes, it is, it's *the* best thing.'

Birkett was speaking from Freddie's *dependence*. He had picked up the horses, fed them and bedded them down for the night. Now at a loss for anything to do he kept Robert on the phone going through all the ups and downs of the day. He had switched the tele on and off a few times, wondering whether Freddie might appear on a French news programme. It was running silently in the background as he spoke to Robert. He had found a third of a bottle of whiskey in the cupboards and was eking it out best as he could with a little tap water added.

'No,' Robert did not know where Freddie kept the keys for the big house. But it did not stop him making a few suggestions, even though he'd never visited the place. Birkett was happy to play along because it kept him occupied. They went back and forth this way, like two teenage best-friends, neither prepared to end the call, as they re-lived every moment of the day over and over again. Occasionally the mood would be brought down as they paused to talk about Freddie and his plight, but within moments it was back up again, neither man capable of keeping a lid on the great ocean of joy that their winning punt had released in them. They talked like that for more than an hour, until eventually Birkett heard a car on the gravel and saw its headlights flash across the windows of the *dependence*. Robert begged to be left live on the phone so that he could witness whatever it was as it unfolded, then told Birkett to hang up and wait for him to ring him back *face-time*. Birkett waited for what seemed like an age for him to do that, anxious somehow that he should intercept Freddie and Grandcollot outside rather than invite them in – just in case. Eventually the phone rang and following a few trial runs, they found a place for Robert to watch from Birkett's breast pocket.

Birkett went out of the dependence onto the drive and on a few paces towards Freddie and Grandcollot, who'd parked outside the front door to the main house. Grandcollot had driven. He had no other officers with him. Freddie wasn't handcuffed. That was a start.

Birkett tried to communicate the success of the operation without revealing it to Grandcollot, but Freddie's blank expression told him that he wasn't ready for that conversation yet.

They had reached a certain impasse in the interview room, at which point Grandcollot made the decision to switch venues to the car. Before setting off, Freddie had cautioned himself to proceed with care and to be wary of the more relaxed direction in which the interview was bound to go, and the almost two-hour journey from that point had passed in a tolerably amicable way.

He'd made progress against the co-conspiracy charge before setting off. Grandcollot had not formally dropped the line but there had come a point in the interview when Freddie knew that he was being played, when he knew that if Grandcollot really believed in the case he would have pressed it home. And he didn't. His persistence had all been about getting Freddie to reveal something that Grandcollot didn't know.

His tone in the car had been conversational, sure, but Freddie soon decided that it was less about tricking him into an indiscretion than it was to mask a sinister threat. Half an hour into the journey, just as they were going through Banneville-la-Campagne when Freddie's auto response made him sing, 'Moi, je suis un marionette' to himself, clarity dawned. The implication of Grandcollot's persistence amounted to this: *not only will I run the co-conspirator argument against you in the investigation into the deaths of Felix and Edward; not only will I make you the key witness in both of those cases; not only will I take over your life in a way that you do not wish me to; I will also bring money laundering proceedings against you, and I will force you to give up your Russian clients. I can force you to do this, or you can cooperate with me.*

What that amounted to in practical terms was that Freddie must turn over to Grandcollot the documents to which, so far, he'd denied him access. That had been the point of the lift home. And the detective was a more informed interrogator on these issues than he'd been when the investigation into Felix's death had first opened.

'So, those documents,' said Grandcollot. Freddie directed him towards the cottage, and once inside, had him sit at the kitchen table in the open plan ground-floor space. He went to the understairs' office he'd set up in the early days after Felix's hospitalisation and pulled four or five slim folders from behind the filing cabinet.

He dragged a chair up to the small, square, pine table, to sit alongside Grandcollot, then asked Birkett to split the remainder of his bottle with them. Grandcollot took his without tap water and so Freddie decided to do the same. Freddie pointed to a set of keys hanging behind the utility room door and asked Birkett to go over to the main house to try and scout out some more bottles. As soon as he left Freddie set to work with the inspector, taking him methodically through the documents, pointing out hidden details and assisting him with his questions and difficulties of comprehension. And this time Grandcollot seemed to acknowledge that he was finally getting closer to the truth.

He was. To Freddie this option was marginally the lesser of competing evils. He tried to console himself with the thought that until a forensic accountant got into the file, he still had some breathing space. Then when he finally handed the folders over to Grandcollot he offered a silent prayer to Felix in Heaven that the real murderer would be discovered before the documents could ever assume any real importance in the case.

Birkett returned from the house with two bottles of wine and something that looked like a bottle of spirits clutched under his arm. He watched as the two of them wrapped up the process, then eventually he said, 'What's all this?'

Before Grandcollot could reply, Freddie answered, 'I still haven't convinced him that I didn't have anything to do with Hamilton's death, or Felix's for that matter. These documents might help me prove that.'

'What!' Birkett exclaimed. 'He should have heard you crying and praying for Felix like I have for the last six months.' Turning to the detective he said, 'And I made sure he didn't go after Hamilton. I'd have killed him myself if he'd tried.'

He was in drink and that last effort at a joke proved it beyond all doubt. *At least there's no doubt that the bet's landed*, thought Freddie, smiling for a moment.

'Are you sure you don't want me to have some officers come and park on your drive tonight? It's easily arranged,' said Grandcollot.

Freddie shook his head. 'We'll be fine, thank you.'

Grandcollot emptied the folders of their contents into his hands. He flicked through the slim pack with his thumb and raised his eyes at Freddie. 'Perhaps then, I'll have another drink and keep you company a little while longer,' he said.

The conversation never really flowed as the three of them sipped their drinks. Freddie tried to make something of Birkett's distaste for Calvados but it didn't really translate three ways, and so they talked awkwardly of the difficulty in making any money out of racehorses to pass the longest half hour of the day. Grandcollot declined a second top up and eventually took his leave.

'He knows,' said Freddie, as he returned from the drive.

'Knows what?' asked Birkett, suddenly losing the glow from his face.

'He knows that I have angry clients on my tail. And he knows that they probably killed them both. But worse, he knows what I used to do for them.'

Birkett stood mute in front of him, then eventually said, 'What are we doing here then? Let's get home and get them paid off. Ring up David and tell him to do it.'

Freddie laughed. 'It doesn't work like that. I have to do it. But that's not the end of it though, Birdie.'

'Why? What is it?' Birkett asked.

Freddie explained how, in getting himself out of the frame, he'd put his clients closer to it. 'I don't feel very safe,' he said.

'Well, what about that guard thing then? Ring him back, that inspector, and tell him we'll have them.'

'...and I just want to stay away from him.' said Freddie. 'He's got enough ammo on me; I don't want him to wheedle out the smoking gun.'

'Ferdy lad, what are you saying? What have you done?' asked Birkett, the colour drained from his face.

'Not that,' he said, 'not a real gun. Don't worry. It's just that I'll be lucky if I get away with money laundering now, never mind that I've given him a leg-up in building a case against my old clients. And they're scarier than prison.'

'You've given him all that?' asked Birkett.

Freddie went in search of a clean glass, then returning to stand next to Birkett, holding out the glass for a splash of the Calvados, said, 'That's what I'm saying. Nearly all,' and winked. Eventually he persuaded Birkett to agree that they and the horses needed a little rest before the final leg of the journey. They finally settled on a plan which saw them packed up and back on the road by three-thirty the following morning, heading to the relative security of Newmarket as fast as they reasonably could with their precious cargo.

They arrived home the following evening. News concerning their winnings had still not arrived from David. Robert confirmed the same as they met. It didn't matter. Freddie was back safe and sound, and they'd pulled off the coup of a lifetime. That meant more than money.

'Come on in, and tell us about it,' he said, 'you know David, he's careful and he covers his tracks, just leave him to it and let him do it his way.'

Freddie and Robert led the coveted mare and her foal off the horse box and put them into temporary boxes for the night. They'd be transferred to stud tomorrow, where they'd soon be joined by her yearling son. They were theirs now, and how it did Robert's heart good to see his old charge again. Even if David had run off with all the money, they still had this family, every member of it. That was enough.

They came into the house, hugged each other afresh and started whooping and hollering, and re-running the video of the race, and reading the great controversy it had caused on the websites of the racing papers.

Robert told them that the landline hadn't stopped ringing since the night before, and Birkett said it was the same with his mobile too, which being in France he felt was reasonable to ignore. He'd left it switched off on the journey up just in case there'd been a development that wrong-footed him. But when it rang again now, despite being a few glasses into the evening, he picked up from the unfamiliar number. The journalist first asked him his reaction to his horse being promoted to first place, and Birkett replied, 'Never? We just got in the box and came home when we saw that we'd got beat. I've just got back from France where I was picking up horses.'

The journalist pressed the point, but Birkett batted away his questions with an innocent nonchalance. Finally, he brought the conversation to an end by saying, 'Look, I'll show you, or your editor, or my lawyer, or the police, whoever it takes, all my bookmaker accounts, and all they'll find in them is what I thought was a small losing bet on Bugbear, and a small winning saver on Submariner; wherever it is you get this thousands of pounds of winnings from, I can't help you. For that you'll have to ask Tara's jockey. He was the one who'd saddled the horse that didn't draw the weight – we've got photos of that we can share with you, if you want. My girl looked after Bugbear and nobody's complaining about him.'

It was beneath the dignity of such an accomplished cheat as Tara Fitzsimmons to complain, that was tantamount to a compliment, but her racing manager had texted Birkett to tell him that unfair fights like this do have repercussions. Freddie texted back on his behalf, to say, 'Ask your own man, he saddled the horses; we were in France at YOUR stud – as you should know.'

'Whilst you have your phone out, let's try David again,' said Freddie, but he didn't pick up, and by the time they'd had enough, even Freddie was coming round to the idea that David and the money had gone.

The next day, Birkett and Freddie excused themselves first and second lots and left Robert to explain the mystery of the win to his eager audience. He was to deliver it in a very low-key way, tell them all, as was well known by everyone, how he'd missed most of the action, being ill, and that this would be the last time they saw him for a while because his doctor had told him to take it easy. They didn't want him around when Brodie started to ask questions. Robert Hamley-Flowers, Bobby Hamley, had been but a fleeting presence who soon nobody would remember if he'd stayed for a week or a month; and who, soon after that, nobody would remember at all. But Brodie Fitzpatrick was never seen at the yard again.

They loaded up the mare and her foal and took them to a local stud, the owners of which Birkett counted as two of his four, in total, friends. Whilst there, Freddie received a text message from a number he didn't recognise. It said, 'One forty grand repaid, yearling paid for. Nice float in your Nationwide account. Be in touch.'

And when they checked, there it was. The balance amounted to no more than about fifty percent of what they reckoned was due, but it was enough to cover their various misdemeanours and was more than they were expecting ever to see again.

It left a slightly bitter taste that a coup so exquisitely executed should ultimately turn out to be a coup against them themselves, but sort of appropriate in a way too. They had never really known who David Spencer was, and at least he hadn't left them bereft. He'd been decent about it.

'He's more my sort of conman,' said Freddie, 'I'd choose him every time over Edward Hamilton and his mates.'

THIRTY-FIVE

The sound of the gates flying back was relayed over the loudspeaker system and the disembodied voice coming from the top of the stands announced:

And... they're off for the Group I, Queen Elizabeth II stakes. Machin et Truc the French horse that has taken all before him this season settles in a tie for second as the Irish pacemaker goes on. It's looking like a re-run of the Queen Anne stakes so far as Lord Nelson leads to Machin et Truc, with Yellow Jersey much closer to the pace this time as they settle down in the early stages. Those two Machin et Truc and Yellow Jersey are content behind the strong pace set by Yellow Jersey's pacemaker Lord Nelson. They're followed in the pack by Napoleon Brandy, with Alhambra, the Guineas winner, and Big Leggy disputing fourth, then comes Woodpecker and Endless Narrative. The stablemates Milksheikh and Slipshod, first and second in the Prix du Pin last time, content to look on from joint last place.

The positions remain unaltered as they head on past halfway. The pacemaker not at all so far in front this time as Yellow Jersey and Machin et Truc keep close tabs on him, and the rest of the field sit quietly and hope.

On they go, and Lord Nelson is not having such an easy time of it upfront today as already Yellow Jersey and the all-conquering Machin et Truc loom large besides him. He's not going fast enough for them today. They are cantering, and the rest of the field knows they're in for a race. Alhambra and Big Leggy can't go with them, as Slipshod moves up from the rear to get involved. Yellow Jersey goes on, trying to outstay this champion but is he playing into his hands? The French horse simply canters in behind. Slipshod is interested in making a real race of it now and he throws down a challenge to the front two, but he's flat out while Machin and Truc just sits and

- 251 -

waits. On they go to the business end of the race and HERE COMES THE MACHINE! Machin et Truc picks up Yellow Jersey, but Slipshod clings to his coattails, and from the back Milksheikh begins to make his move. Machin et Truc it is now, from Slipshod in second, as Yellow Jersey gives way and all the time his stablemate chases him down. What a race this is, as Slipshod drags his mate into the race and both horses make this French champion work for the first time all season.

Machin et Truc it is as they go inside the final furlong, he's beginning to assert as Slipshod gives way, but Milksheikh won't lie down. Well inside the final furlong and Milksheikh is starting to get up. What has the French horse got? And the answer is not enough, as Milksheikh brushes him aside and runs away to win by two lengths. And we have a new champion of Europe, and his name is Milksheikh.

Freddie and Birkett stood side by side on the lawns outside the Royal Box turned to each other, unable to speak, held one another by the arms, shedding tears of joy. They stood like that for minutes on end, quite overcome by what they had witnessed, so grateful to have been part of this great horse's story, so full of joy, that the only thing to do was to cry as if it was the greatest of sorrows.

Penny interrupted them in their tears. She grabbed Freddie by the neck and held him close. He tried to look over her shoulder to check the presence of Jonny but couldn't see him.

She kissed him, on the cheek, but firmly, and it was meant. 'I get you, you know. And I love that you've done this. Thank you for paying. I'm sorry I doubted you.'

Freddie smiled. 'You were right to be angry,' he said. 'But I hope the bailiffs told you what happened to them.'

She laughed and walked back with them under the tunnel to the back of the stands.

Robert intercepted them on the way, with Jules, and rendered mute with emotion, simply presented her to the three of them. Jules immediately gravitated to the not yet met Penny and began to swap notes. 'Was it fun being around men like this, or did they just experience fleeting moments of relief in a life of constant fear and anxiety?' The two were on the verge of becoming the best of friends.

In the winners' enclosure, the first to greet Freddie and Birkett was Tara Fitzsimmons, who embraced them both and said, 'Well done. You played it better than me.' She clung on to Freddie as she held his hand and she too lingered over the kiss she planted on his cheek.

From behind her, a thick-set gentleman appeared. He held out a gloved hand to Freddie, and said, in a heavy Russian accent, 'Many congratulations.'

The sight of him sent a shiver of absolute dread through Freddie's body. He looked down at the gloved hand, and his own bare hand, then back again at the face, still smiling with a sinister insincerity. Tara seemed amused by Freddie's shocked expression as she stood aside to give them room together. Freddie ignored the hand and firmly grabbed the left forearm of the man. 'Thank you, Andrei.'

Andrei nodded without replying.

But Freddie was unnerved, and it showed. He looked around for Birkett, who had remembered to be a good trainer and was speaking with the owners of the third placed horse. Tara moved on too, and so Andrei, looking straight at Freddie, and Freddie, doing anything but look back at him, stayed with each other, in the same space, neither speaking.

There was nothing Freddie could say, he was to effect hardly knowing the man, they were the rules of the game. The gift of speech was with Andrei. Eventually he brought his head closer to Freddie's, taking him by the hand to draw him in as he did, and said, 'Thank you for the payment. It must have been difficult.'

Freddie nodded through a set smile. 'At times, but all that's over now Andrei, I think.' And he looked up to see that Andrei agreed, that all of that – whatever it was – was over now, forever.

'But it will not bring back your partner. I am sorry for this.'

'Oh Jesus,' thought Freddie, 'that was a short-lived moment of joy.' He said nothing.

'It was not expected,' Andrei added. 'Do you know who would do this thing? They cause a great deal of problems for us too.'

Freddie paused. 'Andrei, what was not exp… are you…'

- 253 -

Birkett came from his owners and said to Freddie and Robert who hung at Freddie's shoulder, 'There's only one place to go to celebrate this.' He gestured towards the pub on the High Street, which had been the scene of that pivotal moment in their season.

'I'll follow you,' said Freddie, 'just give me a moment.'

Robert said, 'Let's just wait a minute 'til Freddie's finished, and we'll all go over together.'

Freddie looked around for dangers then quietly asked Andrei if he'd mind sparing him two minutes to chat in a quiet corner. Andrei replied that it must be brief, and they each went into the small room just off the weighing room where winners were toasted by the racecourse, knowing that their party, like the French owners of the second placed horse were all elsewhere. One of Andrei's men followed them to the door of the room, the other stationed himself on the terrace outside the weighing room. Birkett and Robert stood between both sets in the lobby.

After a couple of minutes Freddie reappeared, and beckoned Robert over to say, 'Lead on over to the pub, Tara's lot will follow you – Andrei's man is texting her now. I'll be there in a minute.' Freddie went back and picked up Andrei, then left the course with him. Once they'd arrived at his car, he said his goodbyes and thanks, and set off for the pub.

It was a little like the scene in June. No other customers but them. But this time *them* added up to a dozen or more. The mood was good, and even though the likes of Tara and Alan Halliday rarely, if ever went into a pub, and had nothing to celebrate, somehow had allowed Robert to infect them with his good mood, and it felt like a party.

Only Alan was kept at arm's length, and when you looked at him, he gave off the strong sense of having been tricked into coming here. Freddie noticed that he refused a second drink from Birkett, and his body language seemed to indicate that he was on his way.

Freddie cut off his path to the door. Without looking at him, Alan tried to brush him out of the way, but he met with all Freddie's resistance, and suddenly, the sour note was picked up by everyone else in the pub.

'Well done,' said Alan, 'it didn't turn out such a bad year after all.'

Freddie made himself count to ten, otherwise, despite the foot in height between them, Alan would have been lying on the floor already.

'I might agree with you had I not lost my wife, my fortune, and my business partner.'

Alan shrugged as he attempted to push his way through to the door.

'But I didn't.'

'What?'

'Lose them. You took them from me.'

'Get out my way, you low life,' said Alan, looking back quickly to see who else had noticed their skirmish. They all had and were watching in silence to see how it might end.

'I could sue you for that alone…' he said.

Freddie cut across him and said, 'Sue me for this. You killed Felix, and you employed Edward Hamilton or whoever he is to defraud me of millions of pounds.'

Alan shook his head in disgust at such a preposterous suggestion: 'Sorry, I really have to go now. Perhaps you should go a bit easier on the celebrating?'

Freddie grabbed him firmly by the coat to prevent him going past. Alan bent down his head towards Freddie's and said, 'How? How did I do all these things? And while you're at it, why? Take a close look at me Freddie, I'm a wealthy man. I'm not a money-grubbing back street money launderer. Oh, and with the sort of clients who'd think nothing of rubbing anyone out who got in their way. Try looking closer to home before you start throwing around wild accusations. You could find yourself in a lot of trouble otherwise.' To make his point, he jabbed Freddie firmly in the chest.

Freddie let it go but kept the man in his stare.

'I know, because I've just talked to my client,' he said.

Alan tutted and shook his head.

'And I know now that they'd have accepted the lower offer we were making to them, to keep us in business and to give us time to pay our debt,' Freddie continued, 'the debt created by your fraud by the way. You killed Felix, to make it look like our clients, to take my attention away from what you had done, to make me scared to go looking for Edward Hamilton. Edward Hamilton, the small-time crook, who when he bought one of your cast-offs, to perpetrate a small fraud on me, gave you the inspiration to do it on a massive scale – one which only you could finance.'

'Now, you are being ridiculous. Edward Hamilton owes money all over the market. He owes me.'

'Oh yeah,' said Freddie, laughing, 'the Edward Hamilton that you didn't know, and hadn't seen, who was at your party at Newmarket? I saw him, Alan, lying dead in Birkett's yard, where you had him left to implicate me in his death. Or to make me think that my clients had done it and left the body as a warning to me to stay away and stay quiet. There he was, in the same worn-out shoes, shiny blazer and threadbare tie. That wasn't a man who had enriched himself by millions of pounds in the last twelve months. He was your lackey.'

Alan laughed now. 'OK then, let's find a policeman and you can hand me over to him.'

The door opened behind Freddie and one of Andrei's men came in. 'Now Alan, how am I going to get my money back with you in prison? No, we're going to do it a different way. You are going to go on a short retreat, all expenses paid, with this gentleman, and when you've paid your bills, you will be able to go and see your wife again. I'd text her now to tell her that you'll be away for a while.'

The colour drained from Alan's face.

'Oh, you should know. My clients aren't very happy with the way you've implicated them in this business. If you're lucky, we'll hand you over to the police later. If you're unlucky…' He made a face which indicated that it wouldn't be very nice, whatever it was.

'I did…' Alan began, but he stopped himself from saying more. A brief glance back towards Tara said everything that needed saying.

Andrei's man stepped forward, thrusting a piece of paper into Freddie's hand. 'When you've been paid, text the number written here,' he said.

'Thank you,' said Freddie, then looking again at Alan said, 'I'll text you the bank details.'

The man took Alan firmly by the arm and pushed him onwards, out of the pub.

A silence followed as Freddie looked at the assembled party in front of him, then a small ripple of applause ran through it. He smiled, then everyone came forward and embraced and kissed him again. Apart from Robert, who was so moved by the occasion that he was crying freely.

A few moments later, Slipshod's owners and friends had left; Tara and her entourage too; Jules remained in the background, but Penny had disappeared too. Otherwise just Freddie, Robert, and Birkett remained. No one had volunteered to drive, and they had no idea how they were going to get home. That was a worry for later in the evening.

Then, just as the pub started to fill with other racegoers, he arrived. He came to the front of their table, and there, before them, stood David Spencer, a broad smile etched across his distinguished face.

'I had to play a long game,' he told them, 'To make it safe. But I've got the rest of your money now.'

'Get yourself a drink and join us,' said Birkett, 'the tab's open.'

He returned from the bar a moment later with a bottle of champagne and a handful of glasses, 'That was good fun boys,' he said, 'When are we going to do it again?'

Printed in Great Britain
by Amazon

11047426R00149